She's Got Issues

She's Got Issues

Stephanie Lessing

AVON
TRADE

An Imprint of HarperCollins*Publishers*

HarperCollins books may be purchased for educational, business, or sales promotional use. For information please write: Special Markets Department, HarperCollins Publishers Inc., 10 East 53rd Street, New York, NY 10022.

FIRST EDITION

Interior text designed by Elizabeth M. Glover

Library of Congress Cataloging-in-Publication Data

Lessing, Stephanie.
    She's got issues / by Stephanie Lessing.—1st ed.
        p. cm.
    ISBN 0-06-075696-9 (alk. paper)
    1. Periodicals—Publishing—Fiction. 2. Office politics—Fiction. 3. Fashion editors—Fiction. 4. Women editors—Fiction. 5. Young women—Fiction.   I. Title.

PS3612.E8188S54 2005
813'.6—dc22   2004027398

05 06 07 08 09 JTC/RRD 10 9 8 7 6 5 4 3 2 1

For Dan, Kim and Jesse,
because I'm so not funny without you.

ACKNOWLEDGMENTS

I'd like to acknowledge the most extraordinary human being who ever lived, and I'm not exaggerating even a little. My mother is *that* good. And she's beautiful, too—ravishingly beautiful. I'd include a picture, but you'll just have to take my word for it. And, of course, my incredibly devoted and loving father, who is also uncommonly handsome and brilliant. My equally dazzling and adorable sister and best friend, Robin; my precious niece, Chelsea, who read this and laughed out loud; and my favorite nephew, Zack, who always roots the hardest for all of us.

And what would my days have been like had I not received my daily dose of M&M's via e-mail? God only knows. I also want to thank my Aunt Bert for being such a girly girl and my cousin Randi—you know why . . . for waiting for me.

I wouldn't be writing this if it wasn't for my dedicated, deeply astute, and extremely efficient (and blonde) literary agent, Kate Garrick, and my very funny, warm and gifted editor, Kelly Harms, aka c and d. Thank you both for your superb advice, remarkable instincts, and for remaining calm whenever I switched into panic mode.

I would also like to thank the most gorgeous, inspiring, patient and understanding person on the planet, whom I've been in love with since I was seventeen—thank you, Dan—as well as the insanely talented, beautiful, secretly hilarious and incredibly entertaining Kimmy, who just happens to be my favorite type of girl; and the wittiest, most dashing man alive, who does an absolutely genius impression of "Stuie" and who can get me to do pretty much anything with a two-second hug—Jesse. I want to thank all three of you for your steady flow of love, affection, background music and the occasional wisecrack, while I sat here staring into space, forgetting where I was supposed to be for months on end. You're the reason I do everything, so it was nice of you to let me fall apart in the process. I love you all so much.

CHAPTER ONE

~

Recruitment Tactics

I can't take my eyes off of it. It's everything I would want to be . . . if I were a sign.

Issues Magazine
1026 Madison Avenue
New York, New York 60793

Sigh.

I slowly trace my finger over each perfect word, until I feel a little shiver on the back of my neck. I'd know this lettering anywhere. It's *Coronet,* the ultimate in vintage-chic fonts. The sign reminds me of that time my mom took me to see Audrey Hepburn in *Funny Face* at the *Paris Theater* when I was seven years old. I didn't really want to go at first. I knew it wasn't a cartoon, even though they tried to trick everyone with that name, but I figured, what the hell; I had no other plans and my mom let me bring a pocketbook. I had no idea that I was destined to walk out of that movie theater with the answer to the most puzzling of all life's questions. For the first time in seven years, I knew what I wanted to be when I grew up.

As soon as I got home, I ran upstairs to my room and stood in front of the mirror. It was October of 1982. I was about to turn eight and it was not uncommon for me to polish off an entire box of Sugar Wafers at the drop of a hat. I stood frozen in front of my reflection, evaluating my overall look from an entirely new perspective. The thighs were definitely going to be a problem. The pigtails were all wrong, and I needed to grow at least another fourteen inches. There was no doubt about it; some big changes would have to be made if I, Chloe Rose, was going to make it in the fashion magazine business.

Unfortunately, liposuction was completely out of the question, so I settled for the next best thing—bangs. Back then, the only scissors I was allowed to keep in my room were toenail clippers, but that didn't stop me. They weren't perfect, but the overall effect was there. Now all I needed was a job.

I hired myself for a part-time position after school and for a few hours on Saturday. My job was complicated, because I had to stay focused in a home-office setting, which involved a million and one interruptions, including: making my bed, studying for spelling tests, and, worst of all, distracting play dates with children my own age. I wasn't able to sit down for a minute. I spent hours clomping around my bedroom in my mom's high heels, arranging papers, pinning up pictures of models on my cork board, answering the phone, reapplying my lipstick and firing imaginary people. There were days when I managed to put in three or four hours of paper arranging and lipstick reapplications without stopping, even once, to put out my cigarette/broken TV antennae.

I always wore the same sleeveless cotton nightgown to work, which was cut like an old woman's housedress, allowing me to sit in almost any position without my underwear showing. No matter how far I spread my legs, it would stay hooked around my knees. It even had darts.

Under my nightgown was my mom's stretchy bra with the built-in shoulder pads, which I generously stuffed with two rolls of toilet paper. I didn't even bother to unroll it. I just put a whole roll in each cup. There was always a family member yelling for toilet paper from the bathroom in our house.

"Oh, Mrs. Stevens," I'd say to no one, "can you please bring my mother, Mrs. Rose, this little handful of toilet paper and then meet me back here in my office to line up these lipsticks again? Oh, and Mrs. Stevens, I just love how you reorganized the magazines on the bookshelf, so I've decided to give you a raise. Yes, that's right, a million dollars. And please remember to tell Mrs. Rose I say hello and that I'm sorry but I won't be able to make my bed today. As it turns out, I had to do some last-minute rescheduling. I now have a much earlier lunch date with Christie Brinkley, and I'm all backed up on my steno."

I could have used a few more employees to round things out, but the only other person I enjoyed playing with was my sister, and she found "magazine office," and "make-believe" in general, to be an embarrassment. I offered her several very high profile secretarial positions and the opportunity to work directly with Mrs. Stevens, but she flatly refused me every time.

It was always the same story with her: cashier or nothing. She was completely inflexible, no matter how many times I told her that the cashier position was already taken. Because of our professional differences and her overall lack of enthusiasm for imaginary games, I was forced to resort to playing with inanimate objects.

I could have easily used my dolls and stuffed animals to fill in for people, but I've always felt that stuffed animals look a little stiff in an office setting. Dolls are even worse. They just sit there like a bunch of babies, ridiculously overdressed, with no personality whatsoever. I can't work with people like that. There's no give and take. So I used my shoes. Shoes make excellent employees. They stand on their own two feet, ready to get to work at a moment's notice. After work, they kick up their heels, have a few laughs, and are ready to do it all over again the very next day. Except for slippers. Slippers always look like they have a cold or they're down on their luck, especially my slippers. I've always had the big, furry kind with matted hair and juice stains all over the front. Whenever I needed someone to play a bum, I used my slippers.

Because I worked exclusively with shoes, there was never any question when it came to job casting. Shoes are born stereotypes. Some are tall and bossy, some are old and reliable, some are ugly and supportive, some are trendy and loud, some are sweet and charming, and others are just out and out sluts.

You might, on any given day, walk into my room and see a pair of closed-toe sandals, with their straps Scotch-taped to the keys of the family Smith Corona, typing up a letter to the president of Bloomingdale's, or a tiny white Ked, with a pencil knotted to its shoelace, taking inventory of my closet/storage room. My four pairs of party shoes were always gossiping about how late they stayed up, or they were making personal calls instead of working. Whenever I caught wind of what they were saying, I had to separate them. God knows I loved my work.

Every night I would line up my sneakers, sandals, dress shoes, ice skates, and ballet slippers and rate them in terms of their character, function, and ability to make a nice impression. I used a complicated scoring system that involved twenty, sometimes even thirty, categories. My black patent leather Mary Janes were always in first place with a solid ten. They had pearl buttons. The button alone was worth 4.5 points. I knew my other shoes felt that I was showing favoritism, so I compensated by giving them higher scores than they really deserved.

My Mary Janes were more than my favorite shoes. They were my soul mates. I consulted them before making any major decisions, and I told them every single one of my hopes and dreams. I completely trusted them because I knew we shared the same overwhelming secret desire. We both wanted to look like ladies.

Sometimes I like to think that somehow, somewhere, they are still out there, rooting for me.

For a while there, I gave up my fascination with fashionable career women like Audrey and the rest of the *Funny Face* gang. Once I started watching reruns of *The Dick Van Dyke Show,* my childhood fantasy of myself as a glamorous career woman no longer involved a career. I still had bangs, of course. To this day I have bangs. At the moment, they are a little too short, but short bangs are very in, thank God. At least that's what my hair stylist told me when he sensed that I was contemplating taking my own life in his chair. One thing is for sure; I will never, ever change my hairstyle.

Once I got hooked on *The Dick Van Dyke Show,* I began spending a lot of time staring at women as they walked down the street, dressed in massive sweaters and cigarette jeans, imagining them suddenly transformed into hundreds of Laura Petries in gray pill box hats, gray dresses, pretty gray pumps, and gray pearls. Little did I know, by the time I would be old enough to dress like Laura and pull off a gray mink stole, her entire wardrobe would have been out of style for well over forty years. I think Nick at Nite is the reason that a lot of people my age have no real concept of time . . . or color.

I wonder who picks out the shoes that are featured in *Issues* each month. I hope I'll have the opportunity to at least meet her today. We have so much to talk about.

I can just imagine her desk. It's probably at least eighteen feet long and swarming with rows of shiny new shoes. I'm sure she gets called away on business from time to time and has to bring in a substitute to make critical shoe decisions. Of course I would never say no, even if she asked me to fill in at the last minute.

There I'll be, slowly walking around and around the shoe table, holding my chin, nodding to myself, taking notes: "Two points for heel height, one point for toe cleavage, and six points for necessity to flex calf muscle in order to walk."

If I really love a particular pair, I will, on occasion, agree to bring them home for further evaluation. People will write in with shoe questions from all over the world, and I will pride myself on answering each and every one of them personally.

I hope this interview doesn't take too long. If I get this job, I'm going to need a whole new wardrobe, and I should really start shopping right away. I wouldn't dare call in sick just because I couldn't get everything I needed in time.

The truth is I already started shopping as soon as they called me to set up this appointment. I began by looking around for a new pair of brown boots that can be worn both in and outdoors. I should also start looking for a wallet that holds bills. The hand-stitched wallet I bought a few days ago is really beautiful, but unfortunately, it doesn't open.

I'm also going to need all new underwear and bedding, and I should probably have all of my leather accessories cleaned and reconditioned. I might need a bigger handbag, too, in case I have to bring home daily reports of some kind. And I could really use a new set of pots and pans.

Somewhere in a dark corner of my mind, I keep hearing the words "I work for *Issues Magazine*," followed by a faint clapping of little Mary Jane soles. I hope I'm imagining it and not actually saying it out loud.

I want to touch the sign one more time and let its essence wash over me. I think I'll leave a little token of my appreciation by the door before I go in, as an offering of some kind. Maybe

just a simple strand of bang. I feel as though this is going
the most important, self-defining day of my entire life.

I take a deep breath, close my eyes, open the door, and
walk in.

Wow! There are at least thirty other girls sitting in the reception area. This is so weird. Why did they book all of these other
appointments at the exact same time as *my* interview? I hope
I didn't show up on the wrong date. I did that once before. I
had jury duty and accidentally booked a pedicure for the
same day. It's a long story. I head directly over to the front
desk to clear up the confusion.

"Excuse me, what's today's date?" I ask politely.

The receptionist chooses this exact moment to bend down
and tie her shoe. While she's down there, she mumbles,
"Monday."

I flick my bangs aside, coughing absentmindedly, and tell
her my name. Then I sit down at the edge of my seat between
two other girls. They appear to be about my age, height,
weight, shoe, ring, and bra size. In fact, everyone in this room
looks almost exactly like me. This has never happened to me
before. Usually, when I walk into a room filled with strangers,
they are all different heights. I stay close to the edge of my
seat, as though I might have to suddenly leave.

I feel a little uncomfortable that I didn't know what day it
is, but I keep reassuring myself that it's not uncommon for
very busy people to get confused. For all these girls know, I
could have jet lag or I could have switched time zones so
many times this week that my watch is already set for Tuesday
or even Wednesday. No one can even see my watch. It could
say anything. I'm the only one who knows that it hasn't been
able to tell time for over a year.

I'd love to find out the time, too, but I don't want to call
attention to myself again. I can always figure it out in my
head, based on what hour I left my apartment, how long I

waited for a cab, the length of the cab ride, the amount of time it took me to get up to the sixth floor, and how long I stood there staring at that sign. I must have been standing there for a good ten minutes. There is still a little glimmer of the sign lingering in my retinas, like a little halo. *Issues Magazine.* Pinch.

I would do anything to get this job. I would gladly shave my whole head if they asked me to, although I can't see why they would. Just the thought of working in a place that would define me as a fashionista instead of a person who hoards clothes and shoes for no reason gives me an incredible sense of purpose. I just got another one of those little shivers on my neck. What the hell is wrong with me? It's not even cold in here.

I settle in and immediately pick up an issue of *Issues.*

That's so funny.

I wonder if they named the magazine *Issues* on purpose. I never noticed that before, and I've had a subscription for five years. I guess you have to be an insider to pick up on all the little subtle innuendos of the magazine biz. I love puns.

I adjust my cream wool skirt with the subtle flounce. That's what the sales associate called it, a subtle flounce. I love wearing cream. You can never go wrong with all cream. I roll my head around a little, as though I'm loosening my neck muscles, to get a better look at what everyone else is wearing.

The girl sitting directly to my left is really cute, almost cute enough for me to hope she gets called away by a sudden medical emergency . . . that turns out to be nothing serious, of course. She's got on a pink, silky skirt with tiny black polka dots and a little matching pink cardigan with antique buttons and two strands of long pearls—a pink strand and a white strand. She's even wearing a diamond-bow necklace, which hits her right between the double pearls. And, oh my God, what is that? I think she's got a little lacy black camisole under there.

She's not even looking back in my direction. She did.t even check me out once. She's already confident that I'll never get the job. Maybe she still thinks I showed up on the wrong day and that I'm too embarrassed to leave, or maybe she's wondering why I decided to dress up as a nurse to interview at the coolest magazine in America.

I hope the interviewer realizes I'm wearing *winter* white. It's obviously not *white white*. It's definitely cream. It *is* a light cream, though. I hold the magazine next to my skirt to compare the whites. Well, that's a relief. My skirt is practically brown compared to a page of a magazine. I definitely won't bring it up in conversation during the interview. For instance, I won't say something like, "Well, how about that WINTER WHITE we keep seeing in every single issue of every single magazine? What's that all about?"

The cute girl sitting next to me—the girl who has long ago crossed me off the competition list—is a natural blonde. How is that possible? I can't really see where her hair ends, but no matter where I look, there's more. I should let my hair grow really long and give up the bangs once and for all. They are always in my eyes, even when they are way too short. I hate bangs.

I wonder how I'd look as a blonde.

The receptionist just keeps calling these girls in, one after the other, every few minutes. I hope I get enough time to prove myself. It takes me much longer than a few seconds to warm up to someone. I hope I don't walk in and say something insulting right off the bat. I have been known to just belt one out when I'm nervous.

Like that time in kindergarten, I asked the teacher if she was an anti-Semite on the first day of school. Just like that. That was the first question I asked her. I didn't ask, "Where do you keep the crayons?" or "What time do we eat our snack?" Instead I chose "Are you an anti-Semite?" I had just learned what the word meant, and I was feeling a little insecure about it, but it came out all wrong, almost like an attack on her character. She never really liked me after that.

"Chloe, would you like to follow me in now?"

The receptionist asks this question as though this is the single most boring sentence in the entire English language. Apparently she would rather have her eyelashes electrolyzed than escort yet another girl in and then back out of the exact same door.

She could have also said, "Chloe, would you like to follow me in now, or just get the hell out of here, like everyone else?" It would have felt exactly the same.

I can't blame her for feeling resentful of her situation. She went to all the trouble of dying her hair fuchsia, only to be trapped in a room with thirty indistinguishable girls, each of whom is destined to go home after a three-second interview and never see her or her hair ever again.

Her flair for individuality is completely lost here. It's like that whole "if a tree fell and no one heard it" thing. Under normal circumstances, I love fuchsia, but as a hair color, I think it's very impractical. She must have spent hours gelling all those tiny braided antennae. There is a really huge one, which shoots straight out of the back of her head. I can't even look at that one. It looks exactly like a penis.

Her hair reminds me of something else besides a penis. What is it? Oh, I know. It's my pink satin evening bag. I always wear that bag to black tie affairs, for just a spot of color. I should really give it to her if I get the job. The truth is I've never worn it because I've never actually been invited to a black tie affair of any kind. I'm almost positive she would love it, though. What girl wouldn't want an evening bag that matches her hair perfectly?

I take another look at her to make sure it's the right shade, and then I give her a little half wink. I want to let her know that I have something to tell her later, a surprise. She sort of looks back at me, rolling her eyes in disgust.

She is so far above this whole "pick me" scene. She's more of a "don't pick me" girl. Her whole face is covered in powdery white foundation, and her eyes are rimmed with a thick black liner that's dripping down her cheek on one side, and I think that's blood on her lips. She's wearing black pants and a really cute T-shirt, except that it's ripped and there's a skull on the back. And there are some serious metal studs on her boots and her belt. I bet she smells.

The funny thing is, she's looking at me like I'm the oddball. My skirt *is* a little on the girly side but not girly enough to stare at. I try to look down without moving my head to see if the collar of my matching cream wool jacket inadvertently flipped up on one side. She keeps staring at me. You'd think I was wearing a little bonnet or something.

Am I?

I touch my head for a second, to make sure, but of course that's just ridiculous. I would definitely remember something like that and besides, I don't even own a bonnet. No one does.

I just want to say *fuck* for no reason and catch her off guard. Maybe she'll think I'm a Goth Girl too, but in disguise. I just can't believe how long she's been looking at me. I'm not the one with the infected nostril. I'm sure she takes that nose ring out every morning before work and never bothers to sterilize the area properly. She's probably not even a real Goth Girl. Real Goth Girls do not de-ring themselves for work. Maybe she's more of a Punk Girl. I always get those two styles confused. Goth Girls typically choose jobs that require multiple facial piercings. They work at Starbucks, not girl magazines; I mean *women's* magazines. My sister, Zoe, would call her a Pseudo Goth.

Zoe has a name for everyone. They're always great names, but half the time I have no idea what she is talking about. Take the word *pseudo*, for example. For the longest time, I thought that meant psycho.

I can certainly understand why people dress up like Frankenstein on Halloween, but where's the thrill in startling people when there's no candy involved?

There was a Goth Girl in my high school. Just one. I come from a small suburban town in New Jersey. There was no reason whatsoever to go overboard expressing one's self in our town. Any sort of cry for help through fashion was considered bad taste, and more importantly, no one cared. I never spoke to the Goth Girl. I was scared to death that she would stab me. Actually, that's not true. I did speak to her once, when I bumped into her, by accident, in the school cafeteria. I didn't say much. All I said was, "Excuse me, ma'am."

To this very day, I have no idea what possessed me to call her "ma'am." I guess it was out of respect for her decision to do her own thing in high school, of all places, and my deep-rooted fear of the macabre. She was very insulted when I bumped into her. If I remember correctly, I think she called me something like prissy little pussy. Yeah, it was definitely prissy little pussy. Those were her exact words. I never told anyone about that, except for Zoe, who retaliated by writing the Goth Girl a twenty-page letter.

The letter was all about how Zoe recognized the demoralizing effects that our media-imposed universal standard of beauty has on adolescent girls and how she admired the Goth Girl's attempt to think outside of the box, but that nothing! absolutely! nothing! was worth going out and buying all-black makeup. She also offered to give the Goth Girl psychological and cosmetic counseling, if she agreed to apologize to me in front of the whole school. It was a pretty good letter, but parts of it were impossible to understand.

If you saw Zoe, you would never believe the stuff she writes. She's very petite and pretty, and she has the most amazing hair. Unfortunately, she's extremely opinionated, and she is constantly thinking. I guess you can't have everything.

Zoe writes letters telling people off, on my behalf, on a fairly regular basis. She's a big believer in "the pen is mightier than the sword." You wouldn't expect such a small person to write with such powerful emotions, but Zoe can get upset about pretty much anything. The two things that upset her the most are animal testing and when someone insults me. In her mind, I'll always be her little sister, and she takes that job very seriously.

It can be very embarrassing when she reads one of her letters out loud. She doesn't do it very often. She has to be really mad.

When the captain of the soccer team, Ricky Randall, broke up with me in tenth grade, my sister stormed up to the field in the middle of practice and told him what she thought of him and all the other "insensitive, self-obsessed male athletes of the world" in front of the whole team. Zoe was four feet ten at the time with a thick mane of black curls down to her waist. My boyfriend was six feet six and a complete moron.

You should have seen her standing there, reading from a series of index cards. Every now and then she would flick her hair back, change cards, and look up at him. He probably didn't even understand what she was saying. I never got the chance to tell her that the reason Ricky broke up with me was because I cheated on him. Nor did I get the chance to tell her that I cheated on him on purpose, to prove to him that I was a terrible person, so that he would break up with me. But Zoe totally messed it up. The problem with Ricky was that he was a biter. At one point, when we were making out, I screamed, "Why are you doing this to me?" It's amazing that our relationship lasted a full two and a half months.

After she yelled at Ricky, he tried to get back together with me. She didn't have any of the facts, and yet she still managed to convince him that he was guilty. She should really take up law instead of using her powers of persuasion for the sole purpose of making sure that no one hurts my feelings.

The Goth Girl and I are just sort of standing here, right next to each other. I got up a little too fast when she called my name, and I almost broke into a little sprint. Then I realized that I should be following her, so I made that little "after you" gesture, for her to go ahead of me. I guess she thinks that was funny. In fact, all of the girls in the reception area seem to think it was sort of funny. I wonder if they're laughing at the penis coming out of the back of her head or my flounce. Maybe it's not subtle. Maybe it's hilarious.

I smile back at her and try not to look like I'm afraid to get hit. I adjust my decidedly winter white skirt and notice that it's hiking up a little in the back. I hope I didn't sit on something. Any shade of white is probably not the best color choice for an interview. I think I actually read that somewhere. I should try to remember at least one thing that I've ever read before I get dressed in the morning. I try to calm my nerves by taking a quick peek at my new shoes. I still can't believe that they're mine. Between you and me, I call them my lady shoes.

I am still looking at my shoes when Goth Girl turns around, with her hand on her hip, and says, "I'm waiting, Miss Chloe." Apparently I had come to a complete stop in the shoe-staring/walking process.

Miss Chloe.

I hate when people call me that. I feel my head again for the little bonnet.

I can't help noticing that my lady shoes are really pinching me. It's funny because they hardly pinched at all in the store. They created more of a numbing effect. My sister begged me not to get them when I told her that I couldn't feel my pinky toes, but I knew I had to have them. The heel is just high enough to create a decent arch, yet there is no risk of injury, none at all. This is key. I very rarely buy a pair of shoes that cause me to fall down. I may have, once or twice, but both times were under very extenuating circumstances. Zoe always says, "If the shoe fits, wear it." But I've never been one to limit myself to shoes that fit.

My new lady shoes have "perfect for interview" written all over them. They are alligator, which means they exude just the right amount of confidence and maturity. They are Manolo Blahnik, which proves that I can't possibly afford them, thereby indicating that I am prepared to go out on a limb for something I believe in, a risk taker, so to speak. And they are at least a full size too small, which indicates nothing really— oh, actually it does. It indicates that I am willing to accept unbearable consequences to make a nice first impression.

See? I told you. Perfect shoes.

After Goth Girl calls my name for the third time, I snap back to reality and clutch my new leather portfolio. I am now walking, without stopping this time, toward my dream job. I am so happy. I feel a cold rush of air between my legs. Gee, that never happened before . . . from being happy. But it does feel familiar.

As I am about to enter the interviewer's office, I'm getting a vision of champagne-colored silk moiré walls, a colossal antique-carved desk, and some kind of lavishly upholstered Louis-the-something-teenth chair. But that's not even close to what she's got going on in here. She's got an old white Formica desk and two chairs. That's it. No window, no lounging sofa, nothing. Not even a tall glass vase of French tulips. The only non-work-related item on this woman's desk is a pair of tweezers, with a bunch of little hairs in it. My childhood home office was nicer than this. At least I had a vanity. I try to sit down quietly. I don't want to disturb her. She's on the phone.

I can't imagine what she looks like, because she has her back to me. I, on the other hand, am facing the wall. For some reason, she has positioned my chair to face the wall to the right of her desk. I'm not sure how this is going to work. I can't rearrange her furniture just so that I can see her face, and besides, my chair is so low that I'd never be able to see over her desk anyway. I'll just have to twist my body around and look up, that's all. No big deal.

I just feel so odd, staring at a wall, especially since there's nothing on it.

Oh wait, there's a little photo of Audrey Hepburn up there over the door! Fashion people love Audrey. But that's not the way I remember her bangs. Those are the same bangs Jim Carrey had in *Dumb and Dumber*. Audrey looks like a five-year-old with those bangs—the kind of five-year-old that I never wanted to play with. I hope my bangs don't look like that.

I can just imagine my interviewer calling in the girl with the long blonde hair right after me. I can see the two of them laughing themselves sick, discussing the fact that the interviewer purposely hung up the picture of Audrey Hepburn's bangs for this month's issue on How Never to Wear Your Hair.

I wonder if Goth Girl brought me to the wrong office. This woman can't possibly be expecting anyone. She is not even close to hanging up the phone.

Oh no, stomach cramp! This always happens to me. I live in fear of this. I'm allergic to dairy, and I had a pretty big bowl of ice cream for breakfast. Two bowls, I think. What am I going to do? I can't possibly get up and leave before she even turns around. *Oh! There's another one.* This can't be happening. *I hope I don't make a fuffie. She'll think I did it on purpose to get her off the phone.* My career at this place is about to be ruined and I haven't even had my interview. *Oh, that's better.* False alarm.

I'm starting to feel much better about the fact that I didn't choose cheerful little polka dots for such a strained beginning. I really want to see what she looks like. All I can see is the top of her head, which is peeking out over the top of her chair.

Unfortunately, she's got a very flaky scalp. Selsun Blue. I should jot that down for her before I forget.

I just wish she'd give me a little signal. I have no idea what to do with myself. I've already spent way too much time staring at my feet. I'm beginning to despise these shoes, and I think they might even be the reason I got that terrible stomach cramp before.

It's been about half an hour. I am seriously considering falling off my chair by accident, just to alert her that I am still here.

Maybe the other girls just kept leaving, one after the other, because she never turned around. I *can't* leave. I'd rather die here than leave. No one in their right mind would walk away from the opportunity to land their childhood fantasy dream job. It would be like telling your fairy godmother, "Listen, I don't feel like going out anymore. The pumpkin chariot took too long. I'm going back inside to finish cleaning the fireplace. Thanks anyway, though."

I just heard something drop. She must have kicked off her shoe. Kicking off one's shoe is a sure indication that one is enjoying one's phone conversation. I'm trying not to listen to what she's saying, but she's not exactly whispering. I hate knowing that she finds the interviewing process a complete bore. No wonder she's avoiding it. Oh my God. She just said, "I should go; there's someone in my office."

She knows I'm here after all! She was probably talking to one of those people who just ramble on and on.

Okay, she's swiveling around now. This is it. I'm trying to twist my body around and lift myself up off the seat a little so I can see her, but she's keeping her head down. If she lifts it up for one second, I'll be able to see her perfectly in this position.

She must be reading the résumé that I sent in to Human Resources a few weeks ago. I really wish she wouldn't do that. That thing is just loaded with one huge lie after another. I hope she doesn't ask me anything about it. I can't possibly remember what I wrote.

"So, you are Chloe? Chloe Rose?"

Please let that be the end of the questioning.

"Yes, ma'am."

Damn! I did it again.

It looks like she might be tilting her head to the side a little. I saw her part move. She's probably wondering where I'm from. I bet she thinks I'm from the South. Who else says "ma'am"?

Maybe she'll like me better if she thinks I'm from the South.

I offer to shake her hand, over the desk, which surprises her for some reason. Without even glancing up in my direction, she offers me her fingertips. I'm not sure how to shake fingertips, so I just squeeze them a little. I don't want to hurt her.

"Well, it's nice to meet you, Chloe. Please feel free to call me Ruth. Now, it says here that you were an editorial assistant at *Little Missy* magazine for . . . what is this, nine years? That's quite a long time to be an editorial assistant, don't you think, Chloe?"

"Why, yeiz it is. Thair must be some mistayik. It may very well be a typo of some kand."

That didn't sound very Southern. It sounded like I never learned how to speak properly.

"Yes, I suppose it is. How old are you, Chloe? It's impossible to tell from this résumé. These dates aren't gelling, unless you were working full-time while you were in college."

"I'm twenty-seven. I'll be twenty-eight in November, and I'm a Scorpio."

"You're going to be twenty-eight?"

Is that the wrong age? These questions are tougher than I expected.

"Well, I'm at the point in my life where I need to get on track . . . and . . . um . . . pursue my lifelong dream . . . as um . . . as opposed to . . . something else."

The accent is completely gone now. Finished. I can't even remember how to do it.

"Let's see. It says here that you were born in Trenton, New Jersey."

I admitted that? Why couldn't I have written Trenton, France, or something?

"And then you moved to Short Hills, New Jersey, in third grade, and your favorite teacher ever was Mrs. Marshall."

I could swear I took that out. It's obvious that this woman feels like laughing at my résumé and, to some extent, my life.

Oh no, here comes the coughing. There's no way to control it. I always cough when I get scared or when I think I might be going to jail.

Once, in seventh grade, my best friend Jane Moss stole a lip-gloss. She knew she was about to get caught, so she stuck it in my coat pocket. She didn't want me to get in trouble or anything. It's just that she was always stealing stuff and she knew no one would ever check my pockets. Everyone in town knew I wasn't the type to steal. I'm more of a liar. But still, the fear was overwhelming.

When the manager started walking over to us, my throat closed up immediately. I was choking and coughing at the same time.

They had to take me to the hospital because they thought I was having an asthma attack. I tried to explain to the doctor that I was choking on my own nervous saliva, but he did all these tests. Coughing is a way of life for me.

"Are you okay?" Ruth asks. She looks annoyed. Coughing *is* annoying.

She's giving me her bottle of water. It has an orangey-brown lipstick mark on it exactly where I will have to put my mouth. I've been brought up never to drink from another person's glass, bottle, or thermos cup. I'm in a terrible quandary. I drink it and hope I won't die.

"Thank you, ma'am," I sputter. I realize I can't shake the "ma'am" thing just yet. It just keeps coming out.

"Would you like a cup of coffee?" Ruth asks.

There's something strange about the way she asks me this. She's definitely looking for a specific answer. At least it's a yes/no answer. I have a fifty-fifty chance here. Although it doesn't really matter, because I can't possibly stop coughing long enough to actually drink a cup of coffee, even if I wanted one.

"No, but you go ahead," I say, gasping for air.

"Chloe, before we get started, I'd like to ask you something . . . off the record."

"Anything at all. Ask away." I'm this close to calling her "Your Highness."

"If I were to ask you, for argument's sake, if you would get me a cup of coffee; what would you say?"

Okay, now I get it. She wanted a cup of coffee but she didn't want to be the only one. I can read her like a book.

"I'd say, 'Yes, of course, and . . . um . . . how do you take it?' "

She's shifting around in her seat. I'm almost positive that my answer was not only correct but also very thorough.

I wonder if I will call everyone ma'am from now on.

"Anyway, Chloe, the truth is, résumés bore me. I'm more of a people person. I like to look someone straight in the eye to evaluate them."

I can't help wondering how that would be possible, what with me all the way down here and off to the side, but I'm relieved that she won't see the part on my résumé that had me enrolled in medical and law school at the same time.

"Chloe, a piece of paper is meaningless. This whole résumé could be a pack of lies for all I care."

I try to look confused by that statement to entertain myself. She has no idea what kind of facial expressions I'm making. I could morph into a jellyfish, which isn't really that far-fetched, and she would have no way of knowing.

Oh, look, Ruth is standing up. She's getting up to shut the door. What a cute skirt! It's black wool gabardine with one-inch pleats all the way around. She's moving away from her desk. Oh my God, it's way too short on her! It's practically a tutu, and she's got a huge run in her stocking. A skirt with that many tiny pleats shouldn't be a mini. Everyone knows that. What's going on here?

Should I tell her about the run?

It's the kind with the big oblong hole and the millions of horizontal lines from there down. I never know if it's better to tell someone or to pretend that you didn't notice. How could I let her walk around like that all day? On the other hand, we're not really friends yet. I'll just look at her feet instead.

Oh, look at that. I think that might be an Easy Spirit shoe on her foot. It certainly looks like the ones I've seen on TV. There's really no way to be sure though, and I shouldn't be jumping to conclusions.

She's sort of half looking for her other shoe now—the one she kicked off while I was trying not to pass gas in her office.

There, she found it. There's no denying it now. My glamorous childhood-fantasy dream boss is now wearing a complete set of sensible shoes on purpose. I'm sure that we have plenty of other things in common. I mean you can't judge a boss by her shoes. I hope I don't start crying over this. My eyes are starting to burn. That would be hard to explain, wouldn't it? I couldn't very well say, "Please excuse me for crying in the middle of this interview, Ruth. It's just that those are the most horrible shoes I've ever seen in my entire life, and one of the main reasons that I've wanted to work here, ever since I was seven years old (besides the whole *Funny Face* thing) is that I have a sick obsession with shoes. I always thought that I'd have the kind of boss who wore the kind of shoes that I would look up to and admire."

She definitely senses that I've been staring at her shoes and that they are upsetting me.

Now she's looking at them to see what I'm looking at.

Say something. Quick! Tell her you think she stepped in gum.

"Those shoes look *so* comfortable. Don't you just love that commercial? 'It's like you're walking on air.' Isn't that what they say on TV? Those *are* Easy Spirits, aren't they? I've never seen a pair up close, but I have a certain knack for identifying shoe designers and manufacturers. It's not exactly a talent per se, it's more of a hobby."

I can fix this.

"You know, I would just love to try on your Easy Spirits. My feet are killing me, but then again, I doubt we have the same size shoe."

Bingo! I just offered to try on her shoes and I told her that she has big feet at the same time.

Why must I insist on talking to people?

"These are orthopedic Easy Spirits, Chloe. I have bunions."

"That's terrible. I'm so sorry," I say as sympathetically as possible, trying not to laugh now. The word *bunion* always cracks me up. Always has.

I'm like an emotional seesaw in this room. I wonder which is considered worse: Laughing at someone's foot problems or crying over their shoes?

"Now, Chloe, we actually have two positions open here at *Issues*. I need to check my records to see which job Human Resources sent you to interview for."

I can't believe it. She's considering me for an even higher position than the one I originally came in for. I did spot *those Easy Spirits, in what, two seconds?*

I should have written something about shoes on my résumé. I can always make something up later. She's certainly not a stickler for details.

"Well, I *was* interviewing for the editorial position," I say. I'm about to tell her that I realize I'm the wrong age for that job, but she interrupts me.

"Receptionist or assistant to the assistant?"

What?

"The editorial assistant position," I answer, a little more emphatically this time.

"No, I'm afraid you're mistaken."

"I am?"

"Yes, this is the promotion department."

I'm getting promoted? Is it me, or is she talking in complete circles?

"We create sales support material on this floor."

Sales support material? Hmmm. That's got to be some kind of Lycra. They make stuff here?

"We are business people, not editorial people. Who told you this was an editorial position?"

"Personnel?" I whisper, trying to remember if I was supposed to have gotten off on the seventh floor.

"That's odd. I distinctly sent a memo to personnel stating that there was an opening in the promotion department. Are you interested in promotions at all? If not, what type of work *do* you see yourself doing?"

I can't very well tell this woman that I had hoped to spend the rest of my life pointing at shoes on a table and that I've already been an assistant to my dad's secretary, every summer, since ninth grade, and that I was hoping for a real job this time—not like that job that lasted only nine minutes at *Little Missy* magazine.

I got fired in nine minutes. Can you believe that? I got fired all because I sat at my boss's desk for like one second—the very second she came right back into her office to get her coat, which I was trying on—for one second. I wasn't only trying on her coat when she walked in. I was also twirling around and around on her chair with my arms and legs out. It was a beautiful coat. It was pink cashmere with white fur lapels. I'd never seen anything like it in my life. Anyone would have tried it on. I really saw myself going places in that company. I never would have predicted the way that one turned out. To this day, I don't know whether she fired me for wearing her coat or for twirling.

Regardless of why I was fired, it was just ludicrous of me to write on my résumé that I'd worked there for nine years. From this point on, I will never lie again.

"Chloe, do you have any idea what it takes to run a promotion department?"

"Well, I have done quite a bit of research on promotion departments, in general, over the years, you know, just for fun, because I strongly believe that the . . . the um . . . pro . . . mo— *what the hell was that called?*—pro-mo-ti-a-tion*!* department is the backbone of any successful company."

Wow! That's more like it. Why can't I talk like that all the time? Backbone. That was a good one.

Ruth springs to her feet and looks somewhat in my direction. I can almost see her whole face now. I'm practically standing up, dodging my head back and forth, trying to catch her eye. No wonder she was hiding before. Her mustache is all red, and she only finished tweezing one eyebrow. I feel terrible. Maybe she was hoping the redness would subside while she was on the phone. I've got to help this woman. She should not be tweezing her mustache. She should be going for laser treatments. Does she even read the magazine she works for? A few months ago, the whole issue was devoted to hair removal. How could she have missed the article on mustaches? This poor woman works so hard, she doesn't even have time to read, and it seems as though I've antagonized her in some way. She's bending down and really looking hard at me now. Her mascara is clumpy. What the hell is this, some kind of a joke?

"Chloe, let's put our cards on the table, shall we? You're obviously here for a reason, so let's get down to business. Where do you see yourself in five years? Do you see yourself rising to a position, let's just say, such as mine? Is that what you're thinking, Chloe? Is that what you're hoping will happen? Are you thinking that perhaps you will start at the bottom and work your way up to the head of the department? Because that's perfectly understandable."

I think she suspects something. I wonder if I should just come clean and admit that I got out on the wrong floor and that I haven't got the slightest idea what her job is or what this department is for. I'll just say, *"Ruth, let me be perfectly honest, I got out of the elevator prematurely, and therefore, I do not know where I am. But I'd be happy to work for you, in the meantime, just to get my foot in the door."*

Now I'm making puns!

On the other hand, I don't want her to think that I don't want her job. I feel so sorry for her as it is. I just want to help her out so she'll have some free time to go shopping and get a makeover. I'm beginning to feel very close to Ruth. She obviously needs me, and somehow we found each other. It's fate. I think we both feel it.

"I guess I'm just looking for an opportunity to work hard and help my boss in any way I can. If I can make my boss look good, then I'll be happy knowing that I have accomplished something."

She's smiling at me, and she just whispered, "This might work," under her breath. I think Ruth likes me! I just want to jump up and put my arms around her and tell her to take the rest of the day off!

There's something digging into my lower back, so I have to sort of stand up and turn around to adjust my leather case. I shouldn't have brought it. There's nothing in it. I even forgot my brush.

I hate putting my back to Ruth while she's still whispering under her breath, but I'm in a lot of pain. As soon as I turn back around, I can see that Ruth's eyebrow is twitching.

She can't take her eyes off of me. I wonder if she's going to comment on the fact that I just stood up, out of the blue.

"Well, Chloe, I'd say you got the job! What do you have to say about that?"

"I don't know what to say. I'm so excited, I can hardly speak."

Ouch! There goes my stomach.

I'm in agony again. I'm gripping the desk to avoid running out of her office. She probably doesn't suspect that I'm experiencing severe cramps, or she would at least offer me an ambulance. There it goes. It's gone again. That was weird.

"One thing though; I'm just curious." I can hear myself speaking, but there's no way to prevent it at this point. "Why did you pick me?" I ask.

"That's a very good question, Chloe. I chose you, quite frankly, because I'm looking for an assistant's assistant who understands women and what we need to do to get ahead in the business world. *Issues* is a literary magazine, Chloe. It deals with women's issues."

Has this not been like an entire day of punnery?

"I need an assistant who won't hesitate to put her own needs aside to help me accomplish what I need to do. I also need an assistant who reflects the philosophy of this magazine. You even look like an *Issues* girl, Chloe. I'm sure that I can teach you how to sell our philosophy to our advertisers. *Issues* is all about what it means to be a woman—a woman who knows how to market herself to go out there and bring home her piece of the pie."

Pie?

She is standing up and talking to a spot on the wall far, far above my head. It's like she envisions a much larger audience than the very small, low-to-the-floor audience that she actually has. I think she loves this magazine even more than I do, and I have no idea what she's talking about. I thought *Issues* was a fashion magazine. I really did.

I wonder if I should let the people upstairs know that I've accepted a position elsewhere in the building.

"Those other girls I interviewed today were all wrong. They had the wrong attitude. Wrong, wrong, wrong!"

My God, they must have been terrible people for Ruth to be so badly affected by them. I bet those girls completely ignored Ruth, exactly the way the pink, polka-dotted girl ignored me out there.

"They think they are little know-it-alls, but they know nothing. Nothing! Those smug, bossy, little princesses; what do they think this is? A magazine where girls rule? Every single one of those girls flatly refused to get me so much as a lousy cup of coffee! They won't get anywhere in this world. I can tell you that. Do you have any idea how many cups of coffee I had to bring my boss when I first started out, Chloe?"

I want to say, "Somewhere between a thousand and ten thousand," but I'm terrible with numbers.

"This is a place where women work for women, Chloe. It's not a place where children tell women what they'll do and what they won't do. I know I can count on you, Chloe, just like our readers count on *Issues* every month to give them the support they need to get ahead."

I glance over at the July cover of *Issues,* on Ruth's desk, and read the main headline:

How to Go from a 34 B to a 34 C in Three Weeks with These Simple and Easy Exercises. Suddenly it all makes sense, and I understand what she is talking about. *Issues* is a magazine devoted to helping women enhance their appearance and increase their breast size so that they can get better jobs and, perhaps, if all goes well, take over the world!

I never thought about "women's issues" in quite this way. I always thought *Issues* was a place to find cute clothes and fun makeup. But it's so much more. It's practically a career magazine, and I've always dreamed of becoming a career girl. No wonder I've always loved *Issues.* Somewhere in the back of my mind, I must have sensed what it was all about.

"Chloe, women have always been undervalued in almost every area of their lives. They still receive fewer wages for doing the same jobs as men, and some see marriage as the only way to make a decent living. Most women don't even realize that men only use them until someone younger and cuter comes along."

She's yelling a little now. It's a good thing she shut the door.

"Many women have learned how to use their bodies and their looks to get what they want, and many of them have gotten way ahead of the rest of us by doing just that!"

"Wow," I say, "like how many girls?"

"There are statistics, Chloe, but that's not the point. The point is that some women get further than others, and I think it's unfair! I mean we all deserve a magazine that empowers us to go out there and get what we deserve! In your role as assistant's assistant, you will be helping a fellow woman get ahead, and that's something that should make you very proud. I know you will provide me with the right tools. I'm sure of it."

When she says "tools," does she want me to show her how to do the simple and easy exercises? They look pretty self-explanatory, but I'd be glad to help in any way I can.

"I also need an assistant's assistant who can learn my job well enough to walk in my shoes when I'm called away from my desk."

I hope she doesn't mean that literally.

"And yet, I have to be sure that she doesn't want to *live* in my shoes, if you know what I mean."

Oh my God. No problem!

"Chloe, I need a young woman I can kick around . . . ideas with . . . and mold into a promoter of what I like to call 'WOMEN'S WRITES.' That's W-R-I-T-E-S."

That's very catchy. If I remember nothing else Ruth said today, I should at least try to remember those two words. This place is just filled with people who love to play with words. After all, this is a literary magazine, as we all know.

Ruth is starting to get a funny look in her eye. She's leaning against the wall and she just slipped off her shoes again.

She's rubbing her feet together. I can see them right through her stockings. She wasn't kidding about those bunions, and it's no surprise that she has a run in her stockings. Her toenails are so long, they are ripping them to shreds. I don't know how much more of this I can take and she's not even close to wrapping up her speech about women's rights to writing or whatever the hell that catchy phrase was.

The funny thing is, and I hate to admit this—I've probably neglected to read the more "literary" articles in *Issues*. In fact, I'd venture to say that I've neglected to read all of the articles in *Issues*. I've always felt that a photograph is worth a thousand words, but I can see now that it is impossible to understand the philosophy behind *Issues* simply by looking at the pictures.

"Chloe, I'm sure you are looking at me and thinking, 'Now this is a woman who has it all. The great job, the great office, and, of course, the great clothes.' "

"Don't forget the most comfy shoes in the whole entire world," I chime in like a buffoon.

"But even *I* want more, Chloe. I need a little inspiration every now and then, and I need a girl, I mean, a woman, who will inspire me and excite me when I'm feeling listless and tired. I need a girl who will understand me and take care of my needs. And, of course, I don't mean that in a sexual way," she laughs.

Ew.

"I'm looking for a solid person, someone who is not afraid to disagree with me and yet someone who knows when to agree with me." She's talking directly to the wall again. Ruth must be accustomed to conversing with herself for hours on end.

I wonder if she's an only child.

"I want a woman with whom I can share my vision and who is also willing to share hers with me. Is this making sense to you, Chloe?"

"Absolutely!" I practically salute, wondering if Ruth is suggesting that we swap clothes on occasion. I start to look around her office and try to redecorate it in my mind, but she interrupts my train of thought.

"Chloe? Is it becoming clear why I didn't choose any of those other young women out there?"

"Absolutely," I say, thinking I should have said something else this time and that I might be getting another yeast infection. It's so hard for me to concentrate on her for any length of time.

Finally, Ruth sits back down at her desk. She offers me her fingertips, and says, "Chloe, I'll see you tomorrow morning at nine o'clock."

As I walk out the door, I turn back for a second, and there's Ruth, staring at the back of my skirt. I'm dying to ask her if I look fat, but instead I sort of bend one knee and say, "Tomorrow it is, Chloe!"

Oh my God. I called her Chloe.

My head is spinning. I can't believe I just got the job of my dreams in spite of the fact that I showed up for the wrong interview. And to think that all this time, I had no idea what *Issues* was really all about. If *Issues* is the empowering career manual that Ruth thinks it is, Zoe is going to be so proud of me. She loves manuals! I never dreamed I could land a job at a literary manual.

Zoe couldn't be more wrong about *Issues.* She always refers to it as inane. Inane is another one of those words that Zoe uses all the time, like *pseudo.* It also sounds like it means "psycho," but it doesn't. It means dumb.

I just hope my new job doesn't have anything to do with shipping and receiving. It sounds awfully similar. I'll be so disappointed if I'm going to have to separate and file invoices, like I've done at my father's office all of my life.

As I press the lobby button in the elevator, I can't help thinking that I might have accidentally curtseyed when I said good-bye in the hall. I keep playing that last good-bye over and over again in my head. I did dip down a bit, but it wasn't quite a bow. I might have been pulling at my skirt a little on each side, but it wasn't really a full curtsey. I know that everyone who was still seated in the reception area saw me do the dip, but there's no way I would ever walk back in there and ask any of those girls if it looked like an actual curtsey. I should just try to forget about it.

I hope I can make Ruth happy. It sounds like she wants an assistant who can practically do her job. Maybe I come across a lot more competent and responsible than I really am, in my lady shoes. Part of me is numb, but the other part feels like I just won the Miss America Pageant. I want to call Ruth and thank her or buy her a little gift. Maybe a nice, new, lump-free mascara.

As soon as I leave the *Issues* building, I feel even more elated. Out here in the real world, there's an excellent chance that someone will ask me where I work. Please let somebody ask me. I'd love to walk up to someone and ask them where they work first, just to get the ball rolling, but there's really no way to start a conversation like that on a sidewalk filled with people who are pushing one another.

I head toward the subway and run down the stairs to get a MetroCard. Once I get one, I run back up and hail a cab. I collect MetroCards regularly. I leave them all around the apartment so my sister will think I use public transportation, even though I take cabs everywhere. The one time I tried to use the subway, I ended up in Hoboken.

I hope this job leads to big things. If I do really well, there's always the possibility that I will one day get a promotion. I can just imagine them asking me what title I would prefer, and I'll say, very nonchalantly, of course, "I was thinking that shoe editor has a nice ring to it." Little will they know that I've dreamed of having that title my entire life. I've always wondered why magazines don't have shoe editors. What do they do; just pick the shoes out of a hat? Once I'm shoe editor, I might be asked to do some sort of government-related, shoe-buying project. For instance, someone might say, "Chloe, the president of the United States is going to France on Monday and he wants his wife to be wearing the right shoe. I'd like you to hop on a plane to Paris this weekend and pick out the perfect shoe for the First Lady, and while you're at it, pick up twenty or thirty pairs for yourself, too. God bless you, Chloe, and God bless America."

CHAPTER TWO

~

Never Curtsey in a Junglelike Setting

I rush toward my apartment door, fumbling with my key. I can't wait to tell Zoe that I got the job. When the door finally opens, there she is, kneeling with her hands in prayer, with smoke fumes emanating from her nose and mouth and just about every pore of her minuscule body. Her eyes are closed and her head is back. For some reason, whenever Zoe gets high, she thinks that if she sits in a yoga position, she's meditating, but she's not even close. She has no idea how to meditate. It's the kind of thing that neither of us will ever learn how to do. We're both way too distracted by what's actually going on here, on earth.

As soon as she sees me, she will forget what she's doing and jump up. She always does that. Even if I walk out of the room for two minutes, she'll get all excited when I come back. Sometimes, if she hasn't seen me for more than twenty-four hours, when I walk in the room, she claps. She tries to hide it, but clapping is clapping.

The sad thing is that she is only living with me temporarily until her boyfriend, Michael, finishes the series of seminars that he's giving at a bunch of business schools around the country. Michael went to Harvard, and Zoe went to Sarah Lawrence. I went to the Fashion Institute of Technology. It's funny. We all went to such technical schools.

There is a very good chance that Zoe and Michael will get married, particularly because they share this incredible knowledge of current events. They are both writers, and they both know everything, but sometimes I wonder how it will all work out. They are polar opposites in the political arena. Something like that wouldn't affect any of my relationships, but they watch the news every single day, and then they argue about it. Sometimes they bring up stuff that happened like thirty years ago and argue about that, too. As if something that happened thirty years ago has any bearing on our lives today.

Zoe writes for a magazine called *The Radical Mind,* and Michael wrote a book called *Our Moral Obligation to be Responsible, Successful Hunters.* I doubt it will be a best seller, but it will definitely get talked about in certain circles. Don't let the title fool you. It has nothing to do with hunting. It's a book about why it's important to be rich.

In the book, "hunter" means "person who makes money." There is absolutely no reason for anyone who knows Michael to bother reading it. He pretty much gives the whole thing away every time he talks. Even I have the whole book practically memorized without ever reading it. For instance: Michael believes, and I quote, "it is everyone's moral responsibility to hunt as much as they possibly can in order to stimulate the economy and restore faith in the integrity of our free enterprise system, which has been raped, pillaged and poisoned by an epidemic of greed, spawned by the promise of great, unearned wealth, created and subsequently destroyed by manipulative abusers of the stock market.

"These financial pirates have distorted the natural order and balance of our global economy, and this imbalance must now be corrected through mandatory high school business and ethics courses, stricter punishments for financial criminals, and radical sales tax reforms that would encourage massive, *responsible* hunting and spending."

Of all the books I have ever been forced to read in my lifetime, I'm sure this one is going to be the absolute worst. I'm especially not looking forward to the part where he supposedly goes on for about eighty pages about how "no two humans are created equal in the sense that all humans are predetermined to 'hunt' a certain amount and that it is inhumane and unnatural for the government to attempt to artificially even the score by overtaxing those who are genetically programmed to produce greater wealth." Of course he believes that all human beings should be given equal opportunities, but they will ultimately only hunt as much as they were genetically predisposed to hunt.

He loves to say, "You can tax the superior hunters from now until hell freezes over, but you can't stop them from bringing home the bacon." Michael believes that the moral equivalent of overtaxing the rich would be something like raising the bar for the highest Olympic jumper.

I can hear him in my sleep saying, "It is immoral to try to bind one man to the limits of another under the auspices of an 'equality' that cannot exist so long as each man, woman, and child is created as a unique individual."

However, he also believes that "once we restore our country's faith in our financial system of rewards, those non-contributing members of society who once felt that the odds of success were against them because the game was rigged by thieves will once again become active achievers, thereby reducing the need for social and welfare programs to extend their services to those individuals who had the ability to sustain themselves all along."

He's a very long-winded guy, and I seriously doubt that anyone understands what he's talking about, but for some reason, everything he says gets stuck in my head. Sometimes I just start reciting entire pages of his book without even realizing it. I didn't even memorize it on purpose. Like I said, I never even read it. It just got stuck in there, like the theme song from *Titanic*. I could be brushing my teeth, or something, and I'll start thinking, "Any attempt by underachievers to downgrade or punish an *honest* hunter for achieving 'too much' by calling him immoral, is no different than calling a mother who successfully goes out in search of worms with which to feed her babies an immoral bird."

I would never hurt Michael's feelings, but everyone already knows that it's wrong to be a sore loser. We learned that in preschool. I know he spent a lot of time writing his book, but I still think he should have written something with a plot.

I do think, however, that it was a very good idea to use worms as a metaphor for money, because no one would ever argue that it is immoral to search for worms. And, as far as I can see, there is nothing immoral about finding worms either. However, I do feel, on some level, that eating worms is both wrong and gross.

According to Michael, "Success is the ultimate moral achievement because successful people are not a burden to society." This is the part that drives Zoe wild. You should hear them go at it when she starts yelling stuff like, "Oh! So you're calling cripples immoral because they can't go out there and hunt?"

I never get involved in these discussions, but I'm always surprised that Michael never interrupts her by saying that most people don't really use the word *cripple* anymore. Zoe loves that word. She uses it a lot.

When Michael and Zoe's friends have parties, they don't just sit around getting drunk, telling idiotic jokes. They utilize their party time by splitting up into teams. I'm not exactly sure, but I think the teams consist of those who like the president and those who don't. My sister is always mad at the president. I don't know what's wrong with her. He's definitely the cutest one we've had so far.

I try not to be home when they all get together. I can't stand listening to Michael and Zoe argue about things that mean nothing in real life, like socioeconomics or the exact definition of morality. My sister is more the type to believe that morality and hunting (even in the figurative sense) should never be used in the same sentence. She'd much prefer it if the word *morality* were reserved exclusively for those unselfish individuals who devote their lives to feeding children in Somalia. Every time she brings that up, Michael says, "Feed them with what? It takes money to feed a country."

It's amazing to me that my sister finally met her match, but she still outtalks him nine times out of ten. Even when he has a better argument, he loses because he gets tired way before she does. Zoe has incredible verbal stamina.

I think Michael's theory is going to confuse a lot of people. Most of us don't think of the acquisition of wealth as a morality thing. I think the majority of people are more inclined to associate monetary success with ripping people off—especially those who haven't yet figured out how to make money the *responsible* way. But Michael is as adamant about "the destructive effects of corruption and greed" as he is about "the destructive effects of not making enough money." I know that for a fact because I also memorized the blurb that's supposed to go on the back cover. Sometimes I wonder if Michael voted in favor of the death penalty as a punishment for white-collar crime. Michael calls cheaters and underachievers "The Murderers of Society." (I would never confess this to Michael, but everyone I know, besides Zoe, cheated on their SATs.)

Michael has been called a modern-day Ayn Rand, and some people say that his theory is an oxymoron. I admit that he's boring, but I totally disagree with whoever it was that said that about him. He is *so* not a moron!

I read one Ayn Rand book in college. It was called *The Fountainblue* or something, but I can't remember exactly what it was about. I know that it was about this girl who was always working late and drinking coffee and that somehow in the book it was considered good to be selfish. I never finished it. I never even got to the part about the fountain.

I find it interesting that Michael is considered so controversial. He wrote a six-hundred-and-fifty-page book that boils down to two things: Couch potatoes and cheaters should be killed. What's so controversial about that?

I think, underneath it all, Michael and Zoe agree on everything, and that's what keeps them together. They both want to fix the world. They just can't agree on what's wrong with it or how to go about doing it.

Zoe was destined to find a group of friends, and a boyfriend, who know everything. It's the only way she can get her hands on a steady flow of unpleasant information so she can get upset about something that's beyond her control at least twice a day. Some of her favorite topics are the Middle East, people who wear fur, unfair elections, some accountant who lied at some big company, the entire health-care system, poor health in general, diamond mining, Russian people who own oil companies, certain types of fish, you name it.

My sister would be better off if she made all new friends. She's smart and everything, but there's a whole other girl who lives inside of her. That's the girl I really love. She's the one who starts flipping through the news channels looking for *I Love Lucy* reruns as soon as Michael leaves the room. That girl is my real sister. If you ask me, Zoe shouldn't be allowed to watch the news. All it does is make her cry.

The worst thing that ever happened to Zoe was when they almost legalized marijuana and then they changed their minds. She had about fifty arguments lined up in favor of legalization. That's all she talked about for months, even in public. Michael kept telling her to keep her voice down wherever we went.

Under normal circumstances, Zoe would be considered a huge pain in the ass when she gets fixated on something, but she's the size of an eleven year old. It's hard to take her seriously when she's mad, especially when she's wearing something I know she got from Gap Kids. Poor thing, she really loves pot.

The truth is, she's not nearly as worried about what's going wrong in the world as she is about me. One of her worst fears is that I will go broke. She constantly makes these long speeches about how the system is rigged to suck people like me into going into debt.

How could she think I would let something like that happen? I always have my credit cards to fall back on.

If she weren't so afraid that I would run out of money, she would realize how many years of her life she wasted by not going shopping with me. You should see her when I come home with stuff. The whole time she is telling me that I should take it all back, she's tossing out the tissue paper, trying to get to what's inside. I wish she would just give up this whole "trying to make the world a better place" thing. She can never just be a girl. Her life is so much work.

Her biggest job is protecting me from things that don't even bother me. She can't help it. She needs to be my big sister. Ever since we were little girls, she was always trying to save me. I'll never forget the time we were hanging out on the seesaw (me on the bottom, her on the top) and Zoe overheard some kid call me fat. I think it was pretty obvious why he said it. Zoe's feet never touched the ground once on that seesaw. She was an unusually small child. She probably only weighed about forty pounds at the time. As a fully grown adult, she only weighs about ninety pounds, and that's with a stomach full of plants.

I didn't hear him call me fat, but Zoe did, and she started crying. At first she wouldn't tell me why.

"What's the matter?" I yelled up to her about fifty or sixty times.

"You see that kid over there?" she finally yelled back.

"Yeah!" I answered, "the really cute one?" I must admit, I was a little boy crazy back then.

"He's not cute!" she hollered back. "He called you fat." (So much for him and I becoming a couple.)

"Yeah, so?" I answered.

"Well," she cried, "I didn't do anything about it."

"How could you?" I yelled. "You're ten feet in the air."

"I know," she said, "that's what I mean. I'm too little to be your big sister. Look at me!"

She had a point. You could hardly see her up there.

"You can help me in other ways," I told her.

That night, Zoe wrote a horror story about me and the kid who called me fat on the playground. I'd rather not repeat what went on between us, but let's just say there was some cannibalism involved, and in the end, I got even fatter, and the kid who called me fat didn't exist anymore, if that gives you any indication. That's how the "telling off people on paper" thing originally got started. She's been doing it ever since.

As soon as Zoe hears me come in the door, she yells, "You're home!"

And then I scream, "I got the job!"

She jumps up to hug me. Then she remembers that she is totally against *Issues* and everything that it stands for, so she tries to calm herself down a little, but then she starts jumping again. She's clasping her hands together. "You got it! You got it!" She's making up a little song about it and a pogolike dance (she's a lot more stoned than I thought), but the phone starts ringing, which snaps her out of it.

On her way to answer the phone, she says, "You're not going to use this job as an excuse to go on a mad shopping spree, are you?"

She already found a reason to worry about this. That took no time at all.

"That's ridiculous," I answer as I turn around to make a

mental list of everything I need. Then Zoe says something that I know can only mean that something terrible has happened. She says, "Oh man."

Oh man means trouble.

"Oh man, what?" I ask, not really wanting to know.

"Oh man, you got your period all over that brand-new skirt," Zoe says.

"I did? What do you mean?"

"I mean, either you've been shot or you got your period. There's blood all over that thing." Her hands are covering her mouth. We both hate blood.

"What thing?" I look down, but there's not a trace of anything that even resembles blood, not even a speck of red lint.

"Turn around and look in the mirror," she says. Now she's covering her eyes. I can only assume I've ruined my skirt. Meanwhile the phone is ringing like mad. She picks it up and says, "Hello? Hey! Me too . . . but can I call you right back?" and then slams it back down.

I walk to the full-length mirror in the bathroom and slowly turn around. It's like witnessing a murder.

"Who was on the phone?" I yell from the bathroom while continuing to check out the huge stain on the back of my skirt. It might just be the most awesome stain I've ever seen.

"It was Michael," she answers.

"Why didn't you talk to him?" I ask.

"Because you got your period, Chloe, and I can't talk to anybody, or function for that matter, until I figure out exactly at what point in your day that might have happened."

"Why? What difference does it make?" I ask, but then I quickly understand her concern. Did it happen *before* or *after* the interview? That is the question here, isn't it? I take off my skirt and stuff it into a baggie. Then I put the baggie into a su-permarket shopping bag, and then I put that bag in a nice shopping bag. I'll take it to a dry cleaner in another part of the world. I wrap a towel around my waist and turn on the shower and start retracing my steps, but I don't have to go very far.

I recite the following to her, aloud: "Let's see now, most of the girls in the waiting room sort of giggled when I said, 'After you' to the receptionist as she was leading the way into the interviewer's office, which is obviously not that funny, unless the person who said it has a giant period stain on the back of her skirt.

"After the mysterious giggling episode, and after my interview, I got up off my chair for a second and turned around to adjust my bag. When I turned back around, Ruth was blatantly staring at the bottom half of my body, which could be interpreted in a myriad of ways, unless she was just simply amazed by the amount of blood that was pouring out of me, without my knowledge. Clues, clues, clues, oh here's one; I had a horrible attack of stomach cramps while sitting in my new boss's office, which I've gotten every month of my life, since I was twelve, and there was a familiar, cold breeze wafting from my underpants, which I brilliantly mistook for a wave of happiness . . . just as I was walking into the interview. So I guess that clears everything up. Everyone saw."

Zoe walks into the bathroom and pushes me aside to kneel in front of the toilet. This is the kind of thing that will make her sick with grief. There's an excellent chance that she will throw up. I stay far away from the bathroom because I can't be anywhere near throw up. The thought of me being embarrassed is too much for Zoe. She still believes that it's her job to prevent things like this from happening to me. However, she can't really help me get over the fact that it *did* happen, because she is too busy dry heaving, so . . . I have to help her.

"Maybe the reason I got the job is because it's a company policy to only hire people who show up with a humiliating stain somewhere on their clothing."

No response. More dry heaving.

I try again: "If I didn't have that eye-catching splotch on the back of my skirt, then my new boss would have been staring at me for that *other* reason that girls look at each other. I'd much rather be embarrassed than have to deal with her having a crush on me," I call from the hallway.

More heaving.

Maybe she's really coming down with something.

"I want this job so badly, I'd probably end up marrying her and I'd make a terrible lesbian. You know how squeamish I am about body hair." That did it. She's up!

"Go call Michael back," I tell her.

She's still holding her head, but I can tell she feels better.

Michael would wait forever for Zoe to call him back. He's a really patient guy and extremely cute, in that dark, rumpled, brooding kind of way. He thinks it's so amazing that two sisters could be so completely different. He has no idea that we are almost exactly the same. It would never even occur to him that our names rhyme. Sometimes overly intelligent people are completely oblivious to even the most glaringly obvious rhymes.

I take a shower and wash my hair, trying to figure out what to wear tomorrow. I come out of the shower, put on my robe, and begin to comb out my hair.

I can hear my sister talking to Michael on the phone, mostly about some slanted news story and something about him coming back to New York early. I dread the thought of her moving out, but I know it's only a matter of time. I've never lived alone in the city, and I'm not looking forward to it.

I go to my closet and begin taking out a few things. I've mentally narrowed down my options to either a long black pleated skirt or a short black suede skirt, either to be worn with a short-sleeved black turtleneck or my new black suit with either a black crewneck bodysuit under it or a pinstriped, man-tailored shirt, or just a simple dress. I don't have a dress, so I cross that off the list.

I could forget the whole black-on-black thing and do really

pretty pastels. It's coming up on spring (in a few months) and I could wear something like a baby blue cashmere sweater, my wide-legged navy blue trousers with my new belt with the sterling silver buckle that I love, and my flowered Prada shoes, or I could wear my really short striped brown skirt and a cream T-shirt and that belt with the thick stitching, which I don't really like anymore. Although I could never make it a whole day in the brown boots that go with that outfit, and there's really no time to get a new pair between now and nine o'clock tomorrow morning. I never should have given up my search for brown boots.

I work the pile down to a height and width that allows me to move freely around the room. As I reach for my jewelry bag, the phone rings. It's my mom. She has a sixth sense about me picking out an outfit, and she will undoubtedly give me her opinion.

My mom is five feet eight, and she has recently been inducted into the "looks even better as a blonde" hall of fame. She has this sort of Asian look, which makes no sense at all, considering that we are Jewish. Her cheekbones are so high and prominent that they practically hit her in the eye. She is quite possibly the most beautiful woman on the planet. I'm not just saying that because she's my mom. You'd have to see her to understand. When she decided to go blonde, the combination of the exotic black eyes, the perfect teeth, and the impossible cheekbones put her over the edge. She can't even walk down the street without every head turning. I have to hook my arm through hers and rush her through a crowd while yelling obscenities just to keep her from getting accosted.

She has no idea that she has a devastating effect on people. But I do. When I introduce her to someone, I always feel like saying, "This is my mom; can you believe that?"

I worry about her a lot when she walks alone. She always walks down the street smiling, with her perfect posture, completely unaware of the fact that men are following her and women are subconsciously hoping she'll get struck by lightning. She just walks on, thinking her sweet, innocent thoughts. I can't even imagine what she thinks about. I know it can't be where she's going. She gets lost a lot. She is so spiritually connected to Zoe and me, even though we live thousands of miles away from her. I think she has this internal mental picture of where we are, at all times. If Zoe and I are walking down the street together, in Manhattan, and we make a left turn on Fifty-seventh Street, our mother will automatically make a left turn too, even if she's on Worth Avenue in Palm Beach at the time. I think it's some kind of hazy attempt to follow us, to make sure that we don't get hit by a car. She's always been very distracted by Zoe and me.

She once showed up at my school in a sports bra and panty hose because I forgot my lunch. She probably ran out of the house in a panic, convinced that I would starve to death without my tuna fish sandwich. She used to show up at my school half dressed all the time. My friends got used to it after a while. They'd just point to her out of the school window and say something like, "Oh look, here comes your mom, in a shower cap. She's got your mittens."

It's amazing that two standard, run-of-the mill people came out of that woman's womb. It's also a wonder how much I love her. Technically, I'm supposed to be mad at this woman. After all, she is my mother and God knows I didn't get her cheekbones. I try to get mad at her, but she's so nice to me.

She's equally attached to Zoe, but she keeps it a secret because Zoe is so *independent*. When Zoe moved to Italy for a year to study Italian and write, my mom secretly got an apartment there. No one knows that but me. Not even my dad. To this day, he thinks she was hiding from him because she got a face-lift.

Her preoccupation with Zoe and me leaves her very little time for her friends, but they understand. Most of her friends have known her since college, and they've never been able to relate to her anyway. She never wants to go out for lunch because the only food she really enjoys is pretzels, and she's no fun to shop with because she lives by two rules that just kill the whole experience. Rule Number One: She ignores all trends. She knows what looks good on her, and she doesn't deviate. She has no interest whatsoever in what's "in." According to my mother, "If it's 'in,' it's on its way out." Rule Number Two: She only wears one style shoe. One. She has the same shoe in twelve colors. It's the same Stuart Weitzman pump that she's been wearing since I was a little girl. She doesn't even buy them in a store. She orders them. She also has the same pair of slippers in eleven colors (some of them are doubles) and a butter-soft, suede-driving loafer, in nine colors. Remarkably, she owns a variety of sandals. For some reason, she has never settled on the one and only sandal that she will eventually buy in every color, for the rest of her life.

That shoe thing really bothers me. I would never buy the same shoe twice. Not if my life depended on it. Still, I love her, in spite of our differences.

"Hi, Mom."

"Hi, honey. What are you doing?"

She knows.

"Picking out an outfit to wear for the first day at my new job at . . . wait . . . try to guess . . . go ahead . . . you'll never guess it . . . but go ahead and try . . . and put Daddy on the phone."

"Don't tell me you got the job at *Issues?*" she squeals.

"You knew! How did you know?"

"Your sister told me. I called before, when you were still in the shower."

My dad cuts in because he's already on the phone. "Hi baby, congratulations!"

"Thanks, Daddy."

"Do you need any money?" He asks everyone in the family this same question all the time. I'm the only one who says, "Yes please!" every single time he asks, and I'm about to say, "Yes please!" right this very minute, but my mom is too excited.

"Tell me everything, absolutely everything," she says.

Any minute she's going to tell me exactly what I should wear tomorrow. I can feel it. She's just looking for an opening. She knows every article of clothing in my closet, even things I never showed her. I guess they come up in conversation somehow. She has a memory like a steel trap.

"Well, my boss, Ruth, seems really nice, but she talks a lot and she's got a bit of a mustache, but I really like her and I think the job is going to be great. Are you ready for this? I'm an assistant to the assistant in the promotiation department."

"Oh."

"Oh what?"

"What does that mean exactly? Assistant to the assistant in the promotiation department?"

"I have no idea."

"Well, I guess you'll find out tomorrow all about what an assistant to the assistant does. Come to think of it, what are you going to wear tomorrow?"

TOLD YA.

I list everything on my bed, but she's not biting. She already has something in mind. Something I already know I don't want to wear.

"Why don't you wear that little gray pleated flannel skirt and the ribbed short-sleeve gray turtleneck with that silver-and-pearl necklace that you got at Barney's, and the gray suede pumps with the tiny bow on the back of the heel and that new belt with the silver buckle?"

"I don't have a little gray pleated skirt or gray suede pumps with a tiny bow."

What is she talking about and how does she know about that necklace? I haven't even worn that yet.

"Yes, you do."

"No, I don't."

"Go look," she says.

I put the phone down and go back to my closet. I have no intention of wearing a gray flannel skirt that I don't even own, but my curiosity gets the best of me. I look in the bottom of my closet. I usually find a lot of great stuff hidden in the corners. There's my belt with the stitching that I hate. And look at that, a gray pleated flannel skirt! It's the cutest thing I've ever seen. When did I buy that? I could have worn that skirt so many times this fall, if I'd known I had it. And what's that over there? A shoebox . . . with gray suede pumps inside! I forgot all about these shoes! I'm running to the phone with the gray skirt, the suede shoes, and the box, but I probably won't wear any of this.

"I found the shoes and the skirt," I say, almost out of breath.

"Oh good! Wear that. It's perfect," she says.

"I don't know. I'm still deciding," I say.

In the meantime, my father has hung up, and I can hear my mom's other phone ringing. I know it's her interior designer. She won't answer the phone unless I give her the okay.

"Mom, I hear your other phone ringing. You might as well answer it because I have to finish getting ready for tomorrow anyway."

"Okay, honey. Call me tomorrow, promise?"

It's so funny the way she's always redecorating the house. She's redone my old room twice since I moved out. When my sister moves out, I'll probably go with a floral slipcover on my sofa. I've always loved florals, and I might do a Venetian plaster finish on the walls and wooden blinds instead of . . . oh, that's right, I have wooden blinds. *When did I get those?* I guess it's the color that I can't live with anymore. Anyway, there will be plenty of time to find ways to eliminate that patchouli smell that seems to have taken over.

I go back to my room and laugh to myself at my mom's suggestion to wear all gray on my first day. One color. *Night and day,* I smile to myself.

I wonder how I'd look as a blonde.

I try on everything on my bed until I feel weak and shaky and all out of ideas. I hear my sister coming in from the kitchen, so I throw everything in the closet, shut the door, and sit on my bed.

"Whatcha doin'?" she asks.

"Nothing. You?"

"Nothing." There's a silence.

She's suspicious. She senses an overblown clothing issue of some sort. Her head is motionless, but her eyes are searching for clues. She wants to help me, but I can't let her. I don't want to show up looking like Stevie Nicks on my first day.

She sits on my bed and says, "So tell me about this job of yours. What is your new boss like?"

"Well, it's hard to describe her. Her name is Ruth. She's really nice and she's really into the magazine. At first, I didn't think the interview was going so well, because she was on the phone and because I was in the wrong place and also because my chair was facing the wrong way. I never really saw her face until the very end. She definitely has an issue with facial hair, I'm sorry to say, but I'm just so happy she chose me." I stretch my arms and yawn a little, while Zoe listens intently.

"She interviewed a million other girls, and believe me, it was hard to tell us apart. Luckily, she didn't like any of them because none of them would even get her so much as a lousy cup of coffee. She asked me if I would get her one, 'for argument's sake,' and of course I said, 'Yes!' Oh, and, promise you won't repeat this, but I was so excited after she offered me the job, I think I curtseyed on the way out. What a day."

I'm yawning really loud now. I'll probably fall asleep mid-sentence.

"Anyway, she seems to think that the magazine is some sort of how-to guide for career girls, which is kind of weird. I never noticed that, did you? She thinks it empowers women to use their tools to go out there and get their piece of the pie, but I'm not sure what the tools are. For a while, I was so confused in her office; I actually thought tools were another word for big breasts. She really wants to get ahead, and she thinks I can help her! She even thinks I reflect the kind of girl who reads *Issues*. Let's see, what else did she say? Oh! She said that she wants to teach me how to do her job. She even asked me if I thought I wanted her job. Of course I didn't tell her, 'No way.' I would never insult anyone like that, even if they had the worst job in the entire world. Anyway, I think we really hit it off and. . ."

I am telling Zoe every single thing that I can remember about the interview, but I'm at that point where I can just barely hear a voice echoing in my head. I think it's mine, but I can't feel my mouth moving. I'm hanging on because I want to tell her about "a girl's right to writing" or whatever that catchy phrase was. I know she'll love that one, but I'm already fading away. I'm stringing together a series of unrelated thoughts and realize that I'm pretty much sleeping, but I can still see that familiar crease forming between my sister's eyebrows. I know that crease.

She's mad about something. Who hurt my feelings? What's the square root of my piece of pie. . . . She's rummaging around for a pen. . . . Who did it? Who called me fat? . . . Did I mention that my lifelong dream is to be shoe editor? It's a secret so . . . don't tell Zoe. If she continues creasing up her forehead like that, she's going to need botox. . . . She'll never do it . . . Botox is the ultimate anti-hippie drug . . . Are drugs herbs?

My alarm is ringing and I have no idea where I am. I look around. Oh right. This is my room and I HAVE A JOB! I want to have a nice relaxing morning getting ready, so I get up slowly and head to the kitchen to get a soda. On the way, I look into my sister's room. She is asleep, at her computer, using her keyboard as a little pillow. I pour myself a Diet Coke and bring it back with me to my bedroom. I put it on my nightstand and . . . there it is. The reason Zoe was up all night is on my nightstand. I take a sip of my soda. There are thirteen pages here. I can't read this now, but I can't not read it either.

Dear Chloe,

I realize that you are probably going to read this first thing in the morning, so I'll try to be brief. I know your dream has always been to work for a fashion magazine, and even though I think *Issues* leaves a lot to be desired, I'm still thrilled that you got the job and I am incredibly proud of you. However, there are some serious issues (hey, that's funny) that must be addressed immediately.

Otherwise, there is an excellent chance that you will be completely annihilated by your new boss before you even get settled in.

That's not very encouraging. I really wish she wouldn't say things like that.

On your first day of work, your new boss will appear to be a little angry with you. She will not look at you right away when you address her. She will wait just a few seconds, until you feel completely ignored, and then she will look up, feigning subtle surprise, as though she was so busy concentrating on something else, she didn't realize that there was a living, breathing, human being standing directly in front of her.

Later on, she will sit on your desk, while you are working, even if you have a little lunch bag there. She will sit right on it.

She will, once again, call you into her office while she is on the phone and repeat her performance of laughing and talking as if she hasn't the vaguest idea that you are spending yet another precious hour of your life waiting for her to get off the phone. The worst part is . . . there's no one on the other end.

Bossy Girl will look you over, raise her eyebrows and smirk. She won't be smirking because something funny happened; trust me. And she won't be raising her eyebrows because you did anything wrong either. What you will be witnessing is fear masquerading as disinterest and disapproval because the second you walk through her door, the power struggle begins. Of course you won't realize this because your mind doesn't work that way, but hers does. Yesterday, there was great potential for a power struggle, but you basically surrendered upon entering the room. A woman who uses the sentence "How would you feel about getting me a cup of coffee, for argument's sake?" as a recruitment tactic is making it very clear what she expects from you and your relationship.

In order for her to accept you, she must be reassured that you are one step behind her, in all areas, and that you are at least a little intimidated by her at all times. Since you already have her beat in all the key categories that her favorite magazine taught her are the most important, you are skating on thin ice. Every move you make could be potentially threatening to your career.

In Bossy Girl's mind, the workplace is a jungle, and it's every girl for herself. Survival vs. the threat of extinction is everything.

A girl who gets her period and then curtsies on the way out poses virtually no threat at all. I can honestly say that that was a brilliant career move, innocent as it was. Most people would never curtsey in a junglelike setting of any kind.

The other thing that you did right, without realizing it, is that you actually offered to remain invisible on her behalf. If she suspected for one minute that you have any career goals of your own, she would never have hired you. Don't you realize why none of those other girls got the job, Chloe? They stood up to her, and one by one, she kicked them out the door. You didn't stand up to her. That's why you got the job. But you *will* have to stand up to her in order to keep it. You will have to be prepared to think on your feet every minute of the day. If you keep your defenses up without letting on that you've figured out her strategy, you can easily overcome her.

Now I see what happened. Zoe got stoned again, after I fell asleep, and she got something that I said mixed up with something that she saw on TV. That could happen to anyone. It's almost like that time in fourth grade when we had the Winter Wonderland Poetry Reading Contest. I was so excited to read my poem aloud. After I read it, the teacher said that Emily Dickinson had already written that exact same poem.

I must have memorized Emily's poem instead of mine, by accident. I guess that's not exactly what happened to Zoe, but it reminds me of it. . . . I wonder if Private Benjamin *was on last night.*

One of the most important things to watch is your appearance. It will be monitored daily. Bossy Girl will begin each morning with a split-second assessment of your hair, your shoes, your lipstick, your eyebrow shape, any recent skin eruptions, your nails, the size and shape of your body, an overall height and weight estimate, and last but not least, she'll compile a mental inventory of everything you are wearing and holding. The results of this little morning survey will determine the risk factor you present for that day.

On the days that you wake up with a great idea and you can't wait to get to work to share it with Bossy Girl, make sure you dress professionally. When your outfit is complete, remove your belt and then replace it with the ugliest, brown, cracked, pleatherette thing you can find. Use an old suitcase shoulder strap if you don't have anything else. Make sure it's something that no one in her right mind would ever wear out of the house. Just don't tell Mom. She's never been out there in the trenches and she could never understand the importance of wearing the wrong belt to divert an attack. She'll only try to talk you out of it.

It *was* Private Benjamin!

The reason that Bossy Girl will be so focused on your looks is because she lives by the doctrine of that magazine she works for. One of the principal underlying themes of *Issues* is how women can use their looks to compete for attention and approval in the workplace (particularly male attention and approval). It practically teaches women to prostitute themselves to "get ahead."

I'm not saying that it's not important to be attractive and well-groomed, but an article extolling the virtues of breast implants in the "Your Brilliant Career" column, that's titled "Smart Girls Who Made It Big," is pretty self-explanatory.

Bossy Girl will be watching you to see if you are following the kind of marketing advice *Issues* dishes out each month. You must assure her that you adhere to an entirely different standard. Let me explain: If you wear a horribly dull, brown belt when she least expects it, Bossy Girl will immediately be forced to reevaluate your entire modus operandi.

This is an undeniable fact. She will be so distracted trying to figure you out, she won't have time to resent you or your bright ideas. Instead, she will be consumed with the thought that she misunderstood you all along and she will begin to reflect inward. This is very bad for her but very good for you.

When Bossy Girl reflects inward, the first thing she will see is an image of you staring at a wall, waiting for her to get off the phone with her imaginary friend. She will begin to wonder why she does these things to you. This is good. Try to keep her in this state of self-preoccupation as much as possible. As long as she's only half-listening to what you say, you have a much better chance of getting your ideas approved.

"How could I have deliberately sat on that poor girl's sandwich?" she will ask herself. "I knew the pita was toasted. I knew it would crack. That poor girl who doesn't even have a decent belt."

Not only are you temporarily off the threat list; you are now pitiful. At this point, you must continue to exercise extreme caution, particularly when opening your mouth. You never know who could be on her side. Everyone is guilty until proven innocent. Never say anything to anyone unless you are positive that you want it repeated.

Keep your mouth shut and your head planted firmly on your shoulders at all times. You never want to be out of control and say the wrong thing.

If that woman thinks that magazine is supposed to empower women, you're in big trouble. In her eyes, empowering women means empowering them against one another. That's what *Issues* is all about, Chloe. It seems to me that Bossy Girl thinks you are going to help her compete against the other women at that magazine because she intends to use what you "represent" to represent her. In effect, she plans to market herself in your image because she now owns you. In her eyes, you are nothing but a visual prop. Put it in her words, and you are, in fact, a tool. Sadly, she will eventually realize that it doesn't work that way.

She will undoubtedly use you on the front line to fight her battles, but she will never be able to train you to clear a path for her. On the contrary, she is more likely to find you attempting to help those around you instead of making sure they don't get in her way. This is not what she hired you to do, and she will never understand why you would risk doing it.

In fact, if she does see you wasting her valuable time helping out a coworker, she will somehow interpret your actions as an opportunity to help yourself. That's all she knows. Nothing else makes sense to her. My advice is this: When you find yourself being helpful, try not to get caught.

Eventually, Bossy Girl will realize that you actually make her feel worse about herself than she did before she hired you because you represent something that is not only unfamiliar but unattainable. Inconceivable as it is to her, your "look" is not what will inevitably make you valuable to that magazine. It's the stuff that you can't help thinking about day and night that will prove to be your greatest asset. You belong there because you are legitimately interested in what that magazine was originally intended to be.

I can only assume that *Issues* was initially supposed to be about helping women look and feel good. I'm sure it was never intended to be a how-to-sleep-your-way-to-the-top manual. You'll be fine as long as you stay true to yourself and the things you truly love.

If there had been more people like you around to keep the magazine on track from the beginning, it never would have become the shallow, mind-numbing piece of garbage that it is today.

Apparently Zoe hasn't been reading the more literary articles either.

Bossy Girl can't help but think everything is about looks and competition. She's been brainwashed. But she's wrong. Beauty is the icing. It's not the cake. Since you will never be able to convince her of this, I'm afraid that you are going to have to even the score, so to speak. Here's what you'll need to do: Let's say, for example, that you are sitting at your desk and it suddenly occurs to you how to turn *Issues* into a magazine that actually teaches women how to understand one another and learn to work together, to get ahead, instead of against one another. You are just dying to tell Bossy Girl how this new direction for the magazine translates into a new strategy to sell advertising.

I wish she would just call her Ruth.

You get dressed and you know you look great and you just refuse to mess it up, on purpose, with an ugly belt. You had six cups of coffee and you feel like you could kick all three of Charlie's Angels' asses.

I don't even like coffee.

You hop in a cab, walk into work, whip off your scarf, and head right for her office. (By the way; you can stop buying MetroCards and leaving them all over the place. No one ever said the subway makes sense for *every* occasion!)

What is she? An FBI agent?

There she is, all hunched over, applying that gloppy mascara, and you go right ahead and spell out your new vision for the magazine. You blurt out everything. The way the magazine plays into female insecurities and stereotypes, the way advertisers can potentially tap into millions of readers if they reach out to a more sophisticated and intelligent audience, the whole thing. You tell her that you were going to save the idea and announce it to the whole company, but you decided to tell her first. Can you imagine doing something like that, Chloe?

I can't even imagine thinking of something like that, but if I did, I'd sure want to alert someone.

I hope not. Because if you ever try anything like that, you will have just committed career suicide. Bossy Girl would never let you look that good or that smart in front of the whole company.

When she says you're working for her, she means you're working for her to look smart in front of the whole company. You were hired to assist her and that's it. It's not about you. In her eyes, you exist for her. Never forget that. She has every right to hire someone for that purpose. Unfortunately for her, she made the mistake of hiring someone who has her own agenda. Just don't ever let her know that.

What agenda? . . . Oh my God! I bet Zoe thinks my new leather portfolio is a Filofax. Come to think of it, I could use one of those, too.

Now, if you do blurt out a great idea, by accident, here's what you'll need to do: Go back to your desk and pretend that you got a call from your doctor with terrible news. Tell her that you might have a disease. Don't say that it was your gynecologist who called, because then she will think it's a sexually transmitted disease, and in that case, she won't feel even a tiny bit sorry for you.

Bossy Girl would kill for a sexually transmitted anything.

If Bossy Girl asks you why you look stunned, tell her that you can't talk about it with her because you are too depressed. Then tell her that you will try not to let it affect your work because the last thing you want to do is let her down. Try to irritate the bottom of your nose so it looks like you were crying and then . . . here's the clincher: the very next day, you will have to show up for work with slightly greasy hair. I know this sounds odd, but believe me, I've given this a lot of thought. Just be careful. If your hair is too dirty, you will scare her and she might send you home and call in a temp. If it's just a little dirty, you can make the comeback of a lifetime.

Once again, she will be forced to rethink everything. You are human after all and vulnerable to disease and yes, at times, unkempt. She might even take you under her wing and give you something of hers that she never wears anymore, like a broken pin or a smelly, stained pashmina.

This has got to be the worst advice I've ever heard. She's blatantly encouraging me to lie when she knows damn well I'm trying to quit.

Once you are safe, continue to proceed cautiously and stay on course. You went from threatening to pitiful, then back to threatening, and now you are a virtual charity case.

Eventually, you will have to make up another lie about how the disease turned out to be a lot less serious than you thought, but still, you live in fear. From that point on, your skirts have to be at least two inches longer and your heels at least one inch shorter than hers at all times, or it will be day one all over again.

I can do the skirt but the heels are out of the question.

Be extra careful with the shoes. I can't stress this enough. A woman with bunions the size of fully matured testicles does not want to see you in a different pair of high heels every single day. Go easy on the shoes, Chloe; I'm begging you. She wants to use you to dissect the elements of style, but she doesn't want it rubbed in her face. I know you won't believe what I am about to say but . . . we might need to go shoe shopping. I looked through all of your stuff while you were sleeping, and there's not even one pair of shoes that won't make her feel bad, except for those gray suede pumps with the little bow. Those are perfect. When did you get those? You should definitely wear them on your first day.

And remember, try not to look too cheerful when you first walk in. Play everything down. Go neutral. I know this hurts, but it must be done. You must survive her in order to get to the next step. Tormenting her with stilettos will not get you where you want to go. The idea is to get around her without going into direct combat.

Maybe it was Patton.

Now, let's get back to the notion that all girls exist to compete for male attention. This is what we call a no-win situation because careerwise, you're damned if you do and damned if you don't. At some point, there may very well be a male whose attention you will need to get, in order to have your ideas heard. Bossy Girl will be on the lookout for this. Not to worry. Like all no-win situations, this battle can also be won.

All you have to do is avoid glancing at any and all cute male body parts, in the entire building, at all times. Here's how it's done: When you talk to a male coworker, particularly one who is in a position to have an influence on her or your career, focus on his shoulder (just pick one) or any spot in the air, just to the left of him. If you overhear him say to Bossy Girl, "Gee, I didn't realize that your assistant has strabismus," let it go. Remember your goals. No matter how adorable he is, you are still better off if she thinks that he thinks you have a dysfunctional eye.

One other thing, you may not laugh at any jokes that any male tells you, under any circumstances, particularly if she is watching or within hearing distance—even if he writes cartoons. No matter what he says, you just bite your inner lip and say, "That's funny, that's really very, very funny."

Your shoulders can bounce up and down a little, but no noise can come out at all—even if he's wearing a fake nose. No matter how you look at it, if you laugh, you flirted; if you flirted, you failed. If a tiny giggle does slip out, you can still rebound by looking at Bossy Girl and immediately rolling your eyes, as though you think the guy is a complete bore, but you were just trying to be polite.

This may seem like you are insulting him, but as long as she feels confident that you are not trying to win anyone over, she'll deal with the fact that you can be a little bitchy at times. It will just reinforce her suspicion that you are still young and naive. If, by some chance, you do end up falling for some guy at work, make sure he's worth losing your job over—just in case. Although, I doubt you would ever fool around just for the hell of it anyway. There are very few slut genes in our family, and it's a lot easier to get what you want out of life when you admit what you're not. The truth is a much shorter path.

She's right about this one. Fooling around "just for the hell of it" never works out for me. I don't even get it.

And another thing; try to remember to compliment her at least twice a week. Every day is obvious and it will make you both look bad. You might want to keep a little log. Never use, "Wow! Did you lose weight?" as one of the compliments. It implies that she needed to lose a few, no matter how you look at it.

When you dine with her, always let her take the lead. Never order or eat first. If you suspect that she is on a diet, order exactly what she orders and eat a tiny bit more than her. If you order a cheeseburger and French fries, then she will hate you for eating whatever you want and not getting fat. If you order something less fattening than she ordered, then you are a better dieter than her and you just made her feel weak. If she's a sloppy eater, try to lodge something between your teeth.

Next: Always have extra stuff in your desk. You agreed to support her in every way possible, so that's what you'll do. Stock up on: cigarettes (only if she smokes—tell her you are trying to quit), panty hose, nail polish, and plenty of gum or breath mints, but they can't say the word "breath" anywhere on the package.

She hired you for a certain job and you are going to do it. In the meantime, we'll plan your escape.

* * *

It's very hard to tell when Zoe is kidding around. Sometimes, when she is very upset, her sense of humor confuses me. In this case, I think she may have accidentally slipped an enormous wad of acid under her tongue.

Remember, by virtue of your subordinate position, you are in control here. Bossy Girl is subconsciously questioning how you judge her at all times. All Bossy Girls secretly want to be liked by their assistants. They just don't know it. Give her the impression that you admire her. And never let her smell your ambition. It's a scent she has learned to associate with danger.

What ambition? What is she talking about? I never told Zoe about my shoe editor idea. I'm keeping that one a secret until the day I die.

Her biggest fear is that you will pass her, or worse yet, replace her. Your objective is to reduce her fear. That's why you might be forced to make a lateral move first.

Where does she pick up this army lingo?

Let her use you all she wants for now. You'll have your day. Just play the game for now and keep a copy of every project you work on. Remember that. If it's your work, it goes in your portfolio.

My new Filofax or the portfolio I already have?

The advice I just gave you will serve as a one-year battle plan. This is the year that will challenge your tenacity, your ability to overcome obstacles and stay positive in the face of defeat. I love you and have a nice day.

Love,
Zoe

It's becoming more and more apparent that my sister has a bit of a mental problem. It's not even funny anymore. She's starting to scare me. Zoe can't possibly understand Ruth. You have to see her, in person, to realize how sad she is and how desperately she needs me. And I don't care if she wants me to succeed or not, I just want to live my dream, for as long as I can. I want to be that grown-up girl I fantasized about my whole life. I can't go back to living vicariously through the lives of TV and movie stars who have been dead for hundreds, maybe even thousands, of years. I need to prove to myself that I can work with actual people. I'm tired of throwing my pocketbook up in the air, in lieu of a hat, pretending that I'm Mary Richards after another exciting day in the newsroom. I finally have a real job. And as God as my witness, I will find out exactly what it is.

CHAPTER THREE

~

The Second You Walk Through Her Door, the Power Struggle Begins

If this taxi makes the next light, I'm going to arrive at precisely nine o'clock, which is exactly the time Ruth predicted!

"I'll see you at nine o'clock," she said, not even knowing if there would be traffic or what time I planned to leave my house or anything at all about my regular morning routine.

I look so professional in this all-gray ensemble. Even my ponytail came out right, which it almost never does. I think Ruth is really going to love my practical, no-nonsense approach to clothes. I look like the kind of girl who's not afraid to get her hands dirty, a girl with a solid work ethic. Just look at me in my gray panty hose, gray shoes, gray skirt, and gray turtleneck. That's an awful lot of gray, isn't it? The only remarkable thing about this entire outfit is that I could walk all day in these gray shoes and there would be no pain involved. Painless gray shoes; who thinks of these things?

The only problem with my outfit is this navy pea coat. I thought it would add a little something to the all-gray look, but I can't move in it. I can't even scratch my nose. I bought it over the summer, and I must have tried it on over a T-shirt.

It's really a full size too small. I should have gotten at least a size six or an eight in a winter coat. Whenever I buy a coat in the summer, I always forget to allow room for a thick sweater. I tend to live a little too "in the moment" in shopping situations.

I wonder what size this is. It's really hurting me. If I could just squeeze my arm out of this sleeve, I could take a peek. Oh, here we go. Size zero! That can't be right. Maybe I bought it for Zoe. Of course—that's it! I can almost remember thinking that Zoe would love a little blue sailor coat. I'm trying to get it back on now, but it's almost impossible, and I think the driver is slowing down at this green light. Why do people do that?

"Excuse me, sir? Can you try to make this light? I normally wouldn't say anything, but today is my first day of work and I don't want to be late."

As I am saying these words, it suddenly dawns on me that this is a perfect opportunity to tell someone who is not a member of my family where I work. I'll ask him first.

"So, um . . . sir? Where exactly do *you* work?" I'm easing in. I don't want to brag. It's not bragging if it comes up casually in conversation.

"Where do I what?" he asks.

"I said, 'Where do *you* work?' "

Clearly, he's not paying attention to the road or me.

"Lemme tell ya sumpin' sweethot. I been drivin' dis cab fa ova twenny yeahs. I know dis city like da back a my hand. Sometimes I don't even stop long enough to take a piss and I got a chronic bladda infection that's chewin' up my kidneys. I put a kid tru college doin' dis job, and balee me, dair was plenty a udda tings I couldda done. Dis is honest woik and I got nuttin' a be ashamed of . . . nuttin'. Does dat ansa ya question?"

"Wow! Twenty years! And what did you say the name of the *company* was? What I mean is, where do you actually park the cab when you are not driving it? Isn't there an office/garage type of place where you and all of the other taxicab drivers meet at the end of the day, like on that show with Tony from *Who's the Boss?* What was the name of that show? It's a one-word name. Wait, it's on the tip of my tongue. I used to watch that show all the time . . . *The Cabbie Driver?* . . . No . . . *The Driver of the Cab?* . . . No . . . *The Taxi Driver Cab Show!* . . . Hold on, it's coming to me. . . . It was a very short name, something like . . . *Louie!* No, that's not it either."

"I know dis may come as a shock ta ya, miss, but I'm a real live cab driva. I own dis cab and da name a dat show was *Taxi* . . . fa cryin' out loud."

"I know," I say.

Now he's turned himself around and he's just sort of staring at me. He's probably wondering why I wore this tiny coat. Is he going to say something or just stare at me until he's absolutely certain that I won't ask any more personal questions?

We can't just sit here like a couple of statues. I was only trying to make conversation. Someone has to interrupt this awkward silence.

"Sorry for asking," I mutter.

"Lady, what da hell is wrong witch you?"

"What's wrong with *me*?" I protest. "You're the one who obviously got up on the wrong side of the bed this morning," I say. He's holding his head like he just can't win.

I glance out of my window and realize that we've arrived at the *Issues* building and this man would simply like me to pay him and get out of his cab. I hand him six dollars and step on the sidewalk. Before I walk away, I call to him through the open window on the passenger side, "I'll be right on time for my new job at *Issues*!" while pointing directly at the building with my entire arm. I'm bending my elbow slightly, so my coat won't rip.

"Is dat right?" he yells back. "Dat's fuckin' fantastic. Good luck."

Look at that. He turned out to be very sweet. That Bugs Bunny accent really had me fooled there for a minute.

As soon as I step foot in the lobby, my stomach starts to flip out from excitement. Everything about this building is thrilling. I look around for a minute just to remind myself that I'm not imagining this. I am really here. This is a real magazine and I'm about to start my real job.

If someone came up to me right now and said, "Chloe, you have two choices. You can stay here and work for *Issues* for the rest of your life or you can win lotto," I wouldn't even hesitate. Who cares about a dumb bingo game? I even love the little newsstand/candy store in this building. Look at all these magazines. These big, glossy ones are obviously European. The cover models are practically life-size. And look at all this candy! I wish I'd had time for breakfast this morning. My stomach is growling. I'll never make it to lunch unless I have a little bite to eat, but it's already after nine. I'll just grab something quickly, something light.

"Can I have a bag of M&M's please? Yes, and a bag of Skittles and that big bag of Twizzlers?" I thank the cashier and smile. I want to compliment her on the impressive selection of sugar-free items, but there will be plenty of time for us to get to know one another and there's a little crowd of beautiful people right behind me, waiting for me to pay. The crowd consists of one cute guy surrounded by two blondes and a sort of brunette who looks like she is on the verge of going blonde.

She's still in the heavily highlighted stage, but she hasn't lightened her base color yet. It's just a matter of time. The cute guy is holding about fifty packs of gum. I guess he's treating them all. They all keep saying, "Thankstan," as though *thanks* and *Stan* are one word.

As I turn to walk away with my candy, the cute guy steps out of the crowd and asks me, "Is that your breakfast?"

I look behind me to see if he's talking to someone else.

"I'm talking to you," he says, right to me.

"Oh, no, of course not. This is for my . . . um . . . for a little birthday celebration I'm having later for some of my friends in my office."

"Oh really? Wow. It looks like it's going to be a fun party. Will there be music and dancing as well as candy?"

He knows I'm lying. I wonder why his mother named him Stanley. Maybe she thought it was funny.

I smile at him and walk away. As a rule, I try to eat as much candy as I possibly can. I heard somewhere that candy is a highly effective appetite suppressant.

I walk to the elevator and press Up. I get in and press Six. I'm alone in here, so I take a good, long look at myself in the elevator mirror. I should have known I'd look drab in gray. Everyone looks drab in gray. Why do they even make gray clothes?

Ding!

I quickly step out of the elevator and head directly toward the door, which is being held open by a little rubber wedge today.

Oh look, there's Ruth!

For some reason, Ruth has dressed herself up in a little plaid skirt and matching red suspenders. And she's wearing a very short T-shirt. She looks like a giant toddler who just had lunch. I can't believe she is standing right in front of me with her stomach showing. Her stomach shouldn't be showing. It's . . . um . . . fat. And her lipstick is smeared. I hope I don't have that *What Ever Happened to Baby Jane?* nightmare again. I used to have that dream every time my Aunt Dottie came to stay with us.

Aunt Dottie used to parade around our house wearing red lipstick all over her lips and teeth and a see-through nightgown. Hers was the first vagina I ever saw, and it made me sick to my stomach. I prayed to God every night that mine wouldn't end up looking like Aunt Dottie's. But praying is useless. Trust me. Mine looks exactly like hers.

"Good morning, Chloe," Ruth says, glancing down at her watch.

What a cute red band!

She's walking away already. Where is she going? I'm following her, but it's hard to keep up. She's got quite a stride. Ruth is a surprisingly large woman up close. I really have to jog to keep up. My licorice is flopping from side to side.

"Ruth! Hi! How are you?" I call from behind her. "Twizzler?"

"No, thank you. I'd rather not look at anything like that at this hour. I'll show you to your office," she says, without turning around. I'm running at a pretty good clip now, but she's still way ahead of me.

As we scurry to my office, Ruth keeps checking her watch. It probably wasn't working when she put it on this morning, but who could resist wearing a red band with a red plaid kilt! I feel like telling her that I understand, from a fashion point of view, why she purposely wore a watch that no longer tells time. I mean, my God, we've all done it. There's nothing to be ashamed of. She's so nervous. I'll just put her at ease.

"From now on, we should probably call each other in the morning to make sure at least one of us plans to wear a watch that works. I bet you are a lot like me when it comes to stuff like that. But don't worry. I'm sure we'll figure out a million and one ways to help each other out."

She's probably not a morning person.

"Well, Chloe, this is home. Unpack your things and I'll see you in my office as soon as you're settled."

Where am I supposed to hang my little coat? There's not even a door in this, um, hall area. I don't mind keeping my lunch and my handbag on my lap, but there isn't even a place for me to sit down. At least I have two little desks. I can always use two desks. I'll use one for work-related items and one for personal belongings. This coat might even fit in one of these little drawers.

I look around for a while, wondering how I could spruce up the place. I guess it would be impractical to hang anything of value on these removable walls, but a tiny area rug might work.

"Chloe, I'm waiting," Ruth calls from her office. Ruth's office is right behind mine. If I put my back to my desk and her door is open, I can see her sitting in there.

"Here I am. Sorry. I was just trying to figure out where I could put my things in my, um . . . area," I say, rushing into her office.

"I know it's tight, Chloe, but we have a coat closet in the hall, and a maintenance person is on his way down with your chair. You'll get used to it soon enough. Fortunately, your office mate won't be starting for another two weeks. You'll have the whole cubicle to yourself while you're getting acclimated."

I have to share my hall area?

Ruth has her hands folded on her desk so I fold mine, too.

"Let's get started before we lose any more time," Ruth says. She's talking to her papers again, but at least the little, low-to-the-ground chair is facing her desk today. I can look right up at her without twisting my neck.

Someone must have taken the legs off of this chair. Or maybe it's just a big step stool.

"I'm not sure how they do things at *Little Missy,* but here at *Issues,* we customize our selling materials to appeal to specific advertisers. For instance, look at this piece here."

Ruth is holding up a black folder. It doesn't have a little picture on it or anything. It's just a folder printed with columns of words. It looks like a newspaper. And as far as I can see, it's not even written in English. Between you and me, it's pretty pathetic, as folders go.

"This is a piece that we'll be using to entice advertisers of book-related products to take space in our annual book review issue. We frequently review books, but we do one issue every year that is devoted almost entirely to the literary scene and the current 'it girl,' as they say. In our book review issue, the editors focus primarily on contemporary fiction. They typically feature novels that center around the lives of girls in their late twenties, who are juggling their careers and their love lives. Nothing earth shattering, just your basic Chick Lit," she explains.

"Chick, as in chicken?" I ask bravely. There's nothing like overcoming the fear of asking asinine questions.

"No, 'chick' as in young woman," Ruth responds. She's looking at me like she's not sure if I'm serious. I could make a little joke, but it's not really worth it.

I should have been paying attention. She lost me when she said "it girl." I started thinking about Cousin It and then Grandpa and then Uncle Fester. I kept mixing up the Addams Family with The Munsters, and I couldn't get back on track after that.

"You see, Chloe, with this piece, we appeal to book-related advertisers by creating the image that we are newsy, informative, and literary. That's why we designed this intelligent-looking folder. Our sales force will use a piece like this to approach advertisers who sell books, journals, leather goods, briefcases, luxury pens, anything that would appeal to girls who read."

"I'm sorry, but I don't think I understand. Isn't it obvious that all of our readers know how to read, and in what way does that folder indicate that we are newsy?" I realize that this is a two-part question, but I think Ruth gets where I'm going with this. I feel so relaxed. Ruth is a wonderful teacher.

"When I said, 'girls who read,' I was referring to young women who frequently read for pleasure. And this folder certainly does indicate that we are newsy. It was specifically designed *not* to look like a selling piece. We purposely used this fact-reporting format to prove that we are information-driven. Anyone can easily see that this is a very bookish-looking folder. If one of our salespeople told us that they needed a selling tool to bring to a potential shoe advertiser, then we would create something more. . . . "

"Shoeish?" I offer.

"It's really very complicated and I don't expect you to catch on right away. There are many factors that play into an advertiser's decision to go with one magazine over another, but let's talk about the benefits of advertising, in general, for a minute.

"Try to think of it this way: Every month we feature stories about young, successful career women. In doing so, we are, in effect, teaching our reader what she needs to do to become the kind of woman she sees in our pages. Sometimes our editors will recommend a particular product as part of the educational process. They might suggest a new, long-lasting mascara for an interview or a certain style skirt or low-maintenance fabric for a business trip.

"Our potential advertisers, the people who sell skirts and mascara, would love to have their products recommended by our magazine editors, but we, the salespeople, can't always promise that their products will be chosen by our editors. We can, however, offer potential advertisers another way to be IN the magazine. Our selling pieces explain to our advertisers that their ad pages can influence our reader as heavily as our editorial pages. Quite frankly, Chloe, our editors would be very disappointed to know this, but most readers can't even distinguish between advertising and editorial. If they see it in the magazine, they think they should buy it."

Ruth picks up an old issue of the magazine and flips to the middle.

"Here is last year's book review issue. We did a whole story on books that are perfect to bring to the beach. We happen to have done several articles on eye protection in this issue, as well. The articles stressed the importance of protecting the eyes from lotions, the sun, sand, pollution, and a multitude of other irritants. The editors featured hats, umbrellas, visors, all-natural eye lubricating drops, and a whole array of sunglasses. Do you see what a great opportunity this was for us to pitch

Oakley, Chanel, Gucci, and a slew of other sunglass advertisers? Gucci took five pages in this issue.

"The Gucci ads were placed all throughout this article called 'Look What Our Favorite Shady Ladies Are Reading.' Of course our editors do not specifically endorse our advertisers' brands, but it sure seems that way, doesn't it? Now, if we turn the page again, we see this ad for a Teeny Weeny Book Light, right next to this article on the importance of proper lighting to protect your eyes. As we all know, poor lighting can ruin your eyesight. Is this making sense to you? Can you see how the reader would be affected by these ads while they are reading these kinds of articles?"

"That's actually a fallacy about poor lighting ruining your eyesight, but I totally get what you're saying! When I bought my first pair of sunglasses with those thin rectangular black frames that were just coming into style a few years ago, I suddenly felt like reading. It was weird, but now I see why. I looked so intelligent in my new sunglasses, I just wanted to go out and buy a book. I must have read at least five books that summer. It was so unexplainable at the time, because I couldn't read with my sunglasses on, but now it makes perfect sense."

Ruth is writing down what I'm saying. I must have really hit the nail on the head.

"Well, I must say, that's not even remotely related to what I was trying to explain, but I suppose advertising does have a snowball effect on consumers."

"Totally! For instance, if you buy a new coat, you suddenly realize that you need a new scarf to go with it and then gloves and then a new bag, etc. etc. When you think about it, all of your advertisers are helping each other sell each other's products.

"Wait! I just had a great idea. We should get a bunch of advertisers to pitch in for an ad and do like a group thing."

"That's called cooperative advertising, Chloe, and it's done all the time. It's hardly a new idea."

Now what is Ruth doing? She has her whole head in her pocketbook. She's taking out a mirror, a bunch of rubber bands, and the meanest-looking round brush I've ever seen. No wonder her scalp is flaky. She could easily rake off the top layer of her head with that thing. Oh look, she's making pigtails. See, now that doesn't look good. Why doesn't she know this?

I thought Ruth was finished explaining what our department does, but apparently she is just beginning to scratch the surface. I could really use a soda.

"Here's another example: Suppose one of our salespeople wants to get an appointment with Animal Instinct hair care products. In that case, we might create a beautiful, leopard-print folder and perhaps overlay some fun pictures of hair care products against the leopard backdrop. Inside the folder, we would most likely print our hair care issue rates and research numbers on our readers' hair care buying habits. On the other side of the folder, we might have a picture of one of our models using hair products while she's getting ready for a day at work. This plants the image of our reader using the advertiser's products in the advertiser's mind. We might even slip in a little leopard-print compact as a little gift. Of course that idea just came off the top of my head."

"Or," I interject, "we could write our own article on hair dos and don'ts and call it something like, 'Hair Before and Hair After' and print it right in the magazine. We could design it to look like our editorial pages and show the most amazing hair transformations being created by the top stylists in New York. We could even show photographs of the hairstylists using our advertisers' products. The article will prove how the right haircut, hair accessories, and styling products can totally transform a look. We can also go a step further and include a few tips on how people perceive one another, in the workplace, on the basis of how they wear their hair." *Don't mention her pigtails, no matter what. Just keep talking and forget about them.* "I'm sure that if we offer an advertiser like Animal Instincts the chance to have their products featured alongside the hottest hairstylists in the country, they would buy a ton of advertising."

Ruth's eyebrows are twitching. I messed up.

Did I say pigtails out loud?

"Well, you're certainly not the first person to come up with the idea of an *advertorial* section, Chloe. Plenty of advertising pages are designed to look like editorial pages. Editors don't love that kind of thing, of course. They believe our *advertorial* inserts undermine the integrity of the magazine because they confuse the reader. But advertisers are willing to pay a lot of money for exclusive sections. We did one of those just recently, as a matter of fact. Is that where you got this idea of *yours?*"

"I don't think so. I'm pretty sure it just popped into my head. But don't worry. I think I got the hang of it now. Once that happens to me, the ideas start coming like crazy. I would even be willing to put together one of those adverstories right now," I offer.

"Well, I hardly think you are ready to start a project of that magnitude. We have professionals for that kind of work. *I* do that kind of work, as a matter of fact, and the new copywriter will be assisting me, if I need help. However, it's certainly heartening to hear you thinking promotionally. That's very clever of you, and I'll keep all of your ideas in mind. Just make sure you report them to me and only me to avoid any confusion. I handle things a certain way in my department. We don't just walk around spouting ideas. Projects evolve over time. While an idea is in the developmental phase, I prefer that it be kept private, until it's ready to be presented. That way we don't risk making fools of ourselves."

"I totally agree. It's probably best if we don't spill *any* of our ideas to editorial." I wink. I'm catching on to the fact that editorial is not our friend. It's almost like Ruth and I are in cahoots. Of course it's only natural for the editors to want to do all the talking in the magazine, but I'm with Ruth. I think advertisers have the same right as editorial to express their views and recommend their own products.

"Let's just say that it's in everyone's best interest if all ideas are presented directly to me and leave it at that."

I nod conspiratorially and smile. She's probably had a bad experience in the past.

Pro-mo-tion. *If I say it enough times, I know it will stick.*

I'm getting the feeling that Ruth wants to teach me absolutely everything about the magazine business, even the behind-the-scenes stuff. I guess she needs as many informed people on the promotion side as she can get. I can't believe she's already confiding in me about the editorial people. She must sense my loyalty. I'm probably the right arm she's been searching for her entire life.

I just hope she doesn't give me a ton of projects on my first day, and I hope she doesn't expect me to be able to read that folder they plan to use for the book issue. It's been distracting me this whole time. I should ask her about that before my mind starts to wander again.

"Ruth, excuse me, I hate to change the subject, especially at the risk of sounding like an ignoramus, but what language is that on the book issue folder?"

"Oh," she's laughing. "That's Greek."

"No wonder I couldn't read it." I'm laughing too. "I don't read a word of Greek. Is that for our Grecian advertisers?"

"No, in this case, Greek is just a term. This writing you see here is just a collection of letters strung together to indicate where the words, or copy, will eventually be dropped in. This is just a mock-up of the actual piece we'll be using. This is what we call a dummy. One day, in the future, if you work hard, you will more than likely be asked to write a selling piece yourself," Ruth says.

"Oh, no thank you. I'm terrible with words," I say.

"Excuse me?" Ruth asks.

"No, I mean, if you need me to write something on one of those folders, I'd be happy to do it, but I see myself as more of an idea person."

"Is that so? You see yourself as more of an idea person? Well, it just so happens that I don't depend on my assistants for *ideas*. But you will have to get used to the *idea* of writing. We are always short-handed in this department. At one time, I had three writers under me, but they all quit. One by one, they all walked out for one absurd reason or another. It's just as well. I can't be bothered dealing with the personal problems of three writers every day. The new copywriter will hopefully be able to do the work of all three of them. Writers are a strange breed. You tell them to write one thing, and they hand back something completely different. When you ask them why, they can't answer. It shouldn't be that difficult, but it always is.

"The copywriter we just hired has a degree in journalism from Northwestern. I'm hoping that she'll have the brains to do exactly as she's told. But, if she can't handle her workload, you will undoubtedly be called upon to help her out. She's only one person and this department pumps out a lot of material."

"I'll certainly do my best," I say, already anticipating writer's block.

"I'm glad that we're clear on that, Chloe. I don't tolerate any kind of resistance in my department. We are all working for a common goal, and we all have to pitch in. Everyone starts at the bottom. It's nothing to be ashamed of."

"Thank you. I agree," I say, noting to myself that Ruth probably needs to reevaluate all of her hemlines. So far I've only seen two of her skirts, but they are both too short. I can understand why she chose red tights to carry through the whole red theme, but I'm so not getting the saddle shoes. Wait a minute. I got it. She's dressed up like a cheerleader! Why didn't I see that before? I guess she's just feeling perky today.

There's nothing wrong with feeling perky. It's not like she's *acting* childish. Maybe she just needed a little lift when she got dressed this morning. Who doesn't need a lift every now and then? I know just how she feels. I'm in the same kind of mood.

"Ruth," I say, "how would you like to go out to lunch, just you and me?"

Ruth looks at me for a long time without speaking. I really think I surprised her. She opens her mouth to answer, but her phone rings at the same time. She puts up her finger to indicate that she'll only be a minute, but I'm not dumb enough to fall for that one again. I know my Ruth when she gets on that phone. I'll be sitting here for at least twenty minutes. I'll just go back to my office and put some things away.

I'm beginning to like my office area. True, it's small, but I couldn't help noticing the full-length mirror that's attached to the outside wall of the art department. It's only three steps away from where I sit, and the lighting in here is absolutely perfect.

I take out my table mirror and my makeup case, my hand cream, some mints, nail polish, a brush, and my little suede barrette case. I just love this case. When I bought it, I had no idea what to do with it, and then I thought, *barrettes!* I think I'll wear one now. I should freshen up my makeup, too.

Did I bring my Chanel red lipstick? Yes, I did. Oh! And here's my red nail polish! No wonder Ruth loves red. I feel differently about this whole day now. All gray is the perfect backdrop for bright red lips. And I think I'll just put one coat of polish on my nails. I wonder where Ruth and I will be lunching.

I start to blow on my nails, but Ruth is off the phone already. I hope she didn't rush on my account. Zoe was so wrong about her.

"Chloe, I wasn't finished with you," Ruth calls.

"I wanted to give you some privacy while you were on the phone," I say as I carefully inspect both hands for smudges. I quickly blow on each nail as I walk into her office. Luckily, one coat dries pretty quickly.

"I'll let you know when I need privacy, and what is that smell? Were you polishing your nails, for heaven's sake?" She's practically spitting.

Someone on the phone must have upset her. That just proves she was talking to a real person.

I sit down and Ruth begins jotting something down. She's got a lot on her mind. She's really writing away. How could a woman who thinks that quickly need three writers? Look at her go.

"Okay, Chloe, listen carefully. Number One: All grooming is to be done at home. Number Two: Assistants to the assistants take their lunch when their bosses *return* from lunch. Is that understood?"

"You mean we're not allowed to eat together?" I ask.

"On certain occasions that would be acceptable, but I happen to have a previous engagement today. I'll invite you to lunch when *I* feel it's appropriate," Ruth explains.

"Okay, sure," I say, trying to swallow as though there isn't a huge lump in my throat. I got all ready for no reason. Ruth doesn't like me after all.

What am I doing wrong?

"We have a department meeting every Tuesday at ten o'clock. Of course, we are running very late today," she says, looking at her broken watch again. It's a habit. I do it all the time, too.

"At these meetings, I assign everyone in the art and copy departments their projects for the upcoming weeks, and then we go to work. Lunch is from noon until two o'clock, and the day ends at five o'clock. Again, it's sort of an unwritten policy that noon until two is not for everyone. Try to eat as quickly as possible so that you can cover the phones while I'm gone. Now go fetch a pad and a pencil and meet me in the art department. I'll introduce you to the art staff. This is a great way for you to learn who does what around here."

Ruth points to an open closet in the hall, just outside of my office. The closet is filled with office supplies and promotional pieces exactly like the bookish-looking folder. I grab a pad and a pen. I'm very anxious to meet the girls in the art department. I got a quick look at them before. They are definitely the creative types. They sort of look like Zoe's friends—except they wear jewelry.

We are all seated in the art department. There is a completely different vibe in here. It's like the "I don't care" room. It seems that no one in here pays very much attention to Ruth. She's sort of like a substitute teacher. I hope no one throws a spitball at her.

"All right, people," Ruth says.

They are already laughing through their noses. I wonder if Ruth senses her sudden plummeting status.

"First, I'd like to introduce Chloe Rose. She's the new assistant's assistant, and she'll be reporting directly to me," Ruth begins.

I wish Ruth would cross her legs. Her panties are showing. I wonder if that's why they're laughing. I feel like laughing, too. *Please don't laugh.*

"As many of you know, I've also hired a new copywriter. She'll be starting in two weeks. Chloe and the new copywriter will be sharing the cubicle directly across from the art department."

I look around the room. No one seems particularly overjoyed to meet me, but one girl is smiling, so I smile back at her. Never mind, that's just a little nervous tic there.

There's another girl staring right at me, with her hand on her hip. She's a big girl with a very tiny waist, and she's wearing a gold lamé belt with sparkly sequined flowers all over it. My grandmother had that belt. I wonder if that belt belongs to her grandmother. I wonder if her grandmother and my grandmother were friends.

The girl with the gold belt has long, acrylic nails and she's wearing bright red lip liner, on purpose. She looks like a lady in a beauty parlor, not a girl in an art department. I wonder how old she is. She's got to be close to forty or fifty. She even has "hot roller hair," and that's definitely not an oil-free foundation. I wonder how she fits in here. It's like she's got one foot in the art world and the other foot in Loehmann's.

The girl sitting next to her is the nervous one. She is in her early twenties, blonde and pretty, but every time she touches something on her desk, it drops to the floor. Instead of picking it up, she just stares at it. At one point, her phone rings, and she's so frightened that she picks it up and slams it right back down.

There's another girl sitting on the floor, but she refuses to look up so I have no idea what she looks like. Never mind. She just looked up and she's a boy . . . with really pretty hair. He's wearing his winter coat, which is strange, because it's very warm in here. He's also wearing these really cool, flat, black boots that would look great on me. I can never find boots like that. I can't really see what he's doing, but I think he's cleaning his nails with a pen cap. No, that's not it. He's polishing them. Yes, he's polishing his nails with a black Magic Marker.

And there's one more girl. She's leaning against her desk and scraping the bottom of her yogurt cup with a big loud spoon while Ruth is talking. We're probably about the same age, but I look like a big baby compared to her. Her forehead is enormous. I've never seen one so big. She's wearing a tank top and a big, flowy skirt. Her arms are so skinny that if she weren't moving, I'd swear she was a corpse.

She has that wispy, fine hair that I've always loved, but unfortunately, it's dyed the color of a machine gun. She's really terrifying. She's standing with her legs really far apart, and her eyes are stuck in that thinking person's squint. I feel as though she's just about to throw her spoon at Ruth. I hope she decides not to go through with it. What if she lifts up her arm and flashes a great big ball of hair? If that happens, I hope I don't scream. Wait. She just threw the spoon and the yogurt in the garbage can. It was a real spoon.

Why? Why would anyone do such a thing? I knew there was something wrong with her.

"Chloe, this is Hallie Smyth, the art director," Ruth says.

Girl with the angry spoon.

Hallie waves. I wave.

She's actually pretty nice. I've always said that it's wrong to judge people by their appearances.

"This is Trai, one of our very talented artists," Ruth continues.

Guy on the floor with pretty hair, who apparently has no last name.

Trai doesn't look up. I can't blame him. He's on his last nail.

"This is Ali Rhodes," Ruth continues.

Girl who drops things.

Ali says, "Hi," way too loudly, and then hits herself in the forehead. I wave back and try to say "hi," as loudly as I can.

"And this is Rhonda Gold"—*girl with the small waist, shiny belt, and long nails*— "who has been with us for eleven years."

Rhonda puts her hand back on her hip and says, "How are you?" almost like she's auditioning for *The Nanny*. I give her a little wave but, by accident, I drop my wrist. I hope no one saw.

Ruth begins filling me in.

"Rhonda is working on a beauty tips booklet that we are doing in conjunction with Fragrance Week. Trai is working on a new overall look that we will use to unify all of our selling pieces. Ali is working on a color scheme for the annual spring luncheon, where we plan to promote our spring fashion issue, which features an article called 'Portrait of a Lady.' And last but not least, Hallie is working on our new media kit."

Ruth goes around and talks to each one of them privately. They each show her what they've done so far. As soon as she's finished looking at Trai's work, he waits for her to turn around and then gives her the finger. Hallie acknowledges everything Ruth says by saying, "Exactly, exactly." She shows Ruth what she is working on, and Ruth quietly nods. When Ruth walks over to Ali's table, Ali accidentally cuts her finger with one of those little Exactorama knives.

Ali holds up her bloody finger without saying anything. Then she just turns around and walks right out of the room with about thirty feet of surgical tape trailing behind her. It must have gotten stuck under her shoe. No one even bothers to tell her. They're just letting her walk out the door like that. If I hadn't just seen her hang up the phone immediately upon answering it, I would have found that odd. No one even cares that she is bleeding. I guess she gets hurt a lot. Ruth doesn't seem concerned at all. Nor is she concerned about the fact that none of these people want her anywhere near them. They should call this room "The I Hate Ruth Bloody Horror Show."

Ruth says, "Chloe, I'd like you to take a few minutes to walk around and get a feel for the way we do things here, and then I'd like you to come in to my office."

I want to beg Ruth not to leave me alone with these people, but she walks out of the room before I have a chance. I gently tiptoe around, trying to give the impression that I am interested in what they are doing, and yet somehow invisible, at the same time. I try not to make eye contact with any of them, but when I float over to Hallie's table, she feels obligated for some reason to take out every project she's ever worked on, perhaps over the course of her entire life. I'm not sure what I'm supposed to say. This girl has obviously wasted the best years of her life designing hundreds of identical folders.

"Hmmm," I say, over and over and over again. I try to make it sound a little different each time, but it keeps coming out as, "Gee, now there's something I never would have thought of doing," which is true, because I now realize that the department I work for is pointless.

The salespeople can't possibly find these folders helpful. They probably take turns carrying out as many folders as they can possibly hold so they can dump them in the trash can outside the building. Hallie shows me one folder that's designed to look like a giant price tag and another one that's designed to look like a pair of skis.

"Was this one used for the ski issue?" I ask, not caring.

Hallie says, "Yup," and someone else says "Duh," and then I just get this overwhelming urge to tell them all off so I can get out of here.

"Oh my God. 'Duh'?" I suddenly hear myself say. "It just so happens that I have no idea how any of this stuff could possibly be useful to anyone, nor did I question for one minute that this piece of paper, cut into the shape of a pair of skis, was for the ski issue. I was just trying to make conversation. Nice meeting you all, though."

I can't wait to tell Zoe that I said that! Every now and then, I just stand right up to people. But now I'm hoping that my body isn't found bound in surgical tape, hanging from a hook in one of these hallways, before the end of the day. I also hope I never have to go back in there. As I'm walking out, I hear the guy with the beautiful hair clap and say, "She sure killed your little art exhibit there, didn't she, Hal?"

I wonder if I could move that big mirror into my cubicle by myself. If I just unscrew those little plastic things, I could probably just slide it in here and prop it up against the copywriter's desk, until she comes, of course. Once I have that big mirror, I'll never have to see them again.

"Did you get acquainted with the art folks, Chloe?" Ruth calls to me from her office.

"Sort of," I say, as I slowly walk back into her office.

"Well, that's good. We work very closely with them. Everything we dream up here"— she's pointing to her head—"they make into reality in there."

Those freaks in there are responsible for transforming ideas into reality? They don't even have any manners. One of them is drawing on himself with Magic Marker!

Ruth has a very big pile of files on her desk, and she is taking out more files from her drawers and dumping them on top of the big pile. I guess she's doing some reorganizing or some early spring-cleaning.

"Well, Chloe, I think this should keep you busy for a while."

"Do you want me to read all of those?" I ask.

"No, of course not! I want you to make copies," she says, matter-of-factly.

"Of what?"

"Of these," she says, pointing to the pile.

You would have to see the size of the pile to understand how perfectly my lips formed the letter O.

"I know it seems overwhelming, but don't sell yourself short. I know you can do this. We have a marvelous copy machine, very high-tech, and you don't have to do it all at once. I just want to have a copy of everything I've ever done here. I have a plan, Chloe, and this is part of it. Why don't you hold your arms out and I'll load you up."

"Okay," I say, extending my arms, palms up, hoping that the copier is not as complicated a piece of machinery as it sounds.

Ruth puts a heavy, unwieldy pile of files in my arms. For a second, I lose my balance.

"I'll just leave the rest of this pile in your cubicle. As you finish copying each section, bring it back to my office. How does that sound?" she asks.

I can't tell her that it's the worst idea I've ever heard, so I just say, "Great!"

"Okay, Chloe, you can go now," Ruth says, pointing at the door.

I'm afraid if I take a step, I'll fall over, so I just stand there like a dumb, stubborn mule.

"Go, Chloe! You can do it. Get started so you can get the

rest of these files out of my office. I already wasted most of the morning with you already."

I finally manage to thrust my body forward and drop the pile on the floor in my office. There is hardly anywhere to stand in here now. I should have left myself a little path. I begin to clear an area for myself, but it becomes immediately apparent that my arms are completely numb. I'll have to keep them slightly extended for a while. They won't bend. Poor Barbie; this is how she feels all the time.

I can't imagine how long this copying project will take. I'm estimating a full year. At least I won't have to deal with the art department until I'm finished with all of this.

No sense rushing these things.

~

CHAPTER FOUR

Exercise Extreme Caution, Particularly When Opening Your Mouth

It's only been two weeks but I am really catching on to this copying thing. The trick is to stack your To Do and Copied Already piles very carefully. It's really not a bad project. I've met a lot of very nice people, including Joseph Paglione, the maintenance person. He's this really skinny guy who's always rushing around with a million things on his mind, and yet he's always ready to lend a hand. In the beginning, I was having a little problem with the copier, so now he comes by at least two or three times a day to make sure the paper isn't jammed or to help me reload.

Joe knows everything about this place. He has two little daughters at home, and one of them wants to work here when she grows up. Joe brings her home a copy of the magazine every month. She's only five, but she already knows what she wants to do with her life. I can totally relate to that. I just love Joe. Sometimes I call him Joey. He's pretty much my best friend around here.

As soon as Joe was sure he could trust me, he started telling me all this stuff about Ruth that he thought I should know.

For instance, he thought I should know that Ruth isn't playing with a full deck, as he put it.

He also told me that many, many years ago, Ruth had an affair with the former publisher. He promoted her from promotion assistant to promotion coordinator just a few months after she got hired. But a few months later, that publisher left the company. Apparently, the new publisher is not nearly as impressed with Ruth as the one she slept with many, many years ago. It's just been downhill for Ruth ever since.

Joe is the kind of guy who you can ask just about anything. He loves explaining things. He's a lot like Ruth in that way. I've been dying to find out what the difference is between the publisher and the editor-in-chief, so I just came right out and asked Joe. He wasted no time whipping out the copy of the magazine that he always keeps rolled up in his back pocket. He flipped through a few pages and showed me the masthead. The masthead is where they list every single important person who works for the magazine, including their titles. I was surprised to see that Ruth's name wasn't on it. I was also surprised to see how much information you can find in magazines if you read them.

There is a whole page dedicated to the publisher and his staff, and another whole page dedicated to the editor-in-chief and his staff. Robert Marrow and his staff are in charge of selling advertising space. Daniel Princely and his staff are in charge of creating the editorial pages of the magazine. The word *editor* should have tipped me off right away. Ruth was right about the strict separation between editorial and advertising. They even have separate bosses. It's like two separate teams.

I hate being on the wrong team. I was explaining to Joe that if it was up to me, I would eliminate the promotion/advertising department altogether and forget about trying to get ads. He agreed that my department is getting a little stale, but he disagreed about doing away with our sales staff. Joe explained that magazine sales account for about one-sixth of what advertising dollars bring in. The bulk of a magazine's profits come from ads. Can you believe that? The promotion department *is* the backbone of this company after all. What were the odds of me coming out with something like that? I wonder if Ruth thought I was some kind of a financial genius when she interviewed me. No wonder I got the job! Zoe was way off on that one, too.

Joe said that he overheard the publisher say that if Ruth got a blood transfusion, she would almost be able to qualify as dead wood. According to Joe, the publisher is upset that the backbone of the company isn't supporting the sales staff the way it should, of late. Still, I think that's a terrible thing to say about Ruth. She's not dead.

Joe and I have had some unforgettable moments together. For instance: Today, I pressed *one-zero-zero* instead of *one,* and I accidentally made one hundred copies of a piece of paper that just had one word—Ruth—written on it. Personally, I wouldn't ask someone to make even one copy of that, but Ruth said to copy everything, so I guess she has her reasons.

I really don't mind making copies. It's just that this copier has a tendency to jam as soon as Joe walks away, which is exactly what it's doing right now. It's like the machine knows that Joe isn't here. I saw exactly how he got the paper out of that conveyer belt thing. I know I can do this. Last time it jammed, I waited twenty-five minutes for him to come back. I didn't tell him how long I was standing there doing nothing. I think you just have to open this little door here. . . . Or maybe it was this little door. That's funny, now neither of these little doors will open. Oh, now I remember. Joe sort of pushed on one side of the little doors and they opened on their own. I should be able to do that. Maybe it was more of a little punch than a push. After all, Joe is a pretty big guy. I should probably give it a good solid kick to swing it open. I'm kicking the door pretty steadily now, but it still won't open. What's wrong with this thing? Why is it so mean to me? I kick it one more time. Not because I think it will open but because I hate it. While I'm kicking it, I tell the door that I hate it.

"She's being a little hard on that copier, don't you think?" says a male voice.

It's that cute guy, Stan. He just appeared out of nowhere with one of the beautiful blondes at his side.

"It deserves it. It's jammed and it won't open," I say, giving it one more tiny, hard kick.

"Did you try reasoning with it? Sometimes it's better if you at least try to talk these things out," he says sympathetically.

"I'd hate to see what she would do to *our* copier," the blonde says, sort of to both of us.

"I can't get this little door open," I say, sort of to both of them.

"Did you kick it on both sides?" Stan asks.

"I think so," I answer.

"Let me see what I can do. First things first. Let's give this little door here a chance to recuperate while we find the real culprit," he says. He walks around the copier to the paper tray and pulls it out with one hand. He hands it to the blonde, who finds this to be a huge compliment. Next, he sticks his hand inside the space where the paper tray was, exactly the way Joe did it. It's all coming back to me now. He pulls out a mangled piece of paper. The blonde hands him the paper tray, and he slides it back in.

"Do you want to kick this around for a little while, or can I throw it away?" he asks, holding up the shredded piece of paper that was causing all of my problems.

"You can throw it away, I guess," I answer.

"You don't even want to rough it up a little?" he asks.

"No, not really," I answer.

He crumples the paper into a little ball and shoots it into the garbage pail halfway down the hall. It goes right in.

Nice.

"I could swear I saw Joe open one of *these* little doors," I say, defensively.

"You probably saw him change the toner, which happens to be behind *this* little door here." He points to a third door, which, surprisingly, I neglected to see or kick.

"Oh right, now I remember."

"Can I make a suggestion?" he asks.

"Go right ahead," I answer.

"Don't ever change the toner. I'd hate to have to see that."

"Don't worry, I won't. This is the worst copier I've ever worked with," I say, letting them both know that it's not my fault, even though Stan obviously thinks it is.

"Tell me about it," the blonde says, looking right at Stan. "The one we have on the seventh floor is ten times worse."

At least she understands.

"And, it just so happens, I need to make a copy myself," she continues.

"I'll catch you later," Stan says to the blonde, but by accident, I say, "Okay."

"Promisestan?" she asks, but he doesn't answer.

Instead he looks at me and says, "Keep up the good work. I've always said when it comes to copy machines, you've got to show them who's boss."

"Thankstan," I say, as he walks away.

Now I'm doing it.

It's just the two of us now, the blonde and me.

"I'm Sloane Worthington," she says and reaches out to shake my hand. I shake her hand. It's so small. I wonder if mine feels big and sweaty to her. "Would you mind terribly if I used the copy machine for just a few minutes?"

"No, not at all. Be my guest. I need a break anyway."

"I won't be long. You must have been here for hours," Sloane says, looking at my piles.

"I'm not even close to being finished. I've got a ton more, back in my um, office . . . y area," I say.

I'm not sure why I have decided to call my little nook an officey area, but I want to give the impression that I might have an office but still cover myself just in case this girl ever comes to visit me and sees that I don't.

"Oh, you must be the new assistant's assistant," Sloane says with a knowing, carefree smile.

"I'm Chloe Rose," I respond, with my own version of a knowing, carefree smile.

"Welcome, Chloe. I'm the beauty editor. How are you doing so far? I mean, besides that little battle with the copier. Finding your way around okay? I guess it's not too difficult to figure out where everything is. I'm sure you know that the editorial department is on the seventh floor. At least your copier works *some* of the time. Ours is always broken."

This girl is very pretty. She's not dressed like any of the girls on the promotion/sales floor. She's wearing the kind of flat, beautiful shoes that I always picture myself wearing in another life—a life in which I am very tall and bony and blonde. Unfortunately, I can't wear flat shoes because I have calves, but I can still love them, from afar. In fact, I love everything about Sloane. I love her bouncy blonde, happy hair, and her fresh-scrubbed face. I love her all-cashmere clothing and her tan legs, which are so smooth that, if I didn't know better, I'd think they were both prostheses. Not one freckle; I checked both legs.

I can just picture the whole Worthington family gathered under a white tent in the backyard of their summer cottage mansion. There's Sloane, dressed in a Lilly Pulitzer sundress, standing amongst her three blonde brothers and two little blonde sisters. It's the kind of lavish cocktail party where everyone is drunk out of their minds, and laughing their heads off about some really funny boating incident. Like the time when Uncle Holden's hair was sticking up as he climbed back on the boat after falling overboard because he slipped on, of all things, the tiniest little sliver of a lime peel that you ever saw. I'm watching a whole movie of Sloane's family in my head when she interrupts me.

"Have you heard about Courtney?" she asks, but then adds, "oh, how could you? You just started here, and no one really knows yet."

I have now hopped up onto the heat vent ledge to watch her make a copy of the one piece of paper that she is holding. She's like a little show for me. I've had a very dull day, except for all that fun I had with Joe before. As much as I like Joe, he's pretty boring. This girl is ten times more interesting than Joe.

I've never seen anyone handle a single piece of paper with such incredible delicacy. I could watch her all day.

"Divorce, divorce, divorce!" she starts singing, with an enthusiasm bordering on hysteria. "This is Courtney's third divorce," she adds, holding up three dainty fingers with perfectly manicured fingernails, no polish.

"That's terrible," I say, trying not to acknowledge that her happiness is spilling out all over the place.

"You do know who Courtney is?" she asks, wondering why I'm not reaching the same level of elation over Courtney's third failed marriage.

"Um, I think so, but maybe I have her confused with someone else," I lie, for no apparent reason.

"*Courtney,* Courtney," Sloane says. "From the column *Don't Be Afraid to Ask Courtney.*"

"Oh," I fake.

"You do know the column, don't you?"

"Of course," I say, putting two and two together. There is a girl named Courtney, who writes a column for the magazine that I now work for. Once again, I am amazed at how much information they cram into this magazine. It's like a book.

"Courtney is *Little Miss Know it All* when it comes to everyone else, but we all saw it coming. She's such a flirt and a quack and *a slut*." She mouths the word "slut." Zoe would call Sloane "a spewer," but at least she showed a little discretion with the *slut* word. She must sense that I am very good at keeping secrets or she would never confide in me like this.

"Every time she needs something, she uses that flirty, little girl voice that I can't stand. She's so pathetic. I've never even seen her sharpen her own pencil. The other day, she actually called maintenance because she broke one of her fake nails."

"You mean she flirts with Joe?" I ask, grateful that Sloane didn't see me waiting around for twenty-five minutes the last time the paper jammed.

"Who's Joe?" Sloane asks.

"You don't know Joe? He's one of the maintenance guys. He's really tall and skinny and sweet and he can fix just about anything," I say, happy to add a little morsel of information to the pot.

"Oh, that guy? He has a name?" She throws her head back and starts laughing, I mean really laughing.

My mental movie of *The Life of Sloane* starts playing again. In this scene, Sloane is wearing a shimmering pink gown and a prom queen crown. She rings the bell to her own house late at night. Her butler answers the door and Sloane saunters in, holding the arm of her handsome blue-blood date. Her date nods to the butler and says, "Good evening, James." Sloane looks at her date and throws her head back laughing, "James has a name? A ha ha ha ho ho ho ahhh."

I get a little shiver, but I snap out of it as soon as Sloane begins speaking again, in real life.

"She flirts with anyone who can do things for her, and I mean anyone, including The Prince," she says, gesturing toward the ceiling as though she is referring to God. She's got a pretty big grin on her face. She's probably still recovering from the fact that Joe's mom bothered to name him.

"Who's The Prince?" I ask.

"Oh, it's an inside joke. We all call Daniel Princely, the editor-in-chief, 'The Prince.' But Courtney pretty much hits on every single guy in the whole building. She doesn't care who he is or what he does or what he even looks like. Come to think of it, I bet she does hit on Tom."

"You mean Joe?"

"Whatever. Anyway, I've caught her in some pretty compromising positions. She has absolutely no pride whatsoever. You'll see. She's everywhere. She makes me sick. I once saw her walk into the men's bathroom with two guys from the mailroom."

I'm starting to feel a little guilty about my willingness to drop Joe like a hot potato for this girl just a few short minutes ago.

"I knew her marriage would never last. She doesn't know the first thing about real relationships. I can't believe they let that little b-i-t-c-h actually give people advice."

Oh my.

"Can you believe they gave her the title mental health editor?" Sloane continues. I shake my head like I can't believe it either. I wish I hated the idea, but it sounds like a pretty good title.

"She *does* have some lame degree in psychiatric social work, or something like that, but she quickly gave up that half-ass little career as soon as she caught on to the fact that none of her poor, miserable clients were ever going to make her famous. Then she goes straight from giving people therapy to becoming a makeup artist! Have you ever heard of anything like that in your entire life? She said she became a makeup artist because it's 'the only true helping profession.' Please. And then she gets her own column in *Issues!* And all because she somehow wooed *the powers that be* with her false, fox-fur eyelashes and botched implants." As she mouths the word "implants," she points to her own breasts with her two index fingers. There are certain words Sloane just can't bring herself to say.

I immediately jump in with, "She has false eyelashes made out of fur? That's sick!" I'm just about to get really into it when I blow everything by saying, "But I'm still sorry about the divorce."

As soon as I say it, I realize I've sided with the enemy, and for no reason other than I always say "I'm sorry" about things that couldn't possibly be my fault. Like when someone dies— even though I know it makes it sound like I killed that person.

Sloane looks at me and squints a little. I attempt to distract her from my unexpected sympathy for Courtney by hopping off the vent ledge. Unfortunately, I jump a little too hastily and subsequently twist my ankle. I hate being in pain in front of people I don't know.

"Ouch. Oh my God." *The pain is unbearable.* "I think I broke my ankle and my shoe," I say, desperately trying not to cry.

I look on the floor, and there is the heel to my shoe sitting on its side. It snapped right off. I guess I weakened it when I kicked the copier eight hundred times.

I can't walk around in one shoe. What am I going to do?

Sloane puts her hands together. I can see that she is a worrier and that she has forgiven me for feeling sorry for Courtney.

"I better go and get you some ice. Stay right here. This is terrible," she says.

She truly feels for me, but as I roll my foot around a few times, it starts to feel better.

"No, no, please don't. I'm really fine," I say, brave as a soldier.

"Oh, there's your heel," she says. She bends down and picks it up and turns it over a few times in her hand. She even holds the heel gently. I wonder if she ever spills anything.

"Cute shoes," she says, bringing the heel toward my shoe to see how they look together.

"You think so?" I ask. I hate to admit how much her opinion means to me. This is a girl who knows shoes.

"Sometimes I think I'm the only one left in this entire building who just refuses to run around in heels, but these are just the right height. They are so sweet. Oh, I just love these," she says, sort of to me and sort of to herself.

She can't possibly consider these heels.

She smiles at them and then at me. She's liking me in a whole new way now.

"Whose are they?" she asks.

"The funny thing is, I don't really know. I don't even remember buying them, to tell you the truth."

Then I slip one off to check the inside and say, "Oh right, they're Jil Sander."

She gives me the *Very Nice* face and looks me over again—this time from head to toe. She's really doing some serious thinking now. I feel like telling her, *"These are nothing! You should see some of the shoes that I actually remember buying. These were all the way, I mean, all the way in the back of my closet. I hardly even know these shoes."*

"Well, it was nice meeting you, Chloe. Are you sure you're all right? Why don't I get you some crazy glue for that heel?" She's practically my slave girl now.

"I'm fine, really," I say.

As soon as Sloane walks away, I open the magazine and start looking for Courtney's column. Here it is! It says in bright pink letters,

Don't Be Afraid to Ask Courtney!

Do you have a personal question or problem that you are just too embarrassed to ask anyone? Of course you do. We all do. But you don't have to suffer in silence anymore. You can ask our very own Mental Health Editor/Makeup Artist the most intimate questions imaginable and she'll give you advice that's guaranteed to turn your life around.

Question:
Dear Courtney,

Recently my boyfriend broke up with me and I was thinking that I might slit my wrists. Well, not really slit them, just sort of fake it like I was going to slit them. Do you think that will help us get back together?

Yours truly,
Sort of Suicidal

Answer:

Dear Sort of,

Hmmm, that's a tough one, but no, my answer is no. It has been my experience that boys typically find suicide attempts to be a turnoff. What boys really like is super silky, smooth legs. If you want to get your boyfriend back by using a razor, I suggest that you massage your legs with warm baby oil for at least two to three full minutes before shaving them.

You may have to use two or three blades because the oil and hair tend to ball up and dull the blade, but it is so worth it. Also, it's important to try to get at least 8 hours of sleep every night, but stay away from those sleeping pills! Natural sleep is nature's makeup. And always remember, I love you.

Forever yours,
Courtney

Question:

Dear Courtney,

I have a small cellulite dimple on my ass and my husband said it makes me look fat. Should I get a divorce?

Yours truly,
Dimples

Answer:

Dear Dimples,

Absolutely not! Get a divorce over a silly thing like that? Haven't you heard of "ipecac"? I bet you haven't. You can find it in almost any drugstore. Just get yourself a bottle of that miracle syrup and watch the pounds melt away. In the meantime, why not get a little butterfly or a pretty pink rose tattooed right over that little dimple? It's a lot cheaper than filing for divorce. You can trust me on that one! And always remember, I love you.

> Forever yours,
> Courtney

A tattoo! What a great idea. I can't believe I never even noticed this column.

I have a little dimple, too!

As much as I'd like to sit here reading all day, I've got to get back to my copying.

Some of these papers should definitely be thrown away, but I can't very well make those kinds of decisions. Let's just take this one for instance:

Dear Human Resources Manager:

I am applying for the Director of Creative Services position for the eleventh year in a row and would like to once again reiterate my qualifications. I have been Promotion Coordinator for eleven years and I feel that I have made numerous contributions to this department that have had a significantly positive effect on the overall success of our sales staff.

Although I continue to show an excellent attitude toward fulfilling my responsibilities and have utilized my small staff in a way that has produced remarkable results, I still have not been rewarded the title nor the position I deserve. There is, at present, no one actually holding the position of Director of Creative Services, nor is there, to my knowledge, anyone even being interviewed for that position. Can I please set up an appointment with someone in Personnell to discuss my chances this year?

Sincerely,
Ruth Davis, Promotion Coordinator

Poor Ruth, no wonder she didn't get the job. She spelled personnel wrong. I wonder if she ever gave up trying to win that title. And why would she even want it? It sounds so . . . uncreative. How could they put the words *Creative* and *Director* in the same title? It's like saying: Happy sad person. She's had the same job for . . . *Let's see. If she wrote that letter a few years ago . . . and she had already been working here for eleven years . . . that would mean she started working here somewhere around 1983 or 1984. I wish I was better at math. . . . And let's say she started working here at about twenty-eight years old . . . then . . . Wait a minute, when did she start? 1970, was it? . . . And now it's two thousand and . . . Oh my God . . . Ruth has been working here for thirty-five years?? That means Ruth must be close to seventy years old. She looks fantastic! I'm sure I did the math wrong on that. Still, I'm worried about the fact that she still wears pigtails.*

Let's see . . . this one says Medical File. I can't copy all of these! There must be two hundred forms here. Foot surgery, foot surgery, orthotics, physical therapy, medical pedicure, radiology, acupuncture, chiropractor, another pedicure, it never ends. I wonder if "medical pedicure" means that we can put our pedicures through insurance and get them for free! It's worth working here for that reason alone. I flip through the forms. Poor Ruth has been through hell with those feet of hers. She's a very sickly woman.

I need a break from this. It's almost four o' clock. I should definitely eat something. Candy can only kill an appetite for so long. If I don't eat, I get really irritable. Almost rude. I've been at the copier all day. I'll just stack these files and head back. Tomorrow is another day.

The files I'm carrying reach just a bit higher than my head. I really have to concentrate and walk slowly, especially since I'm only wearing one shoe with a heel. I've got my other heel balancing right here on top of the pile I'm carrying. I'm in a really bad mood now. I'm hungry, I'm limping, and I can't see where I'm going.

"That's quite a load you've got there," someone from behind me says.

Normally I'd turn around and respond, but I don't bother. Only an idiot would strike up a conversation with a starving person who can't see or walk.

"Woops! Don't fall over now," the idiot says, chuckling a little.

Now I have to turn around. To my surprise, it's a small but fully grown man, dressed in a tight black sweater with perfectly tailored cuffed pants and what might even be a suede jacket. Is he going out or just coming in? He's too short to be a model, but he can't be a regular person either. His hair is too neat. It's the wet kind of neat. The kind I don't understand. I would never leave my house with wet hair.

I turn toward him as best as I can. I smile politely and turn away. He chuckles a little and says, "Don't worry, I'm not trying to hassle you. I'm Rob Marrow, and I see you've got a broken heel there."

That name sounds so familiar. Is he famous or something? Oh, right! Now I remember.

He's trying to change the chuckle to more of a chortle. It's the kind of chuckling chortling combo that people use when they are trying not to break down and laugh hysterically at someone who looks completely ridiculous. I just feel like saying, "Hey, I'm not the one walking around with overly neat wet hair, Prince Chuckles."

"Did anyone happen to mention to you that we have plenty

of extra shoes around here for emergencies such as yours? You don't have to walk around like that. There's a closet upstairs with about two hundred pairs. It's perfectly okay for you to borrow a pair. You certainly wouldn't be the first person to break a heel." He's chuckling like mad again. "Go on up to the seventh floor, after you unload that pile, and have a look around. Tell them Rob sent you."

It's quite possible that I just fell in love with this wonderful, little man and that I might faint. I can't believe it! They have a shoe closet here! Filled with shoes! In this building! Normally, I would sense something like that. I feel light-headed. I don't think that I can carry this pile any longer. I've lost all the strength in my arms. I might not make it into my officey area. What if my legs buckle under me and I fall and bang my head on the hard floor and I die without ever seeing the shoe closet? I want to drop everything and grab him by the collar and shake him, yelling, "Where! Where exactly is that shoe closet?" But he's already disappeared around the corner.

My head is spinning. I'm almost positive he's the guy who won't promote Ruth. Oh look, he's coming back. I'll just strike up a conversation and work my shoe into it. The whereabouts of the shoe closet will be uncovered in no time. Maybe I can get Ruth promoted at the same time!

"Oh! Hello again. Did I mention that my name is Chloe Rose? I work for Ruth Davis. Isn't she one of the nicest people you've ever known?" I ask.

He's doing the chuckling thing again, but I'm willing to live with it now. It's sort of cute, in a way.

Oh God, please don't let him say anything funny. If my shoulders start bouncing up and down, I'll drop everything.

"You know, I just love working for Ruth. Isn't she something?" I say, trying to keep my eyes fixated on his small shoulder.

"Yes, she certainly is something. And I bet she's the one who gave you all these files to copy," he says, slipping the top folder out from under my little heel, which is still balancing on top of the pile. He takes a quick look at it, shakes his head, then slides it back under the heel very carefully. He didn't have time to read it. It could have said anything. I know for a fact that it wasn't the paper that just says Ruth. That one is way on the bottom of the pile. When I looked at it again, I noticed that it really only said rut. The *r* wasn't even capitalized. What a waste of paper that was.

"Oh, this is nothing. I have at least ten more piles in my office to copy. Ruth asked me to do these top-priority files first. Ruth is very efficient," I say, as I readjust myself so that I can walk a little more gracefully. I think I changed his mind about her. He seems impressed.

"Right. Well, anyway, welcome aboard, Chloe! I hope you are settling in without any problem," he says and breezes on.

Wait! My shoe!

I make it all the way to my desk without dropping anything and reposition the piles on my desk. I start whispering to myself, "You know, just the other day, my publisher, Rob, told me that—" but Ruth interrupts me.

"Chloe, who are you talking to?"

"Myself," I answer.

"Have you finished all of the copying already?"

"Not exactly, but I just thought I'd get a quick bite of my lunch and see if you needed me for anything else," I say.

"Who were you talking to out in the hall?" Ruth asks.

"Oh, just Rob," I answer.

"Rob?" she asks, obviously not knowing which Rob.

"Yes, my publisher," I respond.

See, now that came out all wrong, almost like I think I own the place.

"I mean, *the* publisher," I quickly fix it.

"You were out there talking to Rob, instead of doing your work?" Ruth asks.

"Oh no, I was on my way back already," I assure her.

Ruth is such a worrier. I hope she doesn't think I was looking directly at him. A tiny shoulder pad can't possibly qualify as a "cute male body part."

"Well, Chloe, I have an appointment with my chiropodist, which will most likely take up the rest of the day. I'd like you to take over the phones until the end of the day, and then I'll see you in the morning. I'm sure you have a lot more copying to do, and now that I see how easily you get distracted, I realize why it's taking so much longer than I had anticipated," she says.

She's putting on her coat. It looks like a varsity jacket, except for the big flower embroidered on the back. I wonder if someone who is trying to break into the fashion business is making these clothes for Ruth. It's very nice of her to wear them. I would never do that for anyone. I would make up some big lie about how I'm allergic to all different kinds of fabrics and that I have to buy my clothes at a special non-allergic store.

I say good-bye to Ruth and look for my lunch, which I've brought in a small bag. I don't mind eating at my desk. It makes me feel like I'm too busy to stop working for something as trivial as lunch. Besides, I don't exactly have lunch plans. Joe probably goes home for lunch. Anyway, I still have a lot of copying to do. I should really eat in this whole week. *I wonder what Sloane does for lunch.*

The thing is, I can't find my lunch anywhere. I could swear that I left it right on my desk, next to my makeup mirror, but it's gone. I start opening every drawer of both desks, but then I spot it in the garbage. It's completely flat. Well, not completely flat, it's really only squashed on one side. I'm trying to forget that Zoe predicted this. Ruth would never sit on my lunch on purpose. She doesn't even come in here. Still, it does look like it's been sat on. I feel so violated.

I'm starving now because I know I have nothing to eat. I guess I could go and see if the oddballs in the art department have anything left over, but it's hardly worth it. They probably only eat spiders or their own hair. I could check to see if the cafeteria is still serving lunch, but I shouldn't leave the phones unattended. Although, the truth is, the phones hardly ever ring on this floor. I wonder if Ruth's phone is even plugged in.

"Wow! This cafeteria is really nice," I say, out loud for some reason.

"It tis beautiful, isn't it darlin'? It's nice to hear someone sayin' it. Most people don't even notice. They take everythin' for granted around here. Imagine callin' a place like this a cafeteria. It's like the Taj Mahal," says a small woman with the tiniest feet I've ever seen. I had no idea cafeterias looked like this these days. I was expecting something more along the lines of my high school cafeteria.

"What can I get fer ya?" the woman with the tiny feet asks me.

"Oh, I don't know. I guess a small salad, or maybe some of that goulash over there. Is it good?"

"I can't say," she says with her head down.

"Why can't you tell me?" I ask.

"Well, for one thing, I made it myself, and for another thing, I've never been much for cookin'. I'm only doin' the cookin' temporarily until they find a decent chef. There's a million other things that need to be done around here, and nobody does any of it, except for yours truly."

"Really? You made that? That's amazing. I could never make anything like that. I'll definitely have some. It looks really delicious."

I sit down with my plate of goulash, but as soon as I take a bite I realize that I've made a terrible mistake. It's really salty. It might even be burning a little hole in the side of my cheek where I'm keeping it.

"Excuse me," I say, careful to keep the goulash tucked neatly under that little flap of skin that formed over the years because one of my molars juts out a little bit. "Could I possibly have another serving of that goulash? I'd like to bring it upstairs to my desk. I have so much work to do," I mumble.

The woman with the tiny feet looks right at me and smiles, "You're a sweet girl. I like you. Now go on and spit that out before you get an upset stomach."

"You don't mind?"

"For heaven's sake, no. I've never been any good at cookin'. How about a piece of chocolate layer cake instead?"

"Did you make it?" I ask.

"No, darlin'. We bring it in," she whispers. She goes into the back room and comes out with a big cake box. She lifts up the top and cuts me a big piece of chocolate cake. Then she cuts another little piece and puts it right next to the big piece. People don't usually do stuff like that for you once you graduate from elementary school.

"None of the women around here would ever dream of touchin' somethin' like this, but I can't stand to see a good cake go to waste, even if it is store bought." She whispers the words "store bought."

"Your secret is safe with me," I whisper back. "You have no idea how much I like chocolate cake," I say, as I start eating.

"You come visit me again and I'll make sure you get a little extra of whatever it is you like. How does that sound?"

I want to tell her that I love her but it's too soon. Instead I just say, "Thank you . . . *nice lady with the small feet*." I say the part about the small feet to myself.

I've been making copies for a month now, and it's starting to sink in that *Issues* isn't the dream job that I thought it would be. I'm very lonely here. The good news is that there is an excellent chance that I will be finished with all of my copying by this afternoon. I know Ruth will give me something more exciting to do next week. I just know it.

I'm so glad it's Friday, but I'm not looking forward to tonight. I have to help Zoe finish packing. I can't believe she's really leaving. It feels exactly like that summer when she went to sleepaway camp. I slept in her bed every night and played with all of her stuff, but it wasn't the same. I missed her so badly that I wrote to her every day about how our mom had turned on me. I explained to her, in great detail, how Mom was not only forcing me to do all of the housework but that she also threatened to give me up for adoption if I didn't become her slave. Zoe wrote back the same thing every day.

"Stop lying. I'll be home in a few days." It felt like I had a fever from the minute she left until the minute she came home. I kept a thermometer by my bed and checked it every few hours. The damn thing was probably broken, and because of that, everyone in the house thought I was faking, including Aunt Dottie.

~

CHAPTER FIVE

The Best Way to Figure Out What You Want Is to Admit What You're Not

Zoe and I are watching The Cooking Channel. Ever since I started working at *Issues,* we've become cooking fanatics. Zoe thought I needed a hobby to get my mind off of Ruth, and I thought Zoe needed a hobby to get her mind off of Ruth.

As I recite the ingredients for a Hearty Chicken Pot Pie, right after The Everyday Chef calls them out, Zoe writes them down. She likes when I repeat everything live. We haven't actually made anything yet, but we've written down loads of recipes. *The Everyday Chef* is our favorite. We both have the apron that everyone wears on the show. Zoe's is so cute. In her size, it came with a ruffle. After every show, we're so hungry that we order in.

We should be packing instead of watching The Cooking Channel, but we're both so tired and there are so many good recipes on tonight.

Michael's book turned out to be a huge success. He's on TV all the time now, and he got this really great apartment for Zoe and him. It's a big loft downtown. I can't wait to go and see it. Part of me hopes that it's this great big, wide-open, sunny space in a cool neighborhood, and the other part of me hopes that it's infested with giant, unkillable cockroaches. I still can't believe I'm going to be living without her. I really hate living alone. I might keep her apron.

I should use this as an excuse to go totally wild and start living my life as though each minute could be my last. My whole problem is that I never really let myself go. I've never experienced a true dark spell or even a mild depression. I never do anything that poses a significant health risk. I've always wanted to live that way, but something always distracts me. Just when I think I'm about to hit on something that will send me into a downward spiral, something great happens, like I'll dream that I got a check for $81,000 and I wake up in the best mood all over again. Just once, I want to pass out drunk on the couch, clutching at my hair in a desperate attempt to hold on to what is left of my shrinking sanity. Is that so much to ask?

I should start planning my first wild adventure right now. My birthday is coming up, and that's always a good reason to start messing up one's life. I'll start with a party.

I'll invite everyone I know. Let's see now. There's Sheryl, but she lives in L.A., so I doubt she'd be able to make it. I could invite Jen, but she's so into her AA meetings, and that whole "refusing to drink thing" sort of defeats my party theme. There's Risa, but I don't really like her anymore, now that she is best friends with Andie and they've merged into one annoying girl, instead of the two annoying girls whom I once loved. I could invite Alexis, but she didn't pick me as her maid of honor or even to be one of her bridesmaids and I considered myself to be one of her best friends. I realize that she has five sisters, but I should try to stay mad at her for at least a few more weeks. She's probably not in the mood for a wild party anyway. Now that she's married and stuck with five boring siblings as her only friends.

What happened to all of my friends? I've basically been working and sleeping for the past few months. I don't have time for anyone or anything anymore. I don't even have time to shop. That's actually not a hundred percent true. I've shopped away my entire paycheck every week since I started my job to cheer myself up. What I don't have time for is socializing. I just sort of exist until it's time to go back to work. You'd think I'd have made a few friends at the office, but I feel like I came in as the new kid in the middle of the year, and somehow I got stuck hanging out with the most unpopular girl in the whole school—Ruth.

After several hours of TV, Zoe and I have finally gotten down to the business of packing, but it's not going very well. Every time I pack something, Zoe takes it back out of the box. Apparently, I don't know how to pack. I'm trying to help her out by reorganizing her things by color, but Zoe wants to organize everything by category. I can't pack by category, so I've decided to think about my party instead. I'll call Jen and tell her what I decided so far.

"Hi. Listen, I decided not to have a party."
   "Okay."
   "No, I mean I was going to have one and then I decided not to, but I still might."
   "I can't drink, you know that, right?"
   "Of course I know you can't drink. I'm hoping the party will be so wild and fun, no one will notice."
   "Wow, who else is coming? Any cute guys?" she asks.
   "Well, I haven't officially invited anyone per se and I can't really think of anyone offhand. Wait, I know one, Aiden! Why didn't I think of him before? He's cute and single and fun, right?"
   "Aiden? Aiden who?" she asks.
   "I don't know his last name. We met him about two months ago. You were sitting on him half the night, or maybe that was

me. Well, one of us liked him. You don't remember him at all? He gave us his phone number and he took ours, too."

"Oh, *that* Aiden!"

"Why are you so surprised?" I ask.

"Because *that* Aiden is in intensive care," Jen says.

"What do you mean? Who told you that? We just saw him a few weeks ago. He looked so healthy, and if I recall, he was partying like a madman."

"That's right. I forgot to tell you. His roommate called me the next day to tell me that Aiden went into a drug-induced coma. His roommate found my phone number and thought I might be a close friend," Jen says, sort of sadly.

"My God! I've never met anyone who was in a drug-induced catacoma. Is it serious?" I ask, crossing him off my mental party list and wondering if I know even one other cute guy.

"Of course it's serious! A coma is the worst thing that can happen to you. It's like getting run over," she explains.

"Is he going to live? I mean, do people survive catacombs?" I ask.

"Some people do, but it's very dangerous. And it's called a coma, not a catacomb. Catacombs are what bees make. Anyway, he might actually be faking. Supposedly his parents were going to put him in rehab and he agreed to it, but then he said he wanted to go out, one last night, and the next thing you know, he's in a you-know-what, or so they say."

"Too bad," I say.

"I know. He was so cute," Jen says sympathetically.

"So cute," I add.

"Oh well," we both say.

"In that case, I guess I should make a less festive party. Maybe I should make a Happy Birthday Chloe/Get Well Soon Aiden party," I suggest.

"Don't bother," Jen says hopelessly.

But now Aiden is the only thing I can think about. In fact,

I think I'm falling in love with him. What if he doesn't make it? I'll just die.

"Why ruin your birthday party by sharing it with a guy who won't even know he's part of it?" Jen says. That wasn't very sympathetic. I'm getting a strange feeling that Jen doesn't even care about the fact that Aiden is in a comb . . . a. She's right, though. I am sort of holding on by a thread. I just can't bear the idea of a wild party without even one cute boy.

"Listen," she says, "how about inviting some people from work? I'll invite some people from AA and Risa and Andie and your sister and Michael and his friends, and that's a party right there."

"I don't want a party anymore. Let's forget it," I say.

"I can't forget it now. I'm already putting together the party music in my head."

Oh God.

"I *really* don't want one," I say. "You don't even drink. You won't dance unless you're drunk, and I never really wanted a party in the first place. I'm just upset because Zoe is really moving out now and I can't even help her pack because I don't know how to pack by category."

"She packs by category?" Jen asks.

"I don't want to talk about it. Everything she does is so complex. She reminds me of that whole Dewey decimal system. Let's just pick a night to go out and have fun before I turn thirty."

"You're turning twenty-eight."

"This year I'm turning twenty-eight. I'm giving myself two years to have one fun night. Just promise me that you'll bring me home if I get drunk and fall asleep without meeting anyone."

"I don't want to be an enabler if you are planning to get drunk."

"Oh really?"

"Really."

"You don't want to enable me to get drunk? Did you learn

that word at a recent AA meeting, or have you been using it all your life but I just never noticed?"

"I wish you wouldn't joke about my addiction or my personal journey towards recovery."

"Oh please. You are so faking this. How long do you plan on going to these meetings? Did you make any friends there yet?"

"Well, there's Mrs. Greenly and her grandson. They're my friends. Mrs. Greenly wears the longest red wig you ever saw. It comes down to her waist. Every time she scratches it, it moves all around, and every time it moves, her grandson turns his head and cracks up laughing. I hate when he laughs at her wig."

"I guess that makes him an enabler, too."

"What makes you say that?"

"Because he laughs behind her back instead of telling her that her wig moves. That means he's *enabling* her wig to move."

"I never thought about it that way. The other thing about Mrs. Greenly is that she has some kind of a problem with her gums. They don't appear to be attached to her teeth in any way. There's a big space where her gums and teeth should meet. It's almost like her teeth are suspended in midair."

"Maybe she has false gums."

"Maybe. Anyway, her other problem is that she smokes. So she always has both of her hands in her mouth. The left hand is for massaging her gums, and the right hand is for smoking. I'm always so afraid she's going to switch hands by accident and catch on fire."

"I can't believe Mrs. Greenly smokes. I can't picture that. Redheads hardly ever smoke."

"I told you, it's a wig."

"Oh right, I forgot. And what about her grandson; what is he like?"

"He's really cute. His name is Cole. He's like sixteen or seventeen and he has blonde dreadlocks and beautiful skin and the most amazing body you've ever seen."

"Jen, you just said that he was like sixteen or seventeen."

"I know, but he's so cute."

"I want to meet him, too. I never had a friend with dreads . . . locks. Which is why I can't just call them dreads."

"Come to an AA meeting and you'll meet all kinds of new and exciting people."

"No thanks. Who else do you hang out with at the AA club?"

"Mostly the Greenlys, but I try to stay away from them because they fight a lot."

"Why is that?"

"Well, Cole is constantly trying to get Mrs. Greenly to come to his Tuesday night devil worship meetings, and Mrs. Greenly keeps refusing because she believes that worshipping the devil can only lead to no good."

"She said that? She said, 'Worshipping the devil can only lead to no good'?"

"Yup."

"What does she think it will lead to? Cigarettes?"

"I have no idea what she thinks. I just know that there's something very wrong with both of them. I hate to tell you this, but sometimes they hold hands."

"I really wish you didn't tell me that."

"I'm sorry. I hope I didn't ruin the nice impression I was trying to create."

"Does the actual devil himself show up on Tuesday nights, or is it just someone who just dresses up like the devil?"

"Chloe, there is no such thing as the devil, and why are you suddenly so interested in my AA meetings?"

"Because I'm bored and I'm trying to picture myself as a wino. Who else do you hang out with?"

"Well, there's another couple. They make out the entire time. They never stop. They both wear the same exact T-shirt to every meeting. It says You Complete on the front and Me on the back. They never stop kissing. Never. Not once. And they're like fifty. Our group leader thinks it's because they feel vulnerable in social settings, and if they stop making out, one of them could easily crumble and look for a drink."

"I can't believe they serve drinks at those meetings."

"They don't serve drinks *at* the meetings. They might crumble and go out drinking *after* the meetings."

"Are you kidding? They go out drinking right after those meetings? Isn't that a little risky? What if someone catches them?"

"It's not like that. They are responsible for themselves."

"Do you?"

"Do I what?"

"Do you ever go out drinking after a meeting?"

"No, of course not! I was never that big of a drinker in the first place. I can't even figure out why they all want to drink all the time."

"Jen, it's because they are alcoholics!"

"I know, but why?"

"Because they can't help it. That's what the word *holic* means. Are you paying any attention at all in those meetings?"

"Not really. I feel completely out of place there."

"I knew it! You've got to stop joining clubs. Remember when you joined Weight Watchers and the group leader said that you needed to gain five pounds and you still insisted on going, so they made you sit in the back?"

"Yeah, that was embarrassing."

"*That* was embarrassing? Jen, you are going to AA meetings and you hardly ever drink! What is wrong with you? How can you possibly keep showing up there?"

"Because I know that *you* think I have a drinking problem. You told me that night I fell off the stage at the Lillypad Lounge. I never even think about drinking unless I'm thirsty, but I always hear you, in the back of my mind, saying 'Jen, you're a terrible drinker.' "

"I never said, 'You're a terrible drinker.' "

"Yes, you did!"

"No, I didn't. I said, 'You are a terrible *dancer.*' You looked like such an idiot that night. I was actually happy for you when you fell."

"You said that I was a terrible *drinker.* I remember it perfectly."

"Well, I meant to say dancer. I was pretty drunk that night. But I would never go and sit in a room with a bunch of alcoholics to try to get over it."

"Well, I'm not going anymore either."

"I'm glad that's settled."

"Me too."

"So I guess you're free every Thursday night now."

"Yeah, I guess I am."

"Want to make that our drinking night?"

"I guess so. Actually, not really."

"Me neither. I always get nauseous when I drink during the week."

"Me too."

"Maybe we can do something else on Thursday nights."

"Something really wild?"

"Definitely . . . What?"

"Let's see . . . Give me a minute . . . I almost had something."

"Anything yet?"

"Not yet. You?"

"Nope."

I wake up Saturday morning and Zoe is gone. She left me a thirty-five-page letter saying that she didn't want to wake me up and that she went to bring her stuff over to the new apartment. I take a quick look around. All of her stuff is gone. There's only one little sock left by the side of her bed. I can't even look at it. It looks like a bootie. It's so lonely.

"I guess it's just you and me now, little bootie," I say. I might as well start talking to myself as soon as possible.

*   *   *

On Sunday morning, my mom calls, but I tell her that I can't talk to her. She sounds too much like Zoe, and I don't want to talk about my birthday. She's too cheerful, and I don't want her to pull me out of what could be a considerable depression.

The phone rings again and I entertain the idea of picking it up and slamming it back down again, like Ali does, but I can't go through with it. Instead I pick it up and say, "Hello?" like I always do.

"How's the wild partier doing today?" Jen asks in her most sarcastic voice, which isn't even remotely sarcastic. "Did you think of anything for us to do on Thursday nights yet?"

"No. And as a matter of fact, I've decided never to go out again. There's absolutely nothing this city can offer me. I need something new and different in my life. I was thinking that I'd like to try speed skiing or mountain climbing and then afterwards go out and have a few laughs with my fellow mountain climbing and speed skiing friends. Something like that might be better for me."

"Chloe, you are deathly afraid of heights."

"True, but I was thinking how cool it would be to meet some new people out on the slopes, or on the top of a mountain, and as soon as we introduce ourselves, we realize that we all speak different languages. But, since we all just happen to be multilingual, we just start chatting away, instantly bridging the gap between our distant and fascinating cultures."

"Wow, I almost forgot that you're multilingual. I guess you're referring to your seventh-grade Spanish dialogue here. So, if one of your mountain climbing friends says something to you in German, for example, you can answer them by saying, '¿A dónde vas Tomas?' 'Yo voy a la oficina de la princípal'?" Jen says, as though she thinks I'm kidding around here. Which I'm not.

"It just so happens that I know a lot more Spanish words than the ones you've heard me recite at parties. I just can't seem to get that line about Tomas out of my head. God knows I've tried. Still, I probably won't be able to keep up, you're right. That's why I don't have any international friends and that's why I never go anywhere mountainous. I've got to conquer my language barrier. *Where are you going, Thomas? I'm going to the principal's office* isn't going to get me where I want to go in this world," I say.

"Chloe, why do you suddenly think that you are supposed to go places and enjoy things that you don't enjoy?" Jen asks.

"Because that's the kind of person I should be. I should be an active, carefree mountain climber who skis and stays up late speaking in a foreign tongue. I've been going to bed at ten-thirty every night since I started this job. I used to go out at ten-thirty!"

"See, that's just not true. You never went out late, not even in college. You always said you were going out late, but then you got tired and cranky right around . . . hmmm . . . let's see if I can remember this right? . . . ten-thirty!"

This is true. I've never been a night owl.

"What's wrong with me?" I say, half to myself and half to Jen.

"Nothing!" she says. "And besides, you *are* active. You play tennis," she adds encouragingly.

"I hate tennis. I only take lessons because I like my instructor," I admit.

"You like that guy?"

"Not really; I'm thinking of quitting," I say.

"You run," she says. She's really groping for wild activities now.

"No, I don't. I jog slower than most people walk and I hate that too. I only do it because I wanted those Juicy sweat outfits in every color. By the way, you can have those."

"You work out." This is what they mean by scraping the bottom of the barrel.

"It just so happens that I haven't been to the gym in three months and I feel like I was just there. I consider myself in great shape if I go once a month. That's not working out. That's pretending," I argue.

"You ice-skate," she says.

"Nope."

"But you have ice skates," she says.

"Yup."

"You like to decorate your apartment!"

"You shouldn't really bring that up when you know I'm upset about not being adventurous enough. I don't go around making fun of you because you were pretending to be an alcoholic."

"What do decorating and alcoholism have to do with one another?"

You'd think she would have learned how to pronounce that word after all those meetings.

"They're both dumb hobbies," I explain.

"You like to read!" she continues, ignoring my attack on her made-up illness.

"I prefer television."

"Okay, Chloe, I give up. You like buying things. There. I've said it. That's the thing that interests you most in life. I'm sorry that you're not a professional athlete or some wild explorer, but you're not, okay? You like buying clothes and pillows. You are who you are, and you like what you like, and you don't have to like things or be things that don't interest you, especially on your birthday."

"You forgot shoes," I mutter.

"What about shoes?" she asks.

"That's another thing that I like to buy, besides clothes and pillows," I say.

"Right. Shoes too. Chloe, you're just in a bad mood because your job is not meeting up to your childhood expectations and your sister is moving out and you want your birthday to be fun and nothing feels particularly exciting right now. Don't make it worse than it is. Want to go shopping?"

"Now? Are you kidding? I just got up. What do you think I am? Some kind of materialistic glutton who can only be cheered up by purchasing meaningless, useless objects?"

"Yes, I do think that. I think that you just described yourself perfectly. It's a good thing Zoe's moving out. You're starting to think too much. So where do you want to go? Barney's?"

"No, I'm not really in a Barney's mood. I almost bought another one of those little leather purse things with the little people embroidered on them, so I'm trying to stay away from that whole part of town for a few days."

"You couldn't possibly want another one of those purses. They don't even open all the way," she says.

"I know, but I love them, and each one is a little different. But don't worry about it too much. My credit card was declined, so instead I ended up with a handmade key chain that doesn't hold keys, and I paid for it with cash," I say, reassuringly.

"So Barney's is definitely out. How about Bergdorf's? Let's get our makeup done."

"I can't," I say.

"Why not?" She's running out of patience, but I can't get my makeup done. I'm too pale. Whenever I'm pale and I get my makeup done, I always end up buying all new makeup that's all wrong for me.

"Why can't you get your makeup done?" she repeats, even more impatiently.

"Because I'm pale right now and I don't want to come home with a bag full of makeup that will make me look ill when my natural color comes back."

She understands this and doesn't argue, but she's not about to give up, either.

"I think I'll just do a little shopping myself then," she says. "I don't know where I feel like going. Maybe Bendel's or Club Monaco. Calypso has some cute things in the window, or maybe . . . Prada. I'll see."

"What time do you think you'll be heading out?" I ask.

It's over. We both know it. I went down on Prada.

"How about if I come by and pick you up in about an hour?" she asks.

"Okay, I guess so," I say, feeling a little rush of serotonin. There's a tiny handbag in pale salmon with suede handles and two strands of fringe that I saw in the Prada window, and it's been keeping me up for two nights.

"I'm actually a little ashamed of you," she says.

"Why is that?"

"Because that was way too easy. I really thought you were in a legitimate slump there for a second."

I'm waiting outside when Jen picks me up exactly one hour later. I feel a hundred times better as soon as I see her in the cab. I think they call this retail therapy. There isn't a thing about my life that I would ever want to change. Isn't life miraculous! I mean, think about it.

As soon as we open the door to Bendel's, I feel my cheeks get hot. This always happens when I haven't been to a particular store in a while. After my cheeks heat up, all these weird memories flood my brain. For example, I once witnessed a pair of shoes kick each other in the closet. I might have dreamed it, but if so, it was a very real dream.

I'm staring at myself in a pair of aviator sunglasses, trying to remember what the circumstances were that led one of the shoes to kick the other, when I look over at Jen. She's trying on a hat. I find this fascinating, because there is a good chance that she will buy that hat. I've never worn a hat. I mean, *besides* my rain hat, but that was forced upon me. Jen wears indoor hats all the time. I could never sit around with something on my head and act like nothing funny is going on.

Jen can easily wear a hat because she pays no attention to

her head. She just ignores her hair and everything. I think it's because everyone is always looking at her body, which is perfect. From the neck up, she's just this pretty, smiley girl with shiny brown hair and lots of freckles, but then, as you move down, it all turns pornographic. Her chest is huge and her waist is tiny and she has no hips. None at all. Like I said, it's a perfect body.

I should get these sunglasses for my mom. They are way out of my league.

Jen and I hit a few more stores, and several purchases later, I suddenly remember that I'm fresh out of bras and panties.

We slip into my favorite lingerie shop, and Jen stuffs all of our shopping bags behind a chair in a corner next to the dressing rooms. She picks up a magazine from a messy pile on the floor and sits down to start reading. It's extremely hot in here. Jen unbuttons her sweater and asks the salesperson, who seems to be hiding behind the register, if the heat is broken.

"No, it's not broken," the invisible saleswoman answers in a gravelly voice, but she doesn't acknowledge the fact that it's about one hundred and ten degrees in here either. When she steps out from behind the counter, I realize that she wasn't trying to hide from us after all. She's just incredibly small. She would probably be about four feet nine if she hadn't teased her hair so high. I've never seen her here before. She must be new. Oh, look at that! She's wearing pink, furry slippers. I used to have those.

It's always so hard to guess the age of short people, but I'd say she's about sixty or seventy. I feel like we walked right into her house without knocking. There's something very unprofessional about her appearance.

"Is there a fan or something?" Jen asks, but the woman pretends not to hear her this time. She's fed up with answering questions. Instead she just stands there mopping up her neck with an old piece of tissue.

A little while later, she walks over to Jen and says, "It starts with hot flashes. You're probably going through your changes. Welcome to the club."

Jen looks at me with a worried look on her face, and I shake my head and mouth the words, "No, you're not."

"It's possible," Jen mouths back, even more worried. "Stranger things have happened, and the elderly can be very wise."

"Yes, that's true," I whisper, "but that woman wore slippers to work today."

"So? What does that have to do with her noticing that I'm experiencing menopause?"

"It means she's senile," I explain.

Jen goes back to reading her magazine, and I begin looking around the store. There is already a nice selection of red silky thongs and lacy bras on display for Valentine's Day. I guess it's never too early to pick up something for the most important lingerie day of the year. I quickly collect a few things and head to the dressing room. I ask Jen if she wants to try on anything, but she just shakes her head no and continues reading.

"Why don't you want anything?" I ask.

"I don't know. I only wear sports bras, and they don't have any regular underwear here."

"What do you mean by regular?" I ask.

"White."

"You wear white underwear?"

"Yup."

"Wow. I never noticed that."

"I'm not into the whole silly lingerie thing," she says and gets up off her chair to show me an example of why she thinks lingerie is ridiculous. She picks up a really cute Valentine's Day promotional bra and panty set and holds it up, swinging it back and forth.

"I always wonder what kind of girls buy this stuff," she says.

I grab it from her and head to the dressing room, but I

don't try anything on. I haven't tried on anything that even resembles lingerie ever since my college roommate got warts from trying on a pair of panties in a store. At first I thought she must have gotten her warts from her boyfriend because he had them too, but I was wrong.

Her boyfriend had a friend who was a pre-med student, and apparently he had studied warts, because he explained to us that there was a ninety-nine percent chance that my roommate got her warts from trying on a pair of panties that had warts—even though she tried them on over her own underpants. You can never be too careful.

I hold up a green-and-black lace bra with embroidered rosebuds on the straps and try to imagine how it might fit. For some reason it doesn't have one single label on it. I'm not even sure if it's a real bra or a prop. It's a good idea for a bra, though, except it doesn't seem to have a clasp.

I wonder how it comes off . . . or goes on. It is pretty, though. And it looks like it might even be my size . . . sort of. I guess it's worth keeping. If it doesn't fit, I can always give it to um . . . Zoe wouldn't wear this, would she?

Oh! I know. I'll use it as a wall hanging and decorate my closet with it! That's what I was going to do anyway, but I forgot. I was planning to put all of my unusable lingerie on pretty hooks and perk up my closet walls months ago. I can't wait to get started. I look at all the beautiful things I brought into the dressing room, and I can't believe how amazing my closet is going to look. I hope none of this fits!!

I thought Jen and I were the only ones in here, but just as I'm about to take all of my new home decorative lingerie pieces off their little hangers, I hear a woman in the next dressing room call out to the saleswoman.

"Excuse me, miss? I think this panty girdle you gave me to try on is defective. It's making my complexion look pasty."

I hear Jen snort a little, trying not to laugh. The saleswoman slowly shuffles over to the customer's dressing room. It sounds like she's taking thousands of incredibly small steps to delay an interaction of any kind, but she makes up for lost time by flinging the curtain open once she gets there, without any warning at all.

"Take that girdle off before you pass out," she says and flings the curtain closed again.

It's a very loud curtain. Every time she flings it, the metal rings clang together and my heart jumps a little. Some women don't care if a salesperson just walks in on them while they are standing there in their underwear, under fluorescent lighting. I keep my curtain closed with one hand, just in case she decides to check on me, too. I don't want her to see that I'm fully dressed in here.

"Something's not right. I always take a medium in any kind of tummy control garment," the woman continues, half to herself and half to the saleswoman, who has no intention of rehashing a problem she's already solved, especially since she's already begun the long journey back to the register.

I'm starting to recognize the voice coming from behind the curtain. It sounds a lot like Nathan Lane—so it's got to be Rhonda.

"Do you have anything with side panels or perhaps a machete?" she calls out again, still unaware of the fact that Jen and I are the only ones listening to her.

"Rhonda, is that you?" I ask, poking my head out of my curtain.

"In the flesh," she answers, without poking her head out.

"Hi! It's me, Chloe Rose. I'm in the next dressing room. What's the matter with your girdle?"

"That's a very profound question. Unfortunately, there's no one here to answer it."

"I think the saleswoman is busy at the register. Maybe I can help," I say.

"If you want to be helpful, get me the name of a surgeon

who removes hips," she says, showing her face from behind her curtain.

"Can they do that?" I ask.

"I was being facetious, Chloe."

"Oh stop it, girdles make everyone look a little facetious. Isn't that right, Jen?" I say to make Rhonda feel better. Rhonda tilts her head with a confused look on her face, and I realize that I never introduced her to Jen, who is sitting right outside our dressing rooms, watching our heads speak. I introduce them to each other, and Rhonda says to Jen, "Is that your real body, or am I hallucinating again?"

I explain to Jen that Rhonda is referring to her five-feet-seven-inch boyish body with the oversize breasts and overly long legs. Jen looks down, as though she is noticing herself for the first time.

"You're not hallucinating. She was born that way," I tell Rhonda.

"Born what way?" Jen asks.

"I've been telling you the same thing since the day we met. God glued your thighs to your body differently than the way he glued the rest of us. He messed up. There's something wrong with you."

"Exactly," Rhonda agrees. "You are supposed to have a ball of fat that attaches each one of your outer thighs to your hips. That's just the way it goes. Otherwise you will always be considered improperly glued by other women, and therefore, shunned."

Rhonda comes out of the dressing room to continue her explanation, fanning herself with the cardboard from the packaging of her panty girdle. She's still wearing the girdle, along with the world's tiniest bra, and I'm still hiding behind my curtain with just my head peeking out.

Unlike Rhonda, I would rather melt or suffocate to death before I would expose myself, in the outfit she has chosen, to entertain a coworker and a girl with no hips.

"If that woman expects me to get this girdle off without a

scissor, she's in for a rude awakening. Once I start sweating, there's no way I can remove any kind of lingerie without a small set of tools. I don't think I have much time left in this thing either. It's cutting off the circulation to my brain. Look at my face. There's no color left at all."

Are girdles lingerie?

Rhonda catches a glimpse of herself in the mirror and says, "You see this body? You can't believe it, right? Well, believe it. Women are *supposed* to be built with the bulk of their weight in the thigh and hip area. Otherwise there's nothing for us to talk about and there is no reason for us to buy foundation garments."

I've never seen a body like Rhonda's. I don't know what to say. She's like two different people stuck together. She's skinny from the waist up, and I hate to say it, but she is more than a little facetious from the waist down. I'm surprised I never noticed that.

The saleswoman reappears with another panty girdle and says, "Try this one on. It's my best seller."

Rhonda goes back into the dressing room, and Jen mouths the words, "I like her. She's so funny." I nod in agreement and go back to collecting the things I'm going to buy.

"What a difference breathing makes," Rhonda yells out after a few minutes, "I'll take two of these."

The saleswoman takes the new panty girdle from her and once again embarks on the long, laborious stroll back to the cash register, which is really only about ten normal steps away from the dressing room.

"I'll take these, too," I say to the saleswoman, but she completely ignores me. She's not about to take on two projects at once in this god-awful heat.

The three of us eventually make it out of there and start to head uptown. It's pretty cold now, compared to the lingerie shop/oven, so we all decide to get something to eat instead of continuing to walk outside.

We decide to eat at a restaurant next door to Dylan's Candy

Bar, which is a complete waste of time because we all know where we're going to end up anyway. Rhonda orders a small salad with some kind of carrot dressing on the side, and Jen and I split a cheeseburger and French fries, and then we each get our own ice cream sundae. When it's all over, we go next door to get some Skittles.

As Jen and I load up our little baskets with all sixteen colors of Skittles, Rhonda asks us if we normally eat like this or if we are both scheduled for a late afternoon electrocution. Jen and I laugh, but then Jen looks at her watch and suddenly gets serious. "I have to go home," she says.

"What? Why? I'm just starting to feel like my old self again, and it's Sunday, and it's almost my birthday, and I don't want to go home to my apartment, where Zoe doesn't live anymore," I plead as she starts taking huge handfuls of stuff out of my basket.

"Fine. You and Rhonda can come to my apartment," Jen says.

"No, thanks," I answer for both of us, while putting everything back in my basket.

"Why don't you want to go to my apartment?" Jen asks at the same time that Rhonda says, "Happy Birthday."

"Because your apartment reminds me of Aiden, and stop touching my candy."

"You're kidding."

"No, I'm not."

"Well, I suggest you forget about Aiden, and that's way too much candy for one person."

"I can't forget about him. He's stuck in my head and you took the exact same amount."

"I'm putting all of my candy back, and so should you. We have to go. I'm sick of this place," Jen says, and she puts both of our baskets up on a shelf that I can't reach.

"Who's Aiden?" Rhonda asks.

"He's the alcoholic liar that Chloe has decided to fall in love with for some reason."

"He sounds adorable," Rhonda says.

"He *is* adorable!" I protest.

"Aiden could be dead for all we know!" Jen says.

"That's why you should be nicer to him!"

"I've never seen anyone so suddenly determined to leave a store. If I didn't know her so well, I'd think she stole something," I say to Rhonda, loud enough for Jen to hear.

"That's very funny. As soon as we get to my apartment, I'll call him," Jen yells back at me.

"Really?"

"No, of course not," she says, as if I should know better.

I really should. What's wrong with me?

It's impossible to keep up with Jen, so Rhonda and I give up and walk together.

"So, happy birthday," she says again.

"Thanks. It's not a big one, but I've decided to have a crisis over it anyway."

"Does that mean you're not even turning thirty yet? Never mind. Don't answer that."

"Not yet, but soon."

"*Soon* doesn't pre-qualify you for a crisis, but just out of curiosity; what type of crisis are you planning?"

"I had the crisis already. It was all about how I'm not adventurous enough, but I'm almost over it now. Actually, I'm not over it at all."

"What type of adventures aren't you having?" Rhonda asks.

"Mountain climbing with bilingual people from other countries."

"That sounds reasonable."

"It's not reasonable at all. I have a fear of mountains."

"Maybe you should try something else. Have you given any thought to Pilates?"

"I can't do that either."

"Why not? You have a fear of lying on the floor?"

"No, I just can't do it. The breathing thing messes me up."

"You can't breathe? Even I can breathe."

"I can breathe. I just can't breathe while I'm exercising."

"Then you shouldn't."

"I shouldn't what?"

"You shouldn't do anything that will prevent you from breathing. Just accept your limitations and go on with your life. If I know anything, and believe me, I know a lot; it's that you should never do anything that could kill you."

I feel like a giant weight has been lifted off my shoulders. I think Rhonda cured me.

I love watching the expression on people's faces when they see Jen's apartment for the first time. Most people don't know what to say, because it looks like a really expensive whorehouse. She has no shame, whatsoever, when it comes to the color pink.

Every room is loaded with lacy, girly stuff, and the whole place smells like a faint, powdery perfume. She decorates her chairs and couches with big enamel-and-rhinestone costume jewelry pins. Who else would do that? She has all of her floppy hats lying all over the place and chiffon scarves draped over her beaded lampshades. It's the kind of apartment that makes you appreciate the fact that you're single and a girl and I guess, on some level, not an actual prostitute. I never realized this before, but Jen's apartment is exactly the opposite of her underwear.

As soon as we get inside the door, Jen rushes into the kitchen, and I quickly show Rhonda Jen's bedroom. Everywhere you look, there are layers and layers of pink lace on top of more layers of pink lace. She even has a lacy garbage can.

"I love this room," I say to Rhonda.

"From the looks of this place, I think your friend might be doing a little entertaining off hours, if you know what I mean," Rhonda says out of the side of her mouth.

"It does look that way, doesn't it? Make yourself at home. I'll be right back; I have to use the bathroom."

When I step foot outside of Jen's jet-black-patent-leather-wallpapered bathroom with the hot pink appliquéd velvet flowers, it's completely dark, except for a blaze of twenty-eight little flames. Under the flames are twenty-eight little pink candles.

I'm pretty sure that's Jen standing there holding what looks like a completely melted ice cream cake that's big enough for at least one hundred and fifty people.

"Is that whole thing for us?" I ask.

"And me!" Zoe says, appearing out of nowhere and trying not to jump up and down.

"It's just the way you like it. Almost soup. I think I timed it perfectly," Jen says.

"Where did you come from?" I ask Zoe.

"I've been hiding in this apartment since one o'clock."

"I thought you were going to spend the day unpacking."

"And miss my sister's birthday?" She's dying to jump.

I hug my sister, introduce her to Rhonda, and blow out the candles. Jen puts the cake down and turns on some lights. The cake says Happy Birthday Tomas. You can tell that it originally said, Happy Retirement and that Jen wrote right over it with her own homemade icing.

"Are you sure we don't have to share this with anyone else?" I ask.

"I'm positive," Jen says. "It's just us this year."

My sister, my best friend, Rhonda, and a cake for one hundred and fifty people; isn't life miraculous? I mean, think about it.

CHAPTER SIX

~

Go Easy on the Shoes, Chloe, I'm Begging You

"Look at that! I broke my heel! I can't believe this!" I say to every single person who so much as glances in my direction as I fly up the stairs, two at a time. Once I make a decision to pursue a particular goal, there's no stopping me. I knew it would happen sooner or later, and today is the day that I reached my breaking point.

Imagine this: I'm just about to go into the ladies' room as two girls are walking out. One of the girls says that she just saw the most incredible shoes in the shoe closet but that they'll probably be gone by lunchtime. She says it like, "ha ha ha, isn't that funny?" Obviously, there's nothing even a little bit funny about that.

At that exact moment, coincidentally, I look down at my feet and see that I'm wearing my ugly gray shoes again. I realize I have to act quickly, so I pull Joe out of the broom closet and ask him if I can borrow a small hammer. Joe doesn't waste time asking questions when he senses an emergency. He hands me a hammer and I get to work. I have to hit my heel at least fifty times before it finally breaks off. I never should have glued it back on the first time. Anyway, Joe just stands there watching me attack my shoe, and he never says a word. That's what I love about Joe.

Still, I feel as though he deserves some sort of an explanation. So I quickly tell him that my heel had a gigantic rusty nail running through it, which was poking me in the foot and that for the life of me, I can't remember when I had my last tetanus shot. Without missing a beat, Joe looks at me and says, "Gottcha. Take that staircase up to the seventh floor and turn left, then make your first right, and then another right, and open the door immediately facing you. Count three doors in from the left, and there you'll find the shoe closet." I grab my handbag and I'm off.

The next thing I know, I'm running up the stairs. I'm almost on the seventh floor when I hear, "Where are you going in such a hurry?"

It's Rhonda. She's going to want to chat. I'll never get there now.

"I broke my damn heel and I've been hearing about some sort of shoe closet somewhere on the seventh floor," I say, trying to sound nonchalant while still remembering how many rights I have to make before I make a left.

"Isn't it more like, you heard that there's a shoe closet on the seventh floor and then you broke your heel?" she asks.

"No! Oh my God. Who would do something like that?" I ask in my best imitation of a horrified person.

"Oh, I don't know, only every single person who has ever worked here since the magazine was launched," she says, like it's really no big deal. There's no sense in lying. Rhonda knows all.

"Really? I can't believe heel breaking is so popular. It's almost impossible to break a heel. You have to bang it with a hammer at least forty or fifty times or jump off a vent ledge," I explain.

"To tell you the truth, no one really does that anymore. Nowadays, we leave our shoes at the gym and say we forgot them because we wore our sneakers back. Although no one really uses that one anymore either. The fashion editors find it annoying when ten girls walk into the shoe closet at four-thirty on a Friday afternoon and then walk back out in ten pairs of stilettos because all ten of them forgot their shoes at the gym.

"Sometimes it's better to just blurt out the truth. You can even show them what you're planning to wear that weekend and ask them what shoes they think you should borrow. If they like you, they'll want to give you their professional opinion. If they don't like you, they'll act like they didn't hear you. But you can still go in there anytime you want, with or without an excuse. It's not like the old days. They can't outwardly refuse any of us anymore. Ever since Rob became the publisher, he made it very clear that the shoe closet was for *everyone*. He's on much better terms with the editorial department than any of the previous publishers ever were. He got permission for us to go in there anytime we want. But don't get me wrong. It's still the editors' turf.

"The only one Rob doesn't want to use the shoe closet is Ruth because she goes up there all the time, wears all the shoes, and then tries to sue the magazine because she claims the shoes they keep in the closet ruin her feet."

"Ruth does that?"

"Oh yeah, she's been doing it for years. She calls a new lawyer every couple of months to see if she can find one to take on her case, but they all just tell her that she doesn't have a leg to stand on. She thinks that Rob will promote her if he's afraid to get sued, but I don't think he's too worried about it. He's not forcing anyone to wear those shoes and besides, most of us can't. All the shoes in that closet are either a sample size five or six or a model size ten."

I feel a sudden urge to drop to the floor and thank God for

all that he has ever done for me, including making my foot a size six, sometimes even a five.

"Well, that explains why I had to copy nearly two hundred medical forms. I can't believe I ruined my shoe. I could have just walked in there like everyone else."

"You should have asked me first. I've been here for eleven years. By the way, there's a big sign-out sheet on the shoe closet door. Don't sign it. It's a fake. Just walk in there and take what you want. They work on an honor system. It's amazing, but they know every single shoe in that closet. It's a big jumbled mess in there, but don't let that fool you. You have to return everything you take," she says. She starts to walk away, but then she turns around again and says, "Have a good time."

"Okay, thanks," I say.

I can't wait. I start taking the stairs two at a time again. As I meander my way in and around the winding halls, I start to feel my internal compass kick in. I feel as though I could find that closet blindfolded. It's almost like I was meant to find it all along. I just needed a little encouragement and a few simple directions. It's practically calling out to me now. I'm walking with a new sense of calm and direction. I'm not even running. I see it! The door is wide open and there's not a person in sight.

I'm striding toward my destiny, swinging my arms, when a wild wind suddenly rushes through my hair. Never mind, that was someone's desk fan.

This moment is bigger than my broken shoe and me. It's bigger than the entire magazine world. It's bigger than this building and all the buildings that have come before it. Bigger than the very country we live in. It's bigger than truth and bigger than the mystery of why we are all here. I feel like Alice in Wonderland when she was way too tall. I feel like the giant hand of destiny is resting weightily and steadily on my shoulder. I feel a blast of thunderous sound fill the air, and I now realize that I've walked all the way into the closet, kicked the doorstop, and the door has slammed itself shut. I feel darkness because there is not one iota of light in here and I feel like screaming because I am afraid of the dark.

I stand still for a few minutes and then feel my way back to the doorknob, which, no matter how furiously I shake it, won't budge at all. I begin to bang violently on the door, but then I stop to collect my thoughts. Do I really want to make a spectacle of myself? I switch to a light tapping, hoping it will attract a very quiet, unassuming person who won't care why I'm locked in here. I tap a little louder because there is always the possibility that I will run out of air, and then I go back to banging. I bang uncontrollably for as long as my stinging hands can take it, but it's hopeless.

The place was deserted when I walked in, and it's still deserted. I start to feel around some more in the dark. Everything I touch is a shoe. I pick up two or three shoes in each hand and, as uncanny as this may seem, I can identify each one of them, even though it is pitch black in here. In fact, I pretty much know the designer, size, color, toe and heel shape of every shoe in this entire closet, solely by instinct. I'm hoping that this qualifies as an actual talent and not a sickness, even though there's no way to prove it to anyone because there's an excellent chance that I will suffocate in here long before anyone finds me.

I sit down and start trying on one pair of shoes at a time and try to imagine how they look on me. For instance, the pair I have on right now makes me look like I have a big nose. Shoes can do that, you know. They affect everything. They affect the way you stand, the way you hold your head, even the way you talk to people, particularly if you are in agony.

The reason these shoes make my nose look big is because they have a round toe and because they're black. I'm pretty sure they are the Costume National pumps that I saw in the Barney's catalogue a few days ago. Oh, and these must be the

Prada silk geometric print pumps that were on the next page. I don't believe it! These are the Alexandra Neel satin and lace d'orsays that I thought would have been perfect if the lace had been black instead of pale pink. I was just thinking about these shoes the other day. In fact, I was thinking about them today, too, and here they are!

I start categorizing each pair by heel height and by the pitch and tone they emit when I tap dance in them. After what may be an hour or two, I have three distinct categories and ten pairs of shoes in each, and I can almost see the outline of my hand.

There's nothing else to do, so I lie down amidst the shoes and call Zoe on my cell phone.

"Hello?"

"Hi. You won't believe this, but I really did break my heel. I really did. I broke it by accident with a hammer. I was only coming in here to find a pair of shoes that I could wear to get me through the rest of the day. A person can't go around in one shoe, can she? And then I got locked in here. Can you believe that?"

"Where?" Zoe asks impatiently, as though she's the one with only a few minutes of oxygen left.

"In here!" I answer.

"Chloe, are you aware of the fact that I can't see you?"

"Of course I know you can't see me. I'm locked in the shoe closet."

"Would you like me to get you out of there?" says a male voice from behind the door.

I quickly disconnect Zoe and feel my way to the door without stepping on anything.

"I'm in here," I yell.

"I realize that. Hold on a second."

"Is that you, Joe?"

"No, it's not Joe, but I can get you out of there," says a helpful, kind, and ready-to-roll-up-his-sleeves type of voice.

"Oh, thank you. I broke my heel and I was told by Rob, the publisher, to come up here and borrow a pair of shoes for one day, which I will definitely return tomorrow, and when I walked into the closet, I must have kicked the doorstop and so I've been locked in here for a very long time. Is it still light outside? It's hard to tell in here," I yell. I don't know why I'm yelling. He barely whispered and I heard him perfectly.

"Well, it's about six o'clock. It's almost dark and everyone is pretty much gone for the day. But don't worry, I'll have you out of there in a couple of seconds," he says and I can hear him put the key in the door. "This is the wrong key. I'll be right back."

"Wait!" I yell. "Why hasn't anyone tried to get in here all day? I've been locked in here for hours." I don't want him to think I was hiding out in here on purpose.

"Unfortunately for you, there was a luncheon for the entire editorial staff. It lasted until about four-thirty, and everyone left right after that. Don't worry, though, I have the right key now," he says. The door swings open and there is light. There are shoes everywhere. I didn't realize how many I took down off the shelves.

"What have you been doing in there all this time? Not that it's any of my business." It's that guy Stan.

"Well, I was just sort of trying to identify all the different shoes," I say, still squinting. *It's just incredible. He gets cuter every time I see him.*

"In the dark?" he asks. His sleeves *are* rolled up! Between my ability to identify all those shoes in the dark and my rolled-up-sleeves prediction, I swear to God, I could be a fortune-teller.

"This is amazing," he says, looking at my shoe piles.

"I know," I answer. I've made a horrendous mess. Neither one of us knows what to say. To the average person, it might look as though I was throwing things.

"It's completely dark in here with that door closed. I had to find *something* to do to keep myself busy."

"I can imagine."

"I knew these were you," I say to a pair of Moschino pumps with three little buttons stitched on the front. "And you!" I say to a pair of Michel Perry black boots with a six-inch heel and a narrow square toe. "I would know you anywhere, but you should be over here with the super narrow leg boots, not the trampy heel boots." Then I turn to one saddle-colored Tod loafer, which is standing all by itself, and whisper, "Don't feel badly about this. None of these other loafers are good enough for you. You'll find someone, you'll see." I want to say a few words to a pair of Christian Louboutin black satin pumps that wrap up the ankle with a three-inch wide sash, but I can't talk in front of this man anymore. I think I'm frightening him.

"Sorry, I know this must seem odd, but I'm just a little overwhelmed. We were in there for a long time, and seeing them all, in the light of day, well, it's just very emotional for me. I'm Chloe, by the way."

I'm speaking to him, but I'm looking at all of my new friends. Seeing them for the first time is just an indescribable feeling. I wish I could take them all home, but I guess that would be taking advantage of an already awkward situation.

"You must really like shoes," he says, jingling his keys. "Do you want to come out now?"

"I just need a minute or two. I've been so busy, I haven't had a chance to choose."

"Choose what?" he asks.

"I came in here to pick out a pair of shoes that I could wear for the rest of the day. I broke my heel. Remember?"

I don't want to keep him waiting, but I don't want to make a snap decision either. I wonder if he'd let me lock up on my way out.

"It's after six. The day is over. Just take anything." He picks up a pair of tan sling backs and says, "Take these."

"I would never wear those."

"Why not?"

"Because they're hideous. I can't believe they are even in here."

I start to look around.

I need something practical that I can wear all evening and then back to work tomorrow. I should probably pick a pair of boots, but there aren't any boots in here that I could wear with this skirt. My skirt is just a little too short for boots. I could wear these little Chanel slippers, but they look too dressy on me. Oh, I know; I'll wear the Gianfranco Ferré vintage velvet. . . . No, I'll save them for another day. . . . I could just throw on these Stephane Kélian platform sandals, but I tend to shuffle in big platforms. . . . Better yet, these pink rosebud Prada mules. They don't go with what I'm wearing, but he'll never know and I can always change tonight before I go out . . . I shouldn't really go out in any of these shoes, but then again, what good are they, if I can't even wear them out? None of these shoes are appropriate for work.

"I choose the vintage velvet Gianfranco Ferré closed-toe-and-back sandal," I announce with conviction, to no one really.

Did he leave?

These vintage velvet sandals are in the "completely impractical and yet incredibly beautiful" pile, but they're the most amazing shoes I've ever seen in my life, and I'd be out of my mind to leave here without them. They tie up the ankle with a frayed, velvet ribbon. *Genius.*

Oh, there he is. He's still loitering just outside the closet. *He's making me nervous.*

His hair is light brown and really wavy. You can just tell that the hair on the back of his neck is baby soft and blonde. I wish he would get the hell out of here; I need to concentrate. I should ask Joe about this guy. Joe probably knows everything about him.

"I was just thinking what a great guy Joe is," I call to him from the closet.

"He sure is. Almost done in there?" he asks.

"Actually, I am. But I have to put the rest of these back now."

I work for a few minutes trying to make some sense out of the mess I created. I can't possibly undo what I've done here in a few minutes. It would take hours. I take a quick break from cleaning up and walk out in the rosebud mules. I'm sure he's thinking that these shoes aren't the best choice for walking home, but he's not the type to pry. I walk up and down the hall to see if I could make it all the way downstairs in them. I turn to look at him, and I see that he is just standing there and staring at the closet floor in utter disbelief.

"What did you do now?" he asks.

"I emptied all the shelves so I could start over."

"I've never seen anything like this," he says.

"I know. This is terrible. I'm going to have to start from scratch in here. You go on ahead. I don't want to keep you."

I start to put the shoes back, but it's really hard to remember where they were. There is no rhyme or reason to any of their previous placements. It's the most disorganized closet I've ever seen.

"This closet was organized all wrong in the first place," I tell him.

"Is that right?"

He's sitting down and watching me. He's got bony knees. Why didn't God give me bony knees? Why did he have to waste them on this guy? He has everything.

"Whoever runs this closet has no feelings for any of these shoes. She put all the hand-stitched, heavy sandals next to these little Kate Spade slip-ons. This may sound overly fussy, but that's not only insensitive, it shows very poor manners."

"Why is that?" he asks with a twinge of interest.

"Because it's like bringing a roast beef sub to high tea. It's just wrong."

I think I've lost him.

"Why don't you just take those?" He's pointing to the pair

of Lulu Guinness black patent Mary Janes with a three-inch pointy heel that I put on a little stool, all by themselves.

"Those? Why those?"

"Because you obviously like them the best or you wouldn't have made a little pedestal for them over there. And you can't possibly walk in the shoes you are wearing. That heel is at least six inches too high."

"I only have to walk a few steps."

"It's more than a few steps just to get to the elevator."

"I would love to wear those Mary Janes, but I would never dream of it. They are strictly show shoes," I explain, as I begin stacking the shoes back on the shelves by color. I should have used the color system in the first place. "They're more like toys. I mean collectibles. They shouldn't be worn under any circumstances. Look at them. They look like little sculptures. They should only be used for display purposes," I continue.

"You'd make some shoe salesperson," he says sarcastically.

"I *would be* a great shoe salesperson!"

"Not if you told people that certain shoes should never be worn."

"Are you kidding? You think people only buy shoes that they intend to wear?"

"I did think that, but if you can convince me otherwise, I'm all ears."

"Sometimes a person, such as myself, will occasionally purchase a pair of shoes with the same intention that another person would use to purchase a piece of art. I buy shoes because they make me feel a certain way or because they remind me of something or someone I love. It could be a friend, a relative, a movie, or even a candy." I hold up a pair of red satin sandals as I say "candy."

"Those do look like candy; you're right about that," he says.

"See? I told you. Now doesn't it make sense that a person might fall in love with a pair of shoes, only to find out that they are not available in her size, but she feels compelled to buy them anyway? I'm not saying that happens very often, but it does happen."

"You've bought shoes in the wrong size because they remind you of candy?"

"On occasion."

"I just want to make sure I got this right. You have shoes in your closet that do not fit you? Deliberately?"

"The truth of the matter is that most of my shoes do not actually *fit* me. I buy shoes for reasons that go much deeper than the exact size of my foot. I'm not bound by numbers. I buy quality workmanship, beautiful materials, updated classic designs, a flattering instep, unique detailing, and they have to give me butterflies."

"Even if they're the wrong size?"

"Even if they're the wrong size. I'm not even sure what size foot I have. It could be almost anything. I can fit into a five and a half, a six, a six and a half, even a seven. I think I'm somewhere in between a six and a six and a half, but honestly, at this point, it doesn't really make a difference."

"Well, in that case, take the ones you're wearing and let's go."

"Okay," I say, "I'm pretty much done here anyway."

"You forgot *your* shoes," he says, as I quickly slip off the mules and retry the velvets with the perfectly frayed ribbon.

"Oh, no thanks. I don't need them," I say, while admiring myself in the mirror.

I thought the mules were amazing, but these shoes give me the legs of a praying mantis.

"That's ridiculous," he says. "These are perfectly good shoes. All you need is a little glue."

"I know, but they are nothing compared to these," I say, and then realize I just insinuated that I'm going to keep them.

"Well, I think you should take your own shoes, too. They look like they've only been worn once or twice. You can still use them."

"But I don't like them anymore," I say, unable to take my

eyes off of my *new* shoes. I wish he'd stop trying to make me feel guilty for not wanting to ever see those frumpy old gray ones ever again. I never even wanted them in the first place. I don't even remember buying them.

"What do you think of these?" I ask, knowing perfectly well how unbelievably sexy they are.

"If you want my honest opinion, I think they're ugly."

"You think they're *ugly*?"

"Really ugly."

"Doesn't this frayed velvet bow remind you of an antique doll's dress?"

"Not at all. I think it looks like it's about to rip right off."

"Well, I think they're beautiful."

"Then take them," he says, a little impatiently.

"I *should* take them, but I still want to leave my options open."

We both sit there not saying anything for a while as he looks around, twirling a shoe in each hand by their straps. I look around, too. I'm not really sure what we're looking at, but there's really nothing else to do. He looks right at me for a second and turns away. Then I look at him. I would turn away, too, but it's almost impossible to stop looking at him once you get started.

"The closet looks great, by the way. You did an excellent job," he says, breaking the silence.

"You really think so? I always organize my own closet by color. At least I try to. Anyway, I'll definitely bring these back tomorrow. I just need *something* to wear home."

"Why don't you leave your shoes in your desk and wear these in tomorrow? You can get glue from the supply closet whenever you need it. The editors do it all the time. No one will say anything," he says.

"Okay, I guess that's a good idea," I say, taking my gray shoes, which he has been holding like a pair of eggs. I don't know why he's holding them so carefully. They're already ruined.

"So, thanks for getting me out of there," I say.

"No problem at all. I'll walk you downstairs."

I don't want him to see me trying to walk in these shoes. He's just the type to suggest that I switch to the gray ones.

"Oh, no, thank you. I'm fine. I have to stop at my desk and take care of a few things."

"Are you sure?"

"Positive," I say, trying not to hobble.

You don't meet people like him very often. He was so patient and appreciative of my ability to organize by color. Everything about him was beautiful: his blue eyes, his soft hair, his blonde eyebrows, his tan hands, and his Crest Whitestrips teeth. Under normal circumstances, like if I hadn't just been hit with over two hundred pairs of shoes all at once, I would have been a lot friendlier.

~

CHAPTER SEVEN

Stay True to Yourself and the Things You Truly Love

These are not my shoes. They belong to the company. I have a responsibility to return them in the exact same condition as I found them. I am a responsible, trustworthy, law-abiding citizen. Always have been. Even if there were a fire in my building, I would not wear these shoes outdoors. I would throw them carefully out the window and run out barefoot. I would.

"Hi, Jen."
  "Hi."
  "What are you doing tonight?"
  "I'm planning to eat dinner, watch TV, and go to bed. You?"
  "I don't know."
  "You don't know? That's impossible. 'I don't know' means you might actually be contemplating leaving your apartment. Are you aware that it's a school night?"
  "I have new shoes on from the shoe closet at work. I don't know what to do. I'm not supposed to wear them out."
  "Hmmm."

"Any suggestions?"

"Bring them here. Wear your own shoes and then change when you get here."

"You're right! That's not *wearing* them out. I'll be there in twenty minutes."

It's almost as if these shoes were specifically designed to be worn in Jen's apartment. Look at them sitting there on her little antique chair, with the casual rip in the upholstery that she ripped herself, with my help. We both can't believe how great they look next to her 1920's dressing room lounger, which she uses as a living room sofa.

We do a little photo session of me and the shoes and then her and the shoes and then just the sofa and the shoes and then we get a few really good shots of the shoes peeking out from a box of ribbons. We take a short break and start shooting again. First we get a few close-ups of one of the shoes lying on the floor next to her bed, and then we get one of both shoes, walking arm in arm, using their ankle straps as arms. After a while, the photo shoot starts to feel like we're playing dress up, and I get another horrible flashback of the summer when Zoe and all of my friends went to sleepaway camp and I stayed home.

At the end of the summer, a couple of my friends came over. Naturally, I went to my closet to take out a few Barbies. I just stood there holding the dolls while all my friends cracked up laughing. You'd think I had inadvertently pulled out a handful of vibrators or something. They were really howling. No one mentioned to me that we were all supposed to grow up and start hating Barbie that summer. I thought it was just a regular summer.

It was so embarrassing. I waited years before I told Zoe about it. As soon as I told her, she wrote this whole big thing about Barbie. It was all about how Barbie was misunderstood and wrongly treated like a trailer park slut because she didn't have cellulite. Barbie was everything to me and Zoe knew it. After I read her essay, I learned that Zoe secretly loved Barbie, too. Although, I must say, she was a little rough on her. As a rule, Zoe hated playing with dolls, but Barbie was more than a doll. She was our big sister. To this day, when I see a Barbie doll, I turn bright red. But I still love her, and I probably always will.

That memory really killed our photo session, though.

CHAPTER EIGHT

~

You Exist for Her

Ruth is in a good mood this morning. Her door is wide open, and I can see that she's wearing a very cute little wraparound dress with a belt. It's not a bad dress for Ruth. It's just that her feet are swollen, and they are oozing out of her high heels like two large, undercooked popovers. One of these days, I'm afraid that a part of her foot is going to lop right off.

She's so busy in there. She's buzzing around like a little bee. I'm glad to see that she's feeling so chipper.

"Chloe? Can I see you for a minute?"

I'm wearing a straight khaki skirt and a lacy tank top. It's Jen's. She let me borrow it last night because it's perfect with my new shoes. Even though I'm going to return them in an hour or so. I feel like an attorney in this skirt. Although this top isn't something I would necessarily wear in a courtroom.

I quickly put my drawstring bag under my desk and appear at Ruth's door. In my bag is a pair of my own shoes and my lunch. I know that sounds odd, but I have to disguise my lunch a little differently every day. Otherwise something will happen to it. The other day, I found my brown lunch bag twisted into a long skinny line, pinned to my bulletin board. It was completely empty. It was like a lynching. There's a side to Ruth that I can't possibly put into words.

I was going to leave my gray shoes here last night, but I finally threw them away . . . by accident.

Ruth is examining me from head to toe.

"Don't we look nice today," she says.

"Thanks! I was just about to say the same thing to you," I answer.

"Since you look like you are ready to get down to business, let's get started. I have two assignments here. Typically, these types of projects would go to the copywriter first and then to the art department, but, as it turns out, the copywriter we hired has taken a position at another magazine. I'm going to have to ask you to pitch in until we resolve the situation."

"How long do you think that will take?" I ask.

"That really shouldn't be any of your concern . . . unless . . . why do you want to know, Chloe?"

"I was just wondering how long I'll be able to use that extra desk," I say.

"Is that your only concern, or are you wondering if you'll be asked to take on projects that are not part of your job description?"

"I have a job description?"

"Of course you do."

"Really? Wow. What is it, if you don't mind me asking?"

"Chloe, I think it's obvious from your title. You are the assistant to the assistant."

"I know, but when you say, 'the assistant to the assistant,' exactly who is the assistant, and who is she the assistant to? I've been meaning to ask you that since the first day, but I keep forgetting."

"Not every position is filled at the moment. For all practical purposes, your job description is that you assist me."

"Well, that's a relief. The last thing I want to do is ignore anyone."

"I'm sure. Now, let's get started. The two projects I have here require immediate attention. Number one: We are doing an issue on ankles, and the advertising staff has asked us to come up with some exciting promotional ideas."

"They want us to promote ankles?"

"Chloe, pay attention. The articles in our ankle issue will deal with ankle-related issues. Our job is not to sell ankles, per se. Our job is to reach advertisers who manufacture ankle-related products: ankle bracelets, eczema creams, foot lotions, anything to do with socks, panty hose, toe rings, toenail polish, toenail polish remover, pedicure sets, spas, foot baths, and of course . . . shoes. I have a list of advertisers here that the salespeople want to get in to see. Have a look at it and then try to come up with some ideas."

"Bear with me a minute here, Ruth. What exactly are ankle-related issues?"

"Women have issues with every part of their body. In order to help them deal with these issues, we highlight a different part of the body each month and teach women how to make that part of their body look better. I believe the editors are doing an article on capri pants and how important it is to combat ankle eczema. We might suggest not wearing ankle-strap shoes because they have a tendency to make the ankle appear larger. The editors might recommend opaque hose or a tattoo to cover a scar. There are a million ways to show women how to love their ankles. We need to let our ankle-related advertisers know that our readers care about their ankles and that they come to us for the best advice on how to beautify their ankles. It's not that complicated, Chloe. You know the magazine. We've done legs, buttocks, stomachs, arms, and cleavage. We even did a whole issue on hair removal."

She did *see that one!*

"I have an idea!" I spring up.

"I doubt that, Chloe. I haven't even finished."

"I'm sorry," I say and sit back down. I really want to tell her my idea before I forget it.

"I was thinking that we should do a folder," Ruth says, "like this one." She holds up a folder with a picture of a pair of gloves on the front cover.

"What was that for?" I ask. "The glove issue?"

"Chloe, why can't you grasp this? It was for the *hand* issue."

I should have known. The folder clearly states, "Slip into our October issue and get your hands on 3.5 million readers."

My idea isn't nearly that good.

"Wow," I say, "who wrote that one?"

"I think it was me, although I can't remember anymore. This one was done way back when I had three writers in my department. It's hard to say exactly who came up with that particular line."

"Well, my idea isn't anything like that, but—"

"Just a minute, Chloe, let me show you the numbers on this." Ruth reads off seven columns of numbers that indicate our readers' buying habits. This information is flowing beautifully in one ear and right out the other, but I'm getting the idea that our readers use a lot of foot cream and they buy a lot of socks.

I wonder if they have any new shoes in the shoe closet.

"Why don't you go back to your desk and rough out some ideas, and then I'll introduce the next project," Ruth says.

"You can just tell me the other project right now. I already know what I'm going to do for this one," I say, trying to take a load off her mind.

"You may think you have an idea, but these things take time. You may need to give me six or seven ideas before I actually bond with one of them. I have to feel it, Chloe. You can't just say, 'This is what I'm going to do.' I have to approve of it *here* and *here*." She points to a piece of paper and her stomach.

"Okay, I'll give you six or seven," I say. "I have about a million up *here*."

"Fine. I have some phone calls to make. Get something on paper and we'll talk in a few hours." Ruth makes a little back-and-forth sweeping motion with her hands. She does this when she wants me to leave.

Here's what I have so far:

1. A fashion show . . . from the calf down. The models come down the runway completely surrounded by individual high-tech mesh barrels or shower curtains on wheels. Only their legs show from the calf down. The fashion show begins with spa items. First the models walk down the runway (completely covered, from the calf up). When they get to the end of the runway, there is a pedicure tub waiting for them with a whole array of beautiful bottles, brushes, foot creams, soaps, foot massagers, polishes, etc.

    Then the next group of models comes out for phase two of the show, which features a whole array of panty hose, novelty socks (with and without toes), foot jewelry, ankle bracelets, henna tattoos, crystals, ankle guards, and anything else that would go on before shoes. The final segment of the show is a shoe fashion show featuring everything from athletic footwear, sports gear and sneakers, to roller blades, ice skates, ski boots, snowboards, skis, and every kind of shoe imaginable, from flats to stilettos.

    We can perform the fashion shows in stores that advertise in our magazine, and the whole fashion show can be shown on huge screens in each of the departments that sell the particular products featured in the show. We can also install screens and play a taped version of the show in sporting goods stores, spas, shoe stores, or any other venue that sells the products featured in the show. We can give any advertiser as much show exposure as they want, based on the amount of advertising they buy.

    We'll advertise the show in May and June. The show will be held in July, just in time for the August Ankle issue. Smart advertisers will want to be in all four issues, because then their products will be seen at the exact same time that our readers are reading and thinking about their ankles. We can even serve all kinds of tofu (which sort of sounds like toe food) to the audience during intermission.

2. The Big Fish Approach. Instead of going after a bunch of advertisers, we go after one big one and offer them a whole section of the magazine. I suggest Dr. Scholl, Nike, Puma, or some other healthy, sporty advertiser. We do an article on the health and safety benefits of certain stretching exercises, breathing techniques, and proper footwear. We can do as many articles as they like for each page of advertising that they buy.

3. Medical Angle. First we get the names of the publicists of big-name female sports medicine doctors and podiatrists. This could be any doctor's big chance to make a name for herself by giving her a niche as *the top female* athlete, *the top female* physical therapist, or *the top female* bone doctor or muscle doctor or bunion doctor, whatever. Just as long as you get the top women in each field. We do a few paragraphs on each doctor, and they all chip in for a page. Then we do the same thing with sports facilities, spas, corrective footwear stores, gyms, you name it. Each category gets a page of editorial and a collectively paid for page of advertising.

4. Cultural Arts Approach. Tie in our ankle issue with the arts. We convince the editors to put a ballerina's ankle in point shoes on the cover of the magazine. The shot would be taken to highlight her beautiful ankles. Then we do an article on a day in the life of five dancers: a ballerina, a tap dancer, a modern/jazz dancer, a hip-hop dancer and a ballroom dancer. We show them stretching and working out at the barre. We show what they eat, how many hours they sleep, etc. The article will stress the health and beau-

tifying benefits of a life of dance and how certain exercises help strengthen bones and muscles at different stages in our lives.

In this case, we will have to approach various foundations or private contributors to the arts for our ad pages, but we'll tell them how the focus of our issue is not only to promote ankle-related products but also to promote the arts. We can also do an article on how badly the arts need funding because of our government cutbacks. Each ad will have a phone number for donations. If we get three or four million readers donating one dollar, that's pretty good. We'll tell them if they donate a dollar and send in their name and address, they can also win season tickets to The American Ballet Theatre.

5. We can do a folder shaped like a pair of feet and ankles and put a really cute pair of socks on it. We can put any designer sock on the folder and put the designer's/advertiser's logo on the sock and do a mailing for them promoting their socks with our name on it. Then we tell them that we'll deduct the cost of the mailing from their ad page cost, because we're sort of promoting ourselves, too, and it wouldn't be right to ask them to pay for our idea to promote both of us.

6. We can put together a little ankle-related spa/beauty package and mail it to potential advertisers as our little gift. We include: a full pedicure kit, a handmade beaded ankle bracelet, foot jewelry, including: toe rings and attached toe ring/ankle bracelets, cute socks, a bunch of different toenail polishes, a foot care booklet, and a loofah. We send it around to every advertiser with a note that says, "Step into Our August Issue and Get a Leg Up on the Competition," or "Our August Issue Is No Small Feat, Get Instep with Our Readers." Or something like that.

7. We can do a folder shaped like an ankle.

★   ★   ★

Ruth comes into my office area at about two-thirty and asks me if I have anything for her. At this point, I've pretty much forgotten about the list of ankle issue promotional ideas because I've been flipping through some old issues of *Issues*, which I found in the bottom of the other desk. Some of these are from the fifties. They are so great. I think we should do something with them, but I'm not sure what.

I wonder if there are any new shoes in the shoe closet.

"Well, Chloe, did you come up with an exciting idea?"

"For what?" I ask.

"For the ankle issue," she says, amazed at my inability to keep up.

"Oh that! Yes, of course. They're all ready. Would you like to see them?"

"Bring them into my office."

I hand Ruth my ideas, and she starts reading what I've written. Either I've made a complete fool out of myself or she likes one of them. It's impossible to tell what she's thinking.

"Did you show these ideas to anyone?" she asks.

"No," I say.

"Fine. I'll take it from here. You don't have to sit here and wait for me to respond. I can't really give this my full attention right now anyway. I'll give you my thoughts as soon as possible."

"Do you want to give me the other project?" I ask.

"What other project?" she asks. She's still looking down. She's completely distracted by what I wrote.

"You mentioned that there were two projects this morning."

"Oh, right," she says, only half listening. "The other one is much more involved." She's reading and talking to me at the same time. "It's for our shoe issue. We need to do something special to attract the European shoe market. I can't go into it right now. Just start thinking shoes. In the meantime, do me a favor and run downstairs and get me a cup of coffee." She reaches into her drawer and takes out a color chart. Without looking up, she says, "I like my coffee camel-colored. Is that understood? Not brown, not beige, camel. If you're not sure what that means, take this with you."

She hands me a strip of paper with several brown squares on it, ranging from dark brown to off-white. She has put a star next to one of the squares.

"Try to match this color as best as you can. I really can't drink it any other way."

I head downstairs with the paint color sample as fast as I can. I can't wait to work on the shoe issue. Ruth is amazing. She's already making my dreams come true. Is she even aware of what an incredible mentor she's become?

The coffee looks like pancake syrup. I could never turn that into camel. It will turn gray. Oh look! There's the lady with the tiny feet.

"Hi! Remember me? I hate to bother you, but do you have any other coffee back there . . . in any other colors? I need to bring a camel-colored cup to my boss. I'm afraid this shade you have here is way off. I need to start with more of a ruddy brown," I say, while looking around the glass shelves for any leftover chocolate cake. Nothing. Damn. I show her the color chart, but she waves it away.

She's wearing a little hairnet and a pink uniform today, and she's got that *You-should-eat-something* look in her eye. I can't wait for her to whip out something from her secret little stash.

"I've seen enough of those color charts to last me a lifetime. You want somethin' for yourself?" she asks me. I'm the only one down here, and you can just tell that she's in the mood to talk.

I wonder where people buy those little hairnets.

"I don't think so. I'm not really hungry," I say, trying not to look as though I could eat a horse.

"How about one of these salads? I made them myself. You want a scoop of tuna in this one?" she asks. "By the way, I'm Liz. I don't think I ever officially introduced myself."

"I'm Chloe Rose, nice to meet you. Do you have anything with icing?" I ask.

"How about a piece of pie, Chloe Rose?"

"Okay, I guess. Pie sounds good."

As soon as I start eating the pie, I get an urge for something sweeter. I choose a small brownie and a bag of chocolate chip cookies, but I only eat half of the brownie. I wonder why I don't come down here more often. The packaged food is very good. Nothing can happen to my lunch if I buy it and eat it here.

As I'm just about to finish my last cookie, Stan walks in. He's with a really pretty blonde, but not the Sloane kind of blonde. This one is the other kind. The kind with roots. She's whispering something in his ear. He's pulling his head away. I wonder if she said something dirty. It sure seems like it. He doesn't seem to like her very much, although he's not exactly running away. Not that it's any of my business.

I hope I'm not going to witness anything obscene. They probably arranged to meet down here at this odd hour to have some time alone. I've got to get out of here. I don't want to be seen sitting here with two empty paper plates, a cookie wrapper, and a half-eaten brownie.

I quickly gather up my garbage and position myself so that I can see them but they can't see me. She's giggling. This is so gross. She's all over him in front of everyone . . . well, just Liz and me, but still. He's very gently taking her hands off his arm. He's holding a little folder. He keeps pointing to it. Does he honestly expect this girl to concentrate on work? She's like a teething puppy. In one minute, she's going to start gnawing on him.

I manage to throw away my garbage, take a napkin, wipe up my table, throw it away, and slip out without being seen, but then I remember Ruth's coffee. I go back in and walk right by them, keeping my eyes glued ahead of me. I don't think I really have to worry about being noticed. His back is to me, and she's practically smothering him anyway.

"Try to focus," he says to her as he puts the folder in front of her face. She should be ashamed of herself.

I see that Liz has made a fresh pot of coffee, so I quietly ask her for a cup. As soon as she hands it to me, I whisper, "Thank you," and begin to add milk. It's not quite camel. It's definitely terra-cotta. It's funny, but I never realized how much red there is in coffee. I add a little more milk, but it's still not camel. Now it's rust. It's not a red rust. It's more of a light brown rust. *There might be something wrong with this coffee.* I try adding some powdered milk and a dash of Half & Half.

"Is this coffee from an unusual country?" I whisper to Liz.

"Not that I know of," she mumbles back. She's very concerned. She comes around to look in my cup. We both hold up the color chart, but it's not right.

"Maybe you need more milk, Chloe Rose," she says.

I can't hold out much longer. Eventually she's got to learn the truth. Maybe I'll just say something like, "You can call me Chloe, for short. I hardly ever use my first and last names."

I add a little more milk, but it's starting to overflow a bit and it's still not a true camel. I hold it over the garbage and add a drop more milk, letting it overflow. Eventually it's got to match the little swatch I've got here, but it's still way off. I reach for the powdered milk substitute, which has a yellowish hue, just as Liz comes back around to check on my progress. I turn to show her, and we bump heads. I attempt to save the coffee by bringing it closer to me and spill it all over my shirt, my shoes (which, of course, do not belong to me), and my skirt, which is now sticking to my body in places that should never be seen in the workplace. It's hot but not scalding, thanks to all the milk. My skirt is soaking wet. You can even see the outline of my panty hose seam. The one right up the middle. My bra is also showing, and I even have a little coffee in my hair. It wouldn't be that bad if my nipples didn't protrude like bullets upon any sort of contact at all. Warm, wet coffee is enough to cause them to erupt to magnanimous proportions.

"Oh, for heaven's sakes, Chloe Rose," Liz says. "Look at what I've done!"

"You didn't do it, Liz. I, *Chloe*, did it," I say, while trying not to move and give her a really big clue at the same time. I look at my hand, which is soaked with coffee. I'm still holding the cup over the garbage can. I turn to see if Stan and the puppy are still in the cafeteria, but they're gone, thank God. I guess they finally noticed that they weren't alone. Liz is trying to mop me up, but I'm beyond mopping.

"You poor dear," she says, over and over again.

"Ruth is going to kill me. I should have had this coffee on her desk a long time ago. I want her to like me, but sometimes it seems like I just can't do anything right."

"I don't want to hear you talkin' like that. You're a nice girl and you'll do fine. I know Ruth all too well, and don't you go worryin' about her. I know everyone around here. You just do your work and you'll be fine."

She's wiping my hand now. I feel like I fell on the playground. She reminds me of my favorite school nurse, Miss June. Miss June believed me when I told her that I felt a heart attack coming on the day we had a mean substitute teacher. She let me lie on the cot and she called my mom and asked her to come get me. I really feel like going home right now. Whenever I think about Miss June, I want to call my mom and tell her to come get me. She can't bring me dry clothes from Florida, but maybe I should call her anyway, just to say hi. I really should go home and change my clothes.

I can certainly call Ruth to explain what happened. I'm sure she'd understand. Oh, never mind; Ruth's here. Although she doesn't look like she's in a very understanding mood. I turn to her with what little coffee is left in the cup and say,

"Would you consider this camel?"

"Chloe, what could possibly be taking so long?"

I gesture toward my clothing to illustrate the point that I'm in a real pickle here.

"Well, no wonder!" she says, focusing on my drenched hand, which is still holding the overflowing cup. "That's way too much milk, and that's obviously decaf. You can't get camel with decaf. You'll end up going too dark or too light. Please be more careful Chloe, really," she says and storms out. Maybe the spillage isn't as noticeable as I thought. She didn't even mention it.

I try to forget about my wet hair and stained clothes and try several more combinations, until I finally create a truly perfect camel color, using Half & Half, skim milk, and a pinch of confectioners' sugar. The sugar sits right on top. It gives the top layer of coffee a nice, tan glaze. I hold up the color swatch, and it's absolutely perfect. Ruth is going to love this. I show it to Liz, and she clasps her hands together. That's the final word, so off I go.

I wouldn't dare take the elevator looking like this, so I carefully tiptoe all the way upstairs without spilling a drop. I'm concentrating so intently that I accidentally walk up an extra flight of stairs, and there's Stan on his way down.

"What happened to you?" he asks.

"Oh, as if you don't know!" I say.

Why am I mad at him? I hardly even know him.

"What are you talking about? How should I know?"

"You didn't see this happen to me?"

"No, of course not! What are you talking about?"

"It doesn't matter. I just spilled some of this coffee on my way upstairs. That's all."

"You spilled *some* of it? Is there anything left in that cup?"

"Of course there is. I only spilled a drop."

"Well, let me help you."

"No, thank you. I'm fine."

"What's wrong with you? Let me help you."

"I'm so late. Please don't help me. Let me just bring this to Ruth before I get in more trouble with her than I already am."

"Chloe, you *have* to change your clothes."

"No, I *have* to bring this coffee to Ruth. But thanks for offering to change my clothes."

What did I just say?

"Anytime."

There's an awkward little silence now because that didn't make any sense, so neither one of us knows what to do.

"Well, nice seeing you," I say. I quickly turn around and walk back downstairs, gently cradling the coffee. I slowly walk down the hall and slip into Ruth's office. I reach over her desk and delicately place the coffee in front of her without taking my eyes off the cup. Then I look up and almost drop the whole thing. Ruth is standing right in front of me, trying on my shoes. We both freeze. My little drawstring bag is on her desk and there she is, trying to fold her foot into my shoe, in broad daylight. I guess I got up here much quicker than she anticipated.

"I thought these were mine," Ruth says.

"Oh! I make that mistake all the time, too. You do have a pair that looks just like those, don't you?" I say, trying not to cough or burst into flames from the humiliation I feel for her.

"I saw that drawstring bag and I thought it was mine because I have the exact same one. Then I looked inside and saw that there was a pair of shoes in there. I thought they looked familiar and I was just checking. But I see now that these aren't mine at all." She takes them and throws them back into the drawstring bag with incredible force. There goes my lunch. It's a good thing I already ate.

I gently pick up the bag and put it on my lap. I try to feel around inside a little to see if any parts of my lunch can be salvaged, on the off chance that I get hungry again later.

We both sit down and try to forget that any of this just happened. Ruth picks up the cup of coffee, lifts the lid, takes a sip, puts the lid back on, and carefully places it in the garbage.

"I didn't do it right?" I ask.

"No, you did not," Ruth says, "but I'm not about to send you down for another one. It's been a half hour already. What happened to you anyway?"

"I spilled," I say.

"Well, I suggest that you try to pay more attention to what you are doing. Now, I guess we should go over some of your ideas. You are almost there, Chloe, but not quite. Over here, in number one, you listed sneakers and athletic footwear. That's redundant. Secondly, we've never done a spa package before." When she says, "spa package," she says it really sarcastically. I think she must have hated that one.

"We'd have to assemble hundreds of packages ourselves, and I'm not sure if the company would be willing to pay you overtime for that.

"Thirdly, and I don't mean to sound too detail-oriented, but you have two folder ideas here, which means you really only gave me six ideas, and I distinctly asked for seven. I'd say, all in all, I like the ankle-shaped folder idea the best, but I'm willing to put these other ideas on the back burner for a while. Just don't discuss them with anyone; do you understand? I might want to rework a few of them, and you know what they say—'Too many cooks spoil the soup.' "

"Isn't it, 'Too many cooks spoil the broth'?" says a voice from out of nowhere. Look at that. It's Rob. He's walked right into Ruth's office. He's wearing the most adorable little suit I've ever seen and a pink tie. I wonder what size suit he wears. I bet he could fit into my jeans.

"I heard there was a little accident in the cafeteria. I just ran into my good friend Liz Jabonowsky, and she filled me in. Where's the young lady who spilled a whole cup of coffee on herself? Ah! It looks like I found her."

Ruth looks over at me as though she is seeing me for the first time.

"My gosh, Chloe. You should have told me. Of course you spilled something! I can see it all over you. I've been so absorbed in getting these promotional ideas tightened up, I must not have realized. Go and get cleaned up this minute. You can't sit here like that."

Finally she realized!

"Why not have a visit to the fashion closet?" Rob says.

What is it with this guy and those closets? He's like my Uncle Jack. Uncle Jack used to go around giving Zoe and me and all of our cousins five-dollar bills if we promised to give him a kiss and a hug. Every one of us took the money, even though we knew we were nothing but a bunch of whores. No one would have hugged him for free. I think Rob just likes the idea that he has something to offer women that no one else in the world can. Unfortunately, I can't risk getting locked in a closet today.

"No thanks, I'm almost dry, but I would like to use the ladies' room," I say.

"I think we can allow that," Rob says and walks around to where Ruth is sitting.

I wonder if I should leave those two alone. I'm really worried about her. She's so nervous around him. I walk out of the room carrying my little shoe bag and hover by the door for a few seconds.

"Can I see what you've got there?" Rob asks her.

"Oh, these are just some ideas I was playing with. To be perfectly honest, I was just brainstorming. I called Chloe in as a sounding board. I'm trying to teach her how to think promotionally, even though some of these ideas are a little over the top; I thought I'd throw them out at her."

"Is that right? I could swear I heard you telling Chloe that she was being redundant by using the words *athletic footwear* and *sneakers*. It sounded like you were discussing Chloe's ideas. You're not taking credit for your assistant's ideas again, are you, Ruth?"

I can't stand what he's doing to her. She's taking the blame for my over-the-top ideas and he's accusing her of stealing them! Poor Ruth.

"Rob, don't be ridiculous. You must have misunderstood. Chloe has only been here a few months. She can barely use the copier," she laughs. "I hope you don't think I was trying—"

"Hello," I say, walking back in the room. "I think I *will* go upstairs and change. I can't really do anything with myself after all."

"Chloe," Rob says, "just a minute. I want to ask you something. Who wrote these?" He puts the paper right in front of me, and I don't know what to say. I look at Ruth and then I look at Rob. He looks at Ruth, who looks like she just saw a ghost. Maybe my nipples are sticking out again.

I start coughing and attempt to cover my breasts with my little bag of shoes. It's the kind of coughing that sounds like I might die. I can't stop. Rob puts his arm around me and leads me outside to the water fountain. He turns it on and holds my hair back. I turn around and see Ruth staring at us with her arms folded. And then I run. Normally, I wouldn't run in an office setting, but I see no way out of this situation. Having a male coworker hold your hair back while you drink from the water fountain is ten times worse than laughing at his jokes or looking at his cute body parts.

I'm still not sure if my ideas were good or ludicrous. I'm not sure if Ruth was protecting me or taking credit for my ideas and the last thing I want to do is make a liar out of her. I also think it was foolish of me to suggest serving tofu at a fashion show, and I'd rather not take credit for that one, under any circumstances. I'm not sure why Rob even cares whose ideas they are, and I'm not sure where I'm going, either.

Before I even realize where I've gone, I'm back at the shoe closet. As long as I'm here, I should probably return the beautiful velvet shoes that I'm still wearing. There are so many people here today. It's like a little social hour. Every single one of these editors looks like a model.

I wish I worked with these girls instead of Ruth. There's Sloane!

"Hi, Sloane," I say, slipping off one perfect velvet shoe at a time. "I was just returning these." I glance at them one more time and see that they are covered with coffee stains. "I brought my own shoes to change into," I say, turning the velvet shoes upside down. She's straining to look at me as though there's something terribly wrong. Then it occurs to me that I must look as though I'm dirty.

"I spilled an entire cup of coffee on myself," I say.

"I can see that," Sloane says, taking the shoes out of my hand. She practically throws them into the closet and says,

"Let's see what we can dig up for you in the fashion closet." Normally a sentence like that would give me intense heart palpitations, but I'm still a little distracted by the fact that I just ran away from my boss and the publisher.

The fashion closet is even messier than the shoe closet. The only difference between this closet and my closet is that this one is loaded with gowns and hats. I don't have any of those things.

Another girl comes in and introduces herself as Blaire, the articles editor. She's about five feet nine, and her skin is the exact same color as peanut butter. She's tall and gorgeous and extremely skinny.

"Sloane just told me that you're working for Ruth," she says. "She's always up to something, isn't she?"

This is like a little dormitory in here. They probably hang out all day, trying on clothes and shoes. I didn't realize how depressing my job is until now.

"How about this?" Sloane says. It's a red suede jacket. I would never wear that. It's the same color as Ruth's sweater coat, the one with the big rip under the arm. I take it from her and say, "It's perfect!" but I don't make a move to go and change.

Instead I start talking. "Ruth has a red sweater coat in this exact same color. It has huge black buttons and a big rip under the arm and she wears it all the time." I'm not sure why I'm telling them this, but apparently they've all seen the sweater coat because they're all laughing. As soon as I say it, I regret it. I don't know what came over me.

I head toward the ladies' room to change into the only thing in that entire closet that I don't like when I hear a voice say, "She should not be wearing red with her coloring." It's the voice of an angel. The angel is rushing toward me.

I've seen this girl before. She's the girl from the cafeteria!

"Oh my, what happened to you?" she asks, as she gets closer.

"I spilled coffee . . . a little while ago. I'd say it was two min- utes ago, at the most."

I don't want her to know that I saw her shamelessly flirting with Stan. She's nice enough to save me from wearing red.

"Well, we have to do something about this. This is just ter- rible," she says.

I feel like Little Orphan Annie.

She walks over to the closet and pulls out a sheer white Dolce & Gabbana shirt and a black-and-white glen plaid skirt. "Put this on," she says. I don't hesitate, because it's perfect, and I don't want Sloane or Blaire coming over with an even better idea, which might involve colorful leather.

I go to the ladies' room and change. I'm wearing the per- fect bra for this shirt. I come out to show everyone, and they all agree that it's great, except for Sloane, who looks in the other direction.

I slip on my own shoes and wonder for a second if I read anything in Ruth's medical files about athlete's foot. I look over at Sloane. I want to ask her what's wrong with what I'm wearing, but I don't know her well enough. As soon as the girl from the cafeteria turns and walks back toward the fashion closet, Sloane points to her and mouths the word "Courtney."

Well, I'll be damned. That's Courtney. She's even more helpful in person.

Courtney comes back from the closet and hands me another skirt, exactly like the one I'm wearing, but in cream-and-brown plaid. She also gives me the exact same shirt in cream.

"Take these, too. The fashion editor is going to clear all of this stuff out of here in a few days, so you might as well have both outfits. You look amazing."

"I love your column," I spit out by accident. Then I quickly recover by making the "yeah right" face at Sloane, and we both smile. I immediately feel guilty, as usual.

"Thanks!" Courtney says. "You're so sweet. Isn't she the sweetest?"

They all hate her. They probably make faces at her all day long and she has no idea. Why do they hate her? Her implants are slightly askew, but that could happen to anyone. She's so nice to all of them and I've got a great outfit on because of her. In fact, I've got two new great outfits because of her. So what if she's a little flirty? Nobody's perfect.

I wonder how I'd look as a blonde?

~

CHAPTER NINE

Sometimes the Wrong Belt
Is the Only Proper Means of Defense

Ruth has her door shut today. She rarely does that. I walk into the art department and ask Trai and Rhonda if Ruth is okay. Trai says that he noticed that her door was closed and that he was hoping I came in there to report that she's offed herself. I stay in the art department for a while, because I don't really know what else to do with myself.

"Did you get that skirt from the fashion closet?" Rhonda asks me.

"How can you tell?" I ask.

"I saw it in there the other day, but I could tell from a mile away that it would be a bad cut for me. I'm an expert at hiding these hips, as you now know."

"You're not hiding anything," Trai says.

"I actually got two outfits like this yesterday," I say quickly, hoping Rhonda didn't hear him. "I wore the black plaid skirt home yesterday, and today I thought I'd wear it in cream, but I feel funny about it, even though Courtney insisted. It feels weird wearing clothes that don't really belong to me. I brought my own clothes to change into, just in case. I'll probably change after lunch or something. They are so sweet up there. I can't believe they just gave me two great outfits!"

"Yeah, yeah, yeah," Rhonda says.

"So what do you think she's doing in there?" I ask. "I'm a little worried about her. She had such a bad day yesterday."

"Who the fuck cares. She's probably jerking off," Trai says. God is going to punish him for his foul language.

Trai is wearing a wool cap today. He'll wear it all day. He doesn't care if his beautiful hair gets all matted under there.

It's very quiet in the art department. Hallie is out of the office, and there are no sounds of crashing art supplies because Ali called in sick again. The drummer who lives upstairs from her plays all night. She calls in sick all the time and says it's because the drummer gives her insomnia. I can't help noticing that Rhonda is quietly working on a folder in the shape of an ankle.

"What's that?" I ask.

"Another fucking folder," Trai answers for her.

"When did Ruth give you that project?" I ask.

"She left me a note about it last night. It was on my desk when I came in. She was here pretty late, I guess," Rhonda says. Rhonda is wearing that horrible belt again. Some of the sparkling sequins are falling off. I want to tell Rhonda what happened with Rob, but there is an overwhelming aura of insanity surrounding Trai, which holds me back . . . but only for a second.

"Yesterday afternoon, Rob came in asking Ruth a lot of questions," I say, out of nowhere.

"Interesting," Trai says, indicating that it's not.

"Actually, that *is* interesting," Rhonda says. "Rob never comes down here. I wonder if he's checking up on her. She's been doing some pretty weird stuff lately."

"Like what? How come I never see her do anything weird? I mean, besides her clothes," I say.

"Because you're never around," Trai says.

"I'm always around," I answer.

"No, you're not. You're never around."

What's he talking about?

"I know you won't believe this, but the past few days she's been calling Rob on the phone and disguising her voice. It sounded like she was choking on something at first, but then I realized she was doing it on purpose. She talks to him in this really raspy voice and asks him all kinds of questions that I'd rather not repeat in mixed company. As soon as he hangs up on her, she calls him right back. You have no idea how frightening she sounds. I'm sure she'll eventually figure out that her sexy routine isn't working and go back to threatening to sue him," Rhonda says.

"Or jerk off in front of him," Trai interrupts.

"Shut up, Trai," Rhonda continues. "Rob hated her from the day he started. But you have to hand it to her. She's hanging in there."

Rhonda really does know everything.

"I wish he'd fucking kill her already," Trai says.

That's the second reference he's made to Ruth and death. I wish someone would come in here and see what kind of a nut they keep on the payroll.

"Chloe, get in here, please."

It's Ruth! She's alive!

"Good morning, Ruth. Sorry about yesterday. That was crazy. I didn't mean to run away, but I didn't know what you wanted me to say to him," I say immediately.

"Don't be sorry, Chloe. I understand what you're all about now. You don't have me fooled for a second. But today is another day, and I need to get something to the ad director for this shoe issue. So instead of spending hours in the cafeteria, why don't you actually do some work? Get me some ideas by lunchtime. Think shoes and don't move from that desk until you've got something. Is that understood?"

"Of course, I'll get started right away," I say.

She's been crying in there. I can tell. I might cry, too. Her life is much harder here than anyone realizes. She needs help. I've got to be strong enough for the both of us so I can pull her out of this mess. No more running away. She hired me to help her, and that's what I'm going to do. It's completely up to me now. I've got to turn this situation around, and I'm going to do it right now. This is it. This is the day that Chloe Rose will learn how to stand on her own two feet. I just have to make one phone call.

"Hi."

"What's wrong?"

"Nothing."

"Chloe, I'm on deadline. Talk quickly, but don't hang up in the middle of a sentence."

"Okay, Ruth hates me all of a sudden."

"You're right, she does hate you, but it's not all of a sudden."

"Yes, it is. She liked me the day before yesterday."

"No, she didn't."

"Zoe, you're wrong. I messed up."

"No, you didn't. She was mad at you at the interview."

"You're not listening and you don't know anything about this. She got caught pretending my ideas were hers to the publisher. When he asked me if they were mine or hers, I ran away."

"You ran *away*? Where did you go?"

"To the shoe closet, well actually, the fashion closet."

"They have a shoe closet *and* a fashion closet at that place?"

"Yup."

"Wow, I was going to suggest quitting, but you just put a whole new spin on things. You're not locked in either of those closets right now, are you? Because I keep the number of a locksmith with me at all times now."

"No! This all happened yesterday and I don't need a locksmith. I need you to help me figure out a way to get Ruth to like me again."

"Okay, reread the letter I wrote to you after your interview. There are tons of ideas in that letter."

"I left it at home."

"Okay, then; have you tried a vinyl belt?"

"No."

"Try that."

"It's too late. I need an idea that I can use right now. It can't involve changing my clothes. I'm already at work, fully dressed, and I'm wearing this great outfit that one of the editors picked out for me. I look exactly like Mom, you should see me."

"How about your shoes?"

"Jimmy Choo."

"Chloe!"

"I couldn't help it. They match my skirt perfectly. It's the most amazing thing I've ever seen. And besides, I really don't think Ruth's problem with me is clothing related. I think the problem is that she thinks I'm a bad person."

"Can you be a little more specific?"

"Okay, she thinks I'm a bad person and a bitch."

"Try the disease thing. Pretend you got a devastating phone call from your doctor, and try to make it look like you've been crying. Make your nose and upper lip all red. Bite it, if you have to."

"Bite my nose?"

"Bite your *lip*. Rub your nose. And do it right now. I have to go. Bye, I love you."

She never said what type of disease I'm supposed to say I have. Wait a minute. I'm starting to remember something from that letter. I think it's something sexual. That's it! I'm supposed to say I have greasy hair and a sexually transmitted disease. I can't believe I remembered that. I usually have a terrible memory!

It would have been a lot easier if I'd let myself cry a few minutes ago, when I actually felt like it. I take out my hand mirror and gently bite my lip, but nothing happens. I take out my red lipstick and dab a little in between my nose and my lip. Then I put a little more lipstick right on my nose, and a tiny bit on each eyebrow. Most people don't realize that crying causes the blood to rush to the eyebrow area, as well as the nose and lips. Now, if I just rub this in a little more . . . I think the effect is fantastic. I definitely look like I've been crying. I'm pretty good at this. I just need a touch under my eyes to create an overall blotchiness, and voila! I feel like going into Ruth's office right now to try this out, but if my memory serves me correctly, I think I'm supposed to wait and let her catch me on the phone with the doctor.

I'll just keep the phone by my ear until she walks in. I can certainly do other things while I hold the phone. I'll just set myself up here with some tissues so I can start wiping my nose as soon as she spots me.

I should think about the shoe issue while I'm waiting.

Shoes, shoes, shoes . . . Let's see now . . . Shoes in Issues . . . Shoes and tissues . . . That's a good one. I hope we do a tissue issue. I'd love to use the headline "DON'T BLOW IT! Get in the Tissue Issue." I wonder if there are any new shoes in the shoe closet.

Oh, wait a minute. It's coming to me, ISSHOES . . . IS SHOES . . . WHAT IS SHOES? WHAT ISSHOES? . . . WHAT ISSHOES IS ALL ABOUT? . . . WHAT IS SHOES ALL ABOUT? . . . It's coming. I feel it. IS SHOES . . .

"Chloe!"

"What!" I yell and slam down the phone. She scared me.

"Ruth, I'm sorry, you surprised me, I was just talking to my doctor. It seems that I have a terrible sexually transmitted disease and look at my hair. Isn't it so greasy?" *She doesn't believe me. Well how could she, really? I washed my hair this morning, twice.*

"Chloe, what are you doing?"

"Nothing, I just got off the phone with my gynecologist."

"What's that lipstick all over your nose?"

"Oh that? I mean, what lipstick?" I pick up my mirror and try to see myself from her point of view. "How did that get there?" I ask Ruth.

There's no denying that it's lipstick.

"Oh, right! Now I remember. I was trying to use my lipstick as blush. Have you ever tried that? Using lipstick as blush? Don't bother. Look how bad it looks. Well, I'll never make that mistake again. Anyway, can you believe that about my sexually transmitted disease? I don't want to talk about it, though. I'm much too upset. Who wouldn't be? Can you imagine how upset you'd be, if you had a sexually transmitted disease? Pretty upset, believe me. Oh God, Ruth. It's just so awful. Can I offer you a breath mint?"

I'm so glad I didn't offer her a pair of panty hose.

"Chloe, perhaps you'd like to take a minute to pull yourself together and then meet me in my office. We have actual business to discuss, and I think you should keep the details of your personal life a little more private from this point forward."

I wish Zoe stayed out of this from the beginning. None of her ideas work. Before I even get all the way into Ruth's office, she tells me to shut the door.

"What do you have for the shoe issue so far? I need something immediately," she says.

"Well . . . um . . . I was thinking, that we could . . . um . . . that we could . . . *oh boy, here it comes* . . . that we could install a retrospective shoe exhibit through The Costume Institute at the Metropolitan Museum of Art, using our advertisers' shoes. It will be the biggest museum event of the year, a huge black-tie gala." *I'll finally be able to wear my fuchsia evening bag!*

"We can design the exhibit ourselves. I'm picturing hundreds of beautifully lit shadow boxes, each containing a single shoe. The landscape of each box is decorated to reflect the time period of the shoe that it holds. I was looking at some old issues of the magazine, from the nineteen fifties, and some of the shoes in those old magazines are amazing, but we can go even further back in history and do 'A Walk through Time' exhibit. We can start with a pair of shoes from cavemen times.

"The possibilities are endless. We can include paintings and photographs, sculptures, and I know this woman named Jane Carroll who makes the most amazing shoes out of flowers. I even have a picture of a pair of baby shoes in my room that we could use. If you like the idea, I'll get started on the invitations right away! It will be the most spectacular event of the year! You'll be famous."

I'm almost out of breath. I never expected that to come out of me. Oh God, what if it was a good idea? I'm not wearing anything vinyl.

"Ruth, can you excuse me for a minute? I just remembered something." I quickly run into the art department and whisper to Rhonda that I need to borrow her belt because my skirt is falling down. She whips it right off and gives it to me. I love her for this, and on some level feel as though I may wind up in hell. I quickly buckle the belt and run back to Ruth's office and sit back down.

"Sorry about that. I had a little emergency. So, what do you think of that idea?" I ask while snapping the belt against my waist a few times.

"Was that the whole thing?" Ruth asks, impatiently.

"Sort of," I say, wondering how long I'm supposed to wear the belt if she doesn't like my idea. "But I also have this drawing that I did of a girl's brain. It shows all the different thought processes that she goes through before deciding what pair of shoes she's going to wear. I have it in my office, if you want to see it. It's not very good, but Trai could probably redraw it, and we can use it as the cover of a folder or something, instead of the museum idea."

"Is that it?" she asks.

"So far," I admit.

"Chloe, I asked for *ideas*. Not one or two. Wipe off your

face, get me a cup of coffee, and go back to work. I have a terrible headache."

I wouldn't dare ask her if I could borrow the color chart again. As I turn to leave, Ruth stops me. "Just a minute, Chloe. Am I seeing correctly? Is your entire outfit from the fashion closet?"

"Yes, but, remember yesterday, I spilled some coffee and I had to borrow something."

"Yes, I remember perfectly, but that was yesterday. It was fine for you to wear something home, but I hardly think it was necessary for you to wear something else from the fashion closet today. That's taking advantage, don't you think?"

"I didn't mean to take advantage, and I brought a change of clothes with me because I knew it was wrong," I start to explain.

"That closet is for emergencies. It's not for fun! And it's really not for assistants at all. Sometimes I wonder who you think you are. I really do. As a matter of fact, forget the coffee. Go change out of those clothes and into your own clothes immediately and make sure that you return *everything* that doesn't belong to you. Honestly, Chloe!"

I walk out of Ruth's office, but I'm not sure how. My legs are numb. I wonder if this is how it feels to have hypothermia. I silently thank God that I am not in a situation where I could potentially freeze to death. I think about this kind of thing all the time. Whenever I have a stomach virus, I try to picture myself in a jail cell, with a toilet in the middle of the room. I do this to force myself into being grateful that I'm having my stomach flu in the privacy of my own home. Right now I'm just grateful that I'm not stuck in a frozen pond. For some reason, this method of reasoning can get me through just about anything.

I walk back into the art department and hand Rhonda back her belt. "Thanks, but I have to change, so I won't be needing this," I say. She takes it back without asking any questions.

Maybe she wears that belt on purpose to help people out whenever they feel an idea coming on. At least I didn't have to wear it for very long or put Vaseline in my hair, which is impossible to get out.

I wish I didn't have to go up there and change right before lunch. The editor girls might think I'm coming up there to look for a lunch date. I don't want to seem desperate. I could always bring my lunch with me, to prove that I already have lunch plans. But I can't even find my lunch, as usual.

Where is it? I put it right here. What the hell is this with my lunch? I can't take it anymore. It's always gone by the time I want to eat it. I wonder if there are any new shoes in the shoe closet?

I walk into Ruth's office and just blurt out, "Do you, by any chance, know where my lunch is today? It's not in the garbage or stuck to the wall. I don't know where else to look."

"Excuse me?" Ruth asks.

"My lunch, I can't find it again."

"Chloe, I haven't the vaguest idea where your lunch is," she says, as though she's the normal one.

"I ate it," Trai interrupts, poking his head into Ruth's office.

"What? Why?" I ask.

"I don't know," he says, slipping off his cap and running his fingers through his incredible hair. "I always do."

"Are you serious? You've been eating my lunch? I thought it was Ruth," I say by accident.

"Why would Ruth want to eat your shitty lunch?" Trai says, in a way that sounds oddly like he's mad at me.

"Why would *you?*" I ask, ignoring the absurdity of this whole conversation.

"It's better than nothing," he says. "And what's that red stuff all over your face?"

"Lipstick!" I yell.

I grab my garment bag with my change of clothes and head toward the ladies' room to wash my face and change. Things can't possibly get any more bizarre around here. I just can't believe this place, and as always, I'm starving, with no lunch, and no one to eat with. I wash my face and check myself in the mirror. My face looks different, even without the lipstick all over it. I think I'm starting to look more like Zoe.

I walk out of the ladies' room and start to walk upstairs, but then I turn around and head to the newsstand to get something to eat. I buy a bag of chocolate kisses and a little package of cheese crackers and some pretzels. Now is as good a time as any to start a diet. I'll eat the crackers for lunch and the kisses for dessert, and I'll save the pretzels for later. Maybe there won't be anyone up there.

Please let there be at least one new pair of shoes in that closet to make this day worth living.

I take the elevator up to the seventh floor. As soon as the door opens, I know I'm alone. You can hear a pin drop up here, it's so quiet. I could change my clothes a hundred times in that closet and no one would ever know.

Before I head over to the fashion closet, I take a quick look both ways and slip into the shoe closet for a peek. Oh my God! There's a ton of new stuff in here! And they are keeping it organized by color. I've instituted a new policy! There must be twenty new boxes up there on the top shelf.

I put my snacks on the floor and bring the little stepladder over so I can quickly check out the new arrivals. I climb up and start taking the lids off the boxes, but I can't really see inside, so I decide to bring them all down, one at a time.

I sit down on the floor and neatly arrange all of the new boxes around me in a semicircle. I can really stretch out and enjoy myself now. I love this closet. I really do. As soon as I finish a cracker, I open a new box. I'm keeping the door slightly ajar with one of my own shoes. This is the best lunch I've had since I started working here. I almost prefer eating alone. It's so peaceful and beautiful in the shoe closet. It's like being on the top of a huge mountain. . . . I would imagine.

"Hello?"

Oh my God! It's him again. I should have locked myself in.

I stand up and quickly start stacking up the boxes, as though I'm here to do a job. There are crumbs everywhere.

"Hello," I say, keeping my back to him and my head down.

"Don't turn around and don't tell me who you are. Let me guess. Chloe. Right?" Stan says.

"Yup, it's me again," I say, wondering what sort of lie would work here. I turn to look at him. *It's mean to be that handsome. It's mean and spiteful.*

"I see you figured out how this is done," he says, gesturing with his head toward my shoe/doorstop. He has both of his hands clasped behind his head. He unlocks his hands and pushes his hair back. He looks like a goddamned movie star and I'm standing here in a pile of crumbs.

"So, are you finding everything okay today?"

It must really look like I've made myself right at home here.

"I just came up here to return this outfit, which the editors gave me, because remember how I spilled all that coffee on my own clothes yesterday? But then my boss, Ruth, said I had to return the outfit right now, which I was going to do anyway, but then I realized that it was almost lunchtime, and someone ate my lunch, so I just got some snacks on my way up to change, and then I just came in here for a second to make sure that it was still organized, you know, the way I organized it last time. And since everything looks fine, I'll just neaten up here and be on my way."

"That's too bad," he says.

"Why?"

"Well, you did such an impressive job organizing this closet last time; I was looking forward to watching you mess it all up and put it back together."

"I know I shouldn't keep coming in here, but the truth is, this closet has gotten to be a bit of a problem for me. I try not to think about it, but it's always there, in the back of my mind. I had no intention, whatsoever, of coming in here today. I was headed straight for the fashion closet. It just happened on its own."

He's looking around. There are boxes stacked everywhere and a lot of crumbs and wrappers.

"You consider this a problem?" he says sarcastically. He's trying to make light of the situation. Once again, I've made an extraordinary mess.

"Well, not a problem, exactly. It's more of an issue."

"What is it about shoes that you love so much?"

He's cleaning up while we talk. He shouldn't have to do that.

"I don't know what it is. They're like miniature people to me. There's something about the size of them and the way they have their own little personalities. I love looking at them and holding them, and it's amazing to me how something as small as a pair of shoes can say so much about themselves and the girl who's wearing them. They can represent a type of person or an entire era.

"Sometimes I go to the shoe department at Barney's and just let myself think about the wonder of it all . . . for hours. When I look at certain types of shoes, they speak to me. When they are made like this"—I pick up a pair of Stubbs & Wooton black velvet slippers embroidered with a gold crest, "I can't help but think that this is a work of art as precious as any other. Look at the craftsmanship that went into these shoes. It's like holding a tiny princess in a castle. I guess I just love them because they are like little treasures."

"Those shoes remind you of a princess in a castle?" he asks.

"Actually, they remind me of a princess in a castle brushing her hair before bed. What do they remind you of?"

"An old lady," he says. But he's not really paying attention. He's getting this place cleaned up in no time.

"Remember these?" I ask him, holding up the pair of Lulu Guinness black patent leather Mary Janes with the white patent leather trim and white button closure. "You know what they remind me of?"

"That pervert in *Lolita?* Who played that? Oh right, Jeremy Irons," he says.

"No, they don't remind me of a pervert. They remind me of a pair of Mary Janes that I had when I was a little girl. I wore them all the time, inappropriately, of course. See how shiny they are and new and partyish? They remind me of how happy I was when I had someplace special to go. Mine had a pearlized button, though. These don't. I really love these, but they could never replace the ones I had. Mine were lined in pink velvet, and they didn't have a heel, of course."

"Wow, pink velvet? That's intense," he says. I know he's not interested, but I love talking about them.

"And yet," I continue, "there's something sort of special about these, too. They have an old-fashioned femininity, yet the classic design, toe shape, and heel height would be perfect to wear with something like a Jackie Kennedyish, Balenciaga cream suit, and, at the same time, you could easily wear them with a sheer polka-dotted black-and-white dress with pearl earrings."

I could have worn these with my interview suit had I known about them!

"I remember these," he says, taking one out of my hand. "They're the display shoes that should never be worn. The ones that were a sculpture and a toy all in one."

"Exactly!"

"Where did you find those?" he asks.

"Up on that top shelf; that's where I got all of these boxes. I brought them down, just to see."

While I'm talking, he's opening up all the boxes, examining all the shoes, and putting them back. I wonder if he's actually in charge of this closet.

"Are you in charge of this closet? Is that your job?" I ask him.

"Not exactly, no."

"What is your job then?" I ask, surprising us both. He's either trying not to laugh at my rudeness, or he's thinking of something funny that happened earlier in the day. Sometimes that happens to me, too. I'll start thinking of something that someone said like two years ago and then just laugh in someone's face while they are talking to me.

"I'm what they call a troubleshooter. I report to corporate," he says.

"You mean you're like a narc?"

"A what?"

"A narc is someone who tells on everyone. I learned that on *The Mod Squad.*"

"You learned that 'narc' means someone who tells on everyone from *The Mod Squad*?"

"I think it was *Mod Squad*. Have you ever seen that show? It's so great. I love old shows. Do you?"

"Probably not as much as you do."

He's not really paying attention. He's looking around at the shoe closet in a whole new way. Before it was just a small room filled with shoes, but now it represents someone's sick fantasy life.

"Since you have this reoccurring shoe problem, you might as well have your own key. This closet is supposed to be locked, believe it or not, and you might need to get in here at some point when I'm not around. Here, take one of mine. Now you can eat your lunch up here whenever you want. Everyone on this floor leaves the building between noon and two. In case you get hungry, or the urge to reorganize, that's the time to come."

"I don't know what to say. Are you allowed to just give out keys?" I'm looking right at him. He's really going out on a limb for me. He's looking right back at me. Either I'm still hungry, or his presence is making my saliva glands burn. I could eat him whole.

"I don't *'just give out keys.'* I just gave one to you. That's all."

No wonder Courtney was all over this guy. He's got some serious testosterone running through his veins. I think I can smell it. I'd love to ask him about Courtney, but I wouldn't dare. The last thing I want to do is come off as a jealous, snooping . . .

"Does Courtney have one?"

Damn! How does that happen! You say to yourself, "Don't say anything," and the next thing you know, you're talking.

He's looking at me a little harder now. I mean, really looking. We're doing that *communicate without talking* thing. He's tilting his head, and I'm tilting mine right back, with one raised, inquisitive-to-the-point-of-pushy eyebrow, which is saying, *"Does she? Does she?"*

"Does Courtney have one what?" he asks.

"A key. Does Courtney have a key?"

"No. Courtney does not have a key."

"Are you sure you didn't give her one?" I ask. This time I meant to say that.

"I'm always sure about everything," he says.

That was too much. My eyebrows are practically dancing now, and I'm in no position to start flirting with guys who work here. Especially narcs. I should go. I can just see Ruth walking in here and finding me on the floor working my eyebrows into a full-scale burlesque show. I get up to leave, but he takes my arm, and I feel my stomach lurch toward my throat. If he touches me again, there's a good chance I will throw up a little.

"Before you run out of here, I really want to see those pervert shoes on you." He bends down and slips my shoes off and carefully puts a Lulu Mary Jane on each of my feet, while I disintegrate into a lumpy little pile of Jell-o.

As beautiful as they are, surprisingly the Lulus don't look right on me at all. There's something clownish about them. They make my feet look childish. It looks almost like I'm wearing my mom's shoes. They're too big for one thing, and they are too stiff, and something's just *off*.

"Something's wrong with these shoes," I say. "I still love them, but there's definitely something very wrong here."

"You're absolutely right. There *is* something wrong with them. You're wearing two left feet. They were probably on that top shelf because they need to be returned," he says. I feel like I touched something that I wasn't supposed to touch.

"Let's not touch these," he says, confirming my suspicion.

He very gently slips both Mary Janes off of my feet and places them back in their box. I put my own shoes on and hand him the rest of the boxes from the floor. He puts them all back up on the top shelf and says, "How about if we meet up here again tomorrow for lunch, my treat? Same time, okay?"

He just assumes I'll say yes, and he obviously wants me out of here now. I wonder if Courtney is due back. They probably work together all day, and when she goes out to lunch, he traps whatever girl he can get his hands on in the shoe closet. I don't want to be one of his little closet girls. I don't need this closet. I can live without it. It's just a room filled with shoes, like any other.

"Okay, great!" I say, marveling once again at how my mouth just refuses to wait to be told what to say.

I should really head back now. I think I hear voices out in the hall. That must be Sloane. She's back from lunch. Yup, that was definitely her. She just looked in here, but I'm pretty sure my head was still down. And I just heard Blaire. She just looked in here, too. They're all back, and I think I made a little eye contact with Blaire. They both saw me! I have to get out of here. They'll think I come in here all the time as soon as they leave and just take whatever I want.

I'm just about ready to dart out of here, but before I can make my move, Stan takes the box of Lulus back down off the shelf and says, "Why don't you hold on to these for a few days? They can always be returned next week. Take them home and talk to them or introduce them to your other shoes . . . or whatever it is that you do with them. Just don't wear them out in the real world," he says jokingly.

We both laugh, even though it's not that funny, and then I escape like a bat out of hell with my garment bag and my two new left shoes. I slip into the ladies' room and change into my own clothes. I can't be caught returning anything to the fashion closet now, so I stuff everything in my garment bag and head back downstairs.

I can't wait to get home and tell Jen and Zoe about Stan. At least I have a reason to start working out again. I'm just about to walk outside when I notice that it's about to pour. I put my garment bag over my head and reach for the door, when I feel a delicate tap on my shoulder.

"Hey, it looks pretty bad out there. You didn't bring an umbrella?" Sloane asks.

"No, but I'm okay. I'm just getting in a cab."

"I just can't believe that you don't have an umbrella. There are so many of them in the fashion closet. I think there are a few in the shoe closet, too."

Well, that settles that. She saw me in there today and she resents the fact that I was in there when no one else was around. I knew that would happen. She looked right at Blaire as she made that remark. Blaire smiled right back at her and popped up her Burberry umbrella without even acknowledging me. I have to stay away from that closet no matter how hard it is.

"Do you take a taxi home every day?" Sloane asks.

"Pretty much. You?" I direct this question at both of them, but apparently Blaire isn't talking to me anymore. Sloane answers for both of them.

"Well, it depends. Sometimes if we work late, we call a car service, which the company pays for, of course, but typically we walk home or take the subway."

"Well, I *would* take the subway, but I don't know how. It's one of those things I can't learn. I might have a learning disability or something. I really tried to understand the schedule and all the different lines, but I'm positive that it can't be done."

"What's in the garment bag?" Sloane asks.

"It's the outfit Courtney gave me yesterday. I wore it to work today, but then I changed into my own clothes."

"You wore that outfit to work today? I'm surprised you didn't throw it away, I would have. Courtney always picks out the worst clothes for everyone," she says, laughing and showing her eyeteeth. She's got a couple of real fangs there. I can't believe I never noticed them before.

"I was actually planning to return it today, but then I stopped in the shoe closet for a second. In fact, I think I saw you guys just as I was leaving. At least I thought it was you. Well, anyway, the truth is, Ruth insisted that I return the outfit. She was really mad at me for wearing it. I'm going to return it as soon as I have it dry cleaned. I never even got the chance to tell her that Courtney gave it to me, but I'm sure she would want me to return it anyway. She probably had every right to be mad at me. I'm just an assistant. I shouldn't be borrowing things from either of those closets, should I?"

"Ruth got mad at you for that? Everyone around here borrows clothes and shoes. Are you sure that's why she was mad at you?" Sloane asks. Blaire is listening with the same intensity that Tom Hanks used on the Apollo 13 mission.

"Well, she's mad at me in general. I'm doing something wrong and I don't know what it is. I think it's because I gave her all these ideas for the ankle issue and she told Rob that they were her ideas and then he asked me, right in front of her, if they were my ideas or hers and I didn't know what to do. I just keep messing up. She really hates me. I just wish I could help her."

"It's just so unfair, isn't it, Sloane?" Blaire asks. "I did an article on this a few months ago," she continues. "The competition between assistants and their bosses is very fierce around here. It would be interesting to do another article that would uncover the inner workings of the assistant's mind for the boss's benefit. Don't you think, Sloane?"

"Yes, Blaire, I do think that would be interesting. You should start working on an article like that right away."

Why do they sound like they're reading off a teleprompter?

"I'm sure if I could just sit down with Ruth and discuss this, we'd be able to work things out. She's so afraid that I want her job, which I don't at all. The funny thing is, I never even knew that magazines had promotion departments. I was supposed to interview for an editorial position, but I got off on the wrong floor."

"Well, you do know that there are no openings in editorial right now," Blaire says as she walks away with Sloane glued to her side.

"Oh, I wasn't suggesting . . . I was just saying that . . . it's very difficult . . . never mind. . . . I guess I'll see you guys tomorrow," I say, but they're long gone.

~

CHAPTER TEN

This Is the Year That Will Challenge Your Tenacity and Your Ability to Overcome Obstacles and Stay Positive in the Face of Defeat

I'm all dressed up today. I couldn't hold back anymore. All that Jackie Kennedy and sheer polka-dotted dress with pearl earrings talk really got me going, so I'm wearing the sheer polka-dotted dress that I bought last night with tiny pearl earrings and my cream jacket from my interview suit. I'm wearing my favorite red lipstick, and I would have worn those Lulu Guinness shoes, except that I promised not to. I brought them, though, just in case something terrible happens to my own shoes. I tried them on again at home, and it's hardly noticeable that there isn't a right foot.

I hope Ruth doesn't think I'm overdressed. Her door is closed again. I brought my lunch, as usual, but I also brought one for Trai. As soon as I hand it to him, he asks me, "What's in yours?"

"Same thing as you," I say.

"Let's see," he says.

I open the bag and show him. We both have a bagel and

cream cheese, an apple, and a Reese's. He wants my Reese's in exchange for his apple.

"What am I going to do with two apples?" I ask him.

"I don't know, give one to the teacher. You haven't kissed her ass all week." He's laughing at his own stupid jokes all the time now. He's in such a good mood for some reason. He probably just went ahead and finally killed someone.

"What are you so happy about lately? Did you commit some sort of heinous crime?" I ask.

"None of your fucking business," he says.

"Then give me the lunch back," I say. I'm not afraid of him anymore.

"Okay, I'll tell you. I like you. I like the way you keep messing up Ruth and you don't even know you're doing it. I like the way you keep changing your clothes and shoes, in the middle of the day, and I like the way you disappear for hours at a time and she can't say anything because you're all she's got. It just makes my job a hell of a lot more interesting. That's all."

"Well, for your information, I never meant to mess Ruth up. I only change my clothes when I absolutely have to, and I only leave my desk when she gives me something to do—away from my desk and if you *like me, like me,* forget it. I think you're the weirdest person I ever met in my life."

"You're also a liar, which I usually find attractive, but you're way too skinny for me."

"Really? Wow! Thanks!"

"I didn't mean that as a compliment."

"Yeah, well, I'm taking it as one," I say, and walk away. I never thought I'd make friends with that guy. You just never know.

I really want to knock on Ruth's door, but I don't have the courage. I hate going in there, but I know she's waiting for more shoe issue ideas.

I go back to my desk and start organizing my pages of

ideas. I've been thinking about shoes all night, but I only have a couple of ideas. It's a lot easier to think about shoes when you're not supposed to be thinking about them.

1. The proverbial shoe obsession has become a source of material for a whole slew of stand-up comedians. I think we should play off of that and sponsor a series of comedy shows in big-city clubs across the country. We invite all the big names in the shoe industry to attend these comedy shows, which we'll call "The Shoe Issue." We can decorate the tables with famous shoe centerpieces: The old lady who lived in the shoe, Cinderella and her slipper, Dorothy and her ruby slipper, Carrie from *Sex in the City,* Imelda Marcos, etc. Advertisers are welcome to set up decorative displays, which can also be used on tables or set up around the room, to promote their new designs.

   Department store buyers will be given front-row tables and VIP treatment, and the shoe designers will be seated at tables with the shoe buyers they want to reach most. In the goody bags, we'll have: shoe soaps, shoe key chains, shoe picture frames, shoe embroidered hand towels, you name it. We can do shoe flowers and shoe cakes and make it the shoe event of the year.

2. We could do a special promotion for athletic shoe advertisers and sponsor a tri-athlete competition between advertisers, department store buyers, and magazine staffers, and the winner wins a free page of advertising for every purchased page, one of which would announce that they won the competition in addition to their regular advertising message.

3. A folder in the shape of a shoe.

I'm still printing a copy of the ideas when Ruth shows up behind me.

"What have you got today?" she asks me.

"A bagel and cream cheese, an apple, and a Reese's," I answer.

"For the shoe issue! What have you got for the shoe issue?" she asks.

"Oh! I'm sorry, I have three more ideas, but I just realized that I didn't really stress the European market thing. I might have to rethink these."

"Just give me what you've got so far," she says and whips the paper right out of the printer. She walks back into her office and slams the door.

Rhonda waits for Ruth to walk away, drops a bag of M&M's on my desk, and continues walking. A few minutes later Hallie walks over and says, "So what's the deal?"

"What do you mean? What deal?" I ask.

"She's not coming in to hound us lately. What's going on around here?"

"I have no idea why she's leaving you guys alone. Maybe it's because she's too busy hating me."

"She doesn't hate you. She's just frustrated. She hasn't had a break in years and you're making her look bad. I wouldn't worry about it too much, though. She can't last much longer. The big guy can't stand her. At least that's what I heard. Have you heard anything?"

Rhonda walks by again, in the other direction, and makes the one-finger-slicing-across-the-throat hand motion behind Hallie's back, thus indicating that she's planning to cut Hallie's throat open or that I should stop talking. I stop talking by putting my hand over my mouth. It's the only way. Hallie hangs around for a few more seconds, waiting for me to answer. Eventually, she walks away. I'm trying to remember what I've said so far, but I don't think I said anything bad. Hallie did most of the talking. *Right?*

A few minutes later, Rhonda is back at my desk.

"Open your M&M's, I have something to show you. And by the way, be careful what you say to Hallie, she's a back-stabber. She's on Ruth's side. She always has been."

"Are you sure?"

"Of course I'm sure. Have I not been here for eleven years?"

She uses that a lot, but you can't blame her. I was a junior in high school eleven years ago. Eleven years is a long time ago. I rip open the M&M's and start eating them.

"Don't eat them all at once. Save some."

"How about Trai? Is he a back-stabber, too?" I ask.

"No, he's just an asshole."

"Thank God. How about Ali? Back-stabber?"

"Nope. But she's not all there, either. I think she might actually be two people. Sometimes she shows up and she looks a little different. For a while there, I thought she was twins."

"That's odd," I say.

"Compared to what?" she asks. "This whole place is odd, but it's in my blood. And it's in your blood, too. Now read this, so we can get past it."

She puts an article in front of me, and then she sits on the other desk in my cubicle. She won't look at me. After a while, she starts swinging her legs. I get the feeling that she'd be willing to sit there all day, waiting for me to need her. It just goes to prove that you should never judge someone by their accessories. Rhonda is an amazing friend.

I'm reading and reading, but I have to say this article isn't that interesting. Halfway through, she turns to me and says, "Keep reading, but know one thing. You're going to get through this, and somehow, it will all be forgotten."

What is she talking about? I've practically forgotten most of what I read already.

Is the Girl Who Works for You Out to Get You?

By Articles Editor Blaire Thompson

You hire a great new assistant and all she wants to do is please you and make your life easier. You can't believe how lucky you are to have found her, and just when things are going great, you realize that she's not working for you, she's working against you.

I recently witnessed this scenario right here at this very magazine. It didn't happen to me, of course. I would have spotted the little "Eve" instantly. Instead, it happened to a very good friend of mine in another department.

The young assistant started out just as sweet and innocent as can be, but after a few weeks, we all started seeing signs of the subtle evil transgression. First came the frail little thing's inability to use the copy machine. She needed a big, strong man to help her change the paper, so she managed to have our company maintenance man at her beck and call at all hours of the day. Before we all knew it, she had him following her around here like a lost puppy. Then came the steady excuses to change clothes in the middle of the day, along with a couple of pairs of choice, Missing In Action stilettos.

This girl visits the fashion and shoe closets more than our very own models, and she comes up with the cleverest excuses. Spilled coffee one day, broken heel the next. She was even caught cavorting with a certain member of the opposite sex, on more than one occasion, in those very closets.

Way to go, sweetheart, nothing like undressing your way to the top. And as if that wasn't enough, she started taking credit for ideas that she couldn't possibly have come up with on her own. How could she? She's way too busy disrobing to put in any real work hours.

Watch out for this babe. Her naiveté is nothing but an act. She's as shrewd and calculating as a cat. The more she compliments you, the more she is laughing behind your back. Watch out when you send her to the copy machine, watch out when you send her downstairs for a cup of coffee, and watch out when she travels in private taxis on company money while the rest of us travel in those dirty old subways that she just can't seem to figure out how to use.

She's trouble and the worst kind. We like to call her "the can you help me? girl." The only help this girl needs is help putting you out of a job.

So the next time some pouty-faced little princess sidles up and asks you the way to the ladies' room, don't give her directions; give her the can.

"Wow! I thought I was the only one who saw that movie *All about Eve*. It's a classic starring Bette Davis or Joan Crawford . . . or Eve Arden. I always get those three confused. Have you seen it? That's what she's referring to when she says, 'the little Eve.' Most people won't even realize that. It's a very old movie. I'm surprised—"

"Chloe, that article is about you! Can't you see it? Ruth, Blaire, and Sloane worked on this together."

"Me? That's ridiculous. How could you think that?"

"Who else do you know around here who is always changing their shoes and clothes? Who else lives five blocks away and takes a taxi to and from work every day? Who else would be stupid enough to confide in those bitches upstairs, who you think are so sweet? And who else still hasn't learned how to change the paper in the copy machine or ride the subway?"

"Well, when you put it that way, it does sound like me. What am I going to do?"

"Nothing. You are going to do absolutely nothing. You just need to be more aware of what goes on around here. You can't tell anybody anything. You can't trust those girls upstairs, and you can't let them bother you, either. Pretend you never read it, but in the back of your mind, remember who wrote it. You are not going to have it easy for a while, but the truth of the matter is that you have really great ideas and you belong here. This is it for Ruth. She knows she's going down, and this was her pathetic little attempt to bring you down with her.

"Ruth probably knew all along that you'd give those editors enough ammunition to create their own little firing squad, but she had no idea that you'd go out in search of them on your own. She didn't even have to throw you to the wolves. You sniffed them out all by yourself. I've never seen anything like it."

"Have you been hanging out with my sister lately? You are really starting to sound like her. Well, I have to say, I still think that article is just a big misunderstanding."

As we sit here discussing the article, Ruth comes out of her office with a big grin on her face. I'm happy to see that she's feeling better.

"Oh, you got a copy of the article. I'm so glad. What did you think of it?"

"I think someone should track down this horrible bitch and fire her," I say.

Ruth looks at me long and hard, but I just turn to my mirror and start brushing my hair. It's the only thing I can think of that will get her to stop staring at me. She turns away and slams the door to her office. Rhonda gives me a high five, and we head out to lunch.

I don't mention to Rhonda that I was supposed to meet Stan in the shoe closet today. I think we've pretty much established that I should stay away from that part of the building for a while, and as much as I trust her, I don't want to make a big deal out of it.

We eat our lunch in the park across the street. Rhonda tells me some pretty ugly stories about girls sabotaging other girls on a daily basis, all around her.

I ask her how she managed to last so long, and she says it's her nature to stay out of trouble.

"Why can't I stay out of trouble?" I ask.

"I hate to say it, but you're a little on the clueless side when it comes to reading people."

"I knew I could trust you," I say, in my own defense.

"Oh please, you trust everyone."

"No, I don't."

"Yeah, you do."

"You're right. I do. How am I ever going to survive at a place like this?"

"You'll be fine. You've got talent, kid, real talent."

I wonder if Rhonda smokes cigars at home.

We eat quickly because Rhonda has to get back, but I stay outside for a while to call Zoe on my cell.

"Hi."

"Hi."

"The article is horrible."

"What article?"

"The one they wrote about me."

"Who?"

"You don't know them."

"Of course I don't *know* them, but you can at least tell me their names . . . and addresses."

"I can't go into it. It's too terrible."

"What is the article about?"

"I told you, it's about me. That's why I'm so upset."

"Chloe, you can't keep calling me up with these catastrophic fragments of information and expect me to help you. I need at least one or two actual facts. Answer these two questions: Who wrote the article and what does it say?"

"Okay. The whole story is that the editor girls wrote this whole big article about me and how I'm exactly like Anne Baxter."

"In *All about Eve*?"

"Oh my God, you read it?"

"Chloe! I'm guessing here!"

"That was an excellent guess."

"I'm getting really good at filling in the blanks. What else did it say?"

"It also says that I don't know how to use the copy machine."

"Do you?"

"Sort of."

"I think you should ignore the article completely and send me a copy of it."

"Really? You think I should just ignore it?"

"Ignore it and it will go away. I promise."

"Just like that?"

"Just like that. And one other thing, don't forget to send me those names and addresses."

As I walk back into the building, I see Stan in the lobby talking to Blaire, Sloane and Courtney. They are all standing around him like he's some kind of god. I duck in and walk past them, but I can't help turning around, and he spots me. We make quick eye contact, but I don't want to talk to him in front of them. I stop at the newsstand, and he's right behind me in a few seconds.

"Where were you?" he asks. "I waited for you in that damn closet for over an hour."

"I had a really bad day. I can't be seen alone with you, especially now," I say, trying not to move my lips in case one of them is a lip-reader.

"What are you talking about? Of course you can be seen with me. Don't be so dramatic."

"Dramatic? Oh my God! You obviously have no idea what goes on around here. This place is horrible. I can't go into it now, but those girls . . . never mind, just leave me alone, okay? Being seen with you is only going to make my life a living hell. And for your information, I! hate! when! people! call! me! dramatic!"

"I'm not going to leave you alone, so why don't you just calm down and tell me what's going on here."

"Oh great, there's Ruth. Go! Please go." He won't leave, so

I walk away from him, and I didn't even have a chance to get any candy. At the elevator, he takes my arm and says, "Where are you going? Don't walk away from me."

"I *have* to walk away from you. And don't tell me what to do, either."

I quickly get in the elevator. He tries to follow me in, but the door closes just in time. It doesn't matter. His harem is swarming around him before he even has a chance to turn around.

When I get back to my desk, there's a huge pile of files on my chair with a note that says,

REFILE IN MY BASEMENT FILING CABINET BY END OF DAY.

RUTH

That should be no problem. There are only about five hundred pieces of paper here and no instructions as to which is *her* basement filing cabinet. I grab the pile and head downstairs. I'm glad she gave me this project. There's nothing I'd rather do than hide in the basement for the rest of the day.

As soon as I make my way down to the basement and open the door, I see Joe, and for some reason, I start crying. I put my head down, but I'm making some pretty loud breathing noises. He's the closest thing I've got to a relative around here, and I always cry when I see my relatives.

I cry until my nose runs and my face is a red, sweaty mess, and I don't even care. He tries to pat my back, but I'm really snorting. I can't blame him for not wanting to get too close to me. He goes to the supply closet and gets me a few napkins, and I start telling him about the article and the editor girls and Ruth. He sits down on a metal folding chair, shaking his head.

"I should have warned you about this stuff. It goes on all

the time. Some of these girls can be pretty nasty. They'll accuse you of anything if they think you are getting in their way. You sure caused an awful lot of trouble in just a few months. From what I hear, Ruth is going nuts again, and the editors think that they caught you fooling around in the shoe closet."

"I would never fool around in the shoe closet!"

"You don't have to tell me that. I'm just telling you what I heard. I don't believe half of what people say around here."

I forgot how much Joe overhears. "What's wrong with Ruth?" I ask.

"She's got problems, real problems, and she wants to be heard. She's been hammered by Rob, but she just keeps at it. She's always looking for a lawsuit or someone to fire for no apparent reason. You're the only one around at the moment. I thought she'd leave a girl like you alone, but having you around is just driving her even crazier."

"How could I be driving her crazy? I was hired to help her, and I'm really trying. Believe me, I'm trying."

"In her mind, you were hired to help her become more like you. She's using you as a front man, but it's backfiring. You're getting all the attention, not her."

Damn, that Zoe is something else.

"She's been sending notes to personnel complaining about you, and it got the publisher's attention. He's been keeping an eye on you, and he likes what he sees. He knows Ruth senses trouble, so he came to see what all the fuss was about."

"I can't believe she's been complaining about me. I'm working so hard to make her happy. For some reason, she's convinced herself that I want her job. What is Ruth's job, anyway?"

"Her job is to come up with creative solutions to help the salespeople sell ads. Mostly she delegates because she's too busy trying to get herself promoted some way or another. But don't worry about Ruth. No one really takes her seriously. If

I were you, I'd be more concerned about the editors. They're trouble."

"I knew they would be mad at me for hanging out in the shoe closet when no one was around."

"The fact that you weren't alone pissed them off even more. They've got it in for you now."

"I know. I know. I wish you would have warned me about all this sooner."

"I wish you would have asked."

"So, what about the publisher? What did you mean when you said, 'he came to see what all the fuss was about'?"

"He's been checking up on you because he knows you make Ruth nervous. He's been telling everyone that you pump out ideas like water from a well. He talks about you all the time."

"I can't believe this. Poor Ruth. I don't know what to do."

"Just keep pumping out those ideas. That's my suggestion; and stay away from 'The Girls.' Eventually, they'll move on to someone else. They always do."

"I wish they would move those closets to another floor."

"They're gone between noon and two every day," Joe says with a smile.

I remind him that two hours is not a lot of time. Apparently he has never seen how many shoes are in that closet.

"Any idea where these go?" I ask, showing him the pile of folders Ruth gave me to file.

He takes them from me and opens the top folder. He starts reading it and says, "I remember this particular lawsuit like it was yesterday. Ruth claimed that she was reaching up for something on the cafeteria line and that Liz Jabonowsky, the cafeteria worker, moved it away from her, which caused her to trip and break her foot. Somehow she managed to convince some doctor friend of hers to give her a bogus cast. She hobbled around here for weeks. Poor Liz, I thought she'd never get over it. She really believed it was her fault. That woman runs the whole cafeteria, all by herself, and she never gets so much as a thank-you. And then Ruth has to go and blame her for something she would never do in a million years. Liz worried herself sick over that damn lawsuit. Sometimes I wish they would promote Ruth, just to keep her off everyone's back for awhile."

Joe slides open a drawer of a massive filing cabinet. He takes the whole pile of files and dumps it.

"This whole cabinet is Ruth's. If she gives you any more files like this, just throw them in here and forget about it. You better go upstairs now and get back to work. The last thing you want is to be caught down here with me." Joe puts his arm around me, and we walk to the elevator together. It's amazing how certain people hang in there, knowing everything that's going on, and somehow manage to stay out of trouble.

"Do you know Rhonda?" I ask, before I open the door.

"Do I know Rhonda? Only for eleven years."

CHAPTER ELEVEN

If You Feel You Must Express Yourself with Clothing, Wear Fun Underwear

The invitations are on everyone's bulletin boards and desks. Everywhere you look, there are giant, hot pink hearts that say Love Is in the Air! I can't help but run to my desk to see if I got one too, but I didn't. Where's mine?

I've been looking forward to this for so long. It's the Valentine's Day Ball. It's one of the biggest events in New York. Every model, designer, photographer, writer, and celebrity on the planet will be there, and the entire company is invited. Everybody has been talking about it for months.

I know exactly what I'm going to wear, right down to my new bra and panty set. I know what Rhonda is going to wear. I even know what Trai and Joe's wife are going to wear.

It's been a pretty brutal couple of months, and I know this night will put everyone in a much better mood. Even Zoe is excited for me.

Zoe wrote a nice little piece called "Gossip Girls" when I told her about the article the editors wrote about me. It's a good thing I didn't give her their real addresses.

It was all about why some girls gossip and how it's nothing

but a harmless method of bonding, much like when vampires suck the blood out of their victims. It was really well written, but it gave me the chills. I should have never told her about the article. She told me to ignore it and I did, but she couldn't eat or sleep for two weeks.

~

CHAPTER TWELVE

If the Shoe Fits . . .

I can't believe it. Today is Friday and tonight is the Valentine's Day Ball and I'm still the only one without an invitation. Why would they invite everyone except me? I'm trying to concentrate on this Fragrance Week copy, but I don't feel like writing a "What Does Your Scent Say about Your Sexuality?" booklet. Every time I try to write something, my mind wanders.

Obsession: You're passionate, addicted to love, and willing to risk it all for that special someone. You like to make a dramatic entrance.
Translation: You have a tendency to stalk people and boil their pets.

Helmut Lang: You love classical music, poetry, and your idea of love is traditional and pure.
Translation: You are not gay.
But every now and then, you are wooed by the unexpected.
Translation: Maybe you are gay.

Chance: You are a dreamer. You believe in miracles and live
for the unknown.
*You have no problem sleeping with strange men as long as they
buy you perfume.*

Truth: *You're a liar.*

Beautiful: *You have black streaks in your white hair and words
can't bring you down.*

I can't concentrate on this. They should do something different this year. Why can't they get twenty male models to line
up in a row wearing twenty different colognes? People can
walk up to them and try to guess what fragrance they're wearing. If someone guesses correctly, they get to keep the model
for a month and he has to promise not to talk.

Happy: *You enjoy show tunes and Prozac.*

Passion: *You're addicted to porn.*

Or . . . we could create a collection of hand-embroidered
handkerchiefs with our logo stitched on the front, and spray
each handkerchief with a different fragrance, and package
them in beautifully carved wooden boxes and call them our
exclusive *Box of Issues.*
Or not.
I can't think of anything even remotely creative. All I can
think about is the Valentine's Day Ball.
"Well, Chloe, I see you're in the mood for Valentine's Day,"
Ruth says, noting the gigantic hearts on both the front and the
back of my pink turtleneck, my ruby beaded necklace, and my
clear Moschino bag with the HUNDREDS and THOU-
SANDS of hearts all over it. Not to mention my silver Jeanine

Payer heart earrings with the little pictures of babies with angel wings dangling from my ears.

"I guess I couldn't stop thinking about the BALL," I say, hoping that Ruth will suddenly say, *"Oh that reminds me, here's your invitation."*

"Oh that reminds me," she says.

Here it comes, Finally!

"I need you to do a little personal project for me. I'd like to get my Christmas card list updated and organized a little early this year. I know it seems premature, but one of my New Year's resolutions last year was to tackle this list. My goal is to have all of my cards addressed and ready to go by the end of this weekend. What I'd like you to do is combine all of the names from these old address books into my new address book and then type up a copy of the entire list and keep it on file. Can you do that for me?"

"Sure," I say, glancing at my calendar to make sure it's still February 14 and that I haven't accidentally lost track of the nine months that will pass before the rest of the world begins thinking about Christmas.

Ruth hands me her old address book, which is the size of an actual phone book, the kind with yellow pages. She can't be serious. There are hundreds of pages in here. She's got lots and lots of little phone books tucked inside the big phone book, and at least one hundred pages of loose numbers on napkins, stick 'ums, and maybe three hundred business cards in rubber bands, all throughout the main book. The big book is tied together with a bigger rubber band. I can see that it was once leather, but somehow it disintegrated into cardboard.

She must bring it into the bathtub with her all the time. It's like holding someone's old bra. It's full of old perfume and house smells. I hate the idea of holding something so intimate that belongs to someone who is so not a part of my life. How could she give me this?

"Oh and Chloe, don't start this yet. I'd like you to spend the morning on that fragrance booklet."

"I think I'm almost done with that. How many fragrances did you say you wanted me to include?" I ask.

"How many do you have?"

"I guess five or so," I say, forgetting that only two or three of them are usable.

"Give me ten more. Oh, and one more thing, unfortunately, I won't be able to look at what you've got until at least two or three o'clock. So, if you finish early, just tweak it until then. And don't worry if you can't finish the address book by the end of the day. I'll send a messenger over to your apartment sometime on Saturday. How does that sound?"

"It sounds okay," I say.

Well, it's coming up on four o'clock. I haven't seen Ruth all day and I guess I should start the address book project, in case she comes back and says I can go to the party.

It's eight-thirty now, and I'm pretty sure I'm the only one left in the building. I pinned someone else's invitation to my bulletin board, just to look at it.

It doesn't look as though I'll ever get out of here. I'm only up to the letter P. By the time I finish and start the file copy, it will be way past midnight. It's so quiet in here. I can feel the weight of my own body on this chair. I can hear the air move when I turn my head. I can even hear the heat coming out of the vent.

No wonder it's so goddamn hot in here all the time.

I can actually hear the electricity running through the cords. And I think I just heard somebody call my name.

That's weird. I'm probably just imagining it.

Oh my God; there it is again. There's definitely somebody in here!

I quickly dial Zoe's number, but there's no answer. I whisper a message in her voice mail to come get me and gently replace the receiver. There it is again. No one even knows I'm here. I wonder if I should hide. I pick up the big stapler on my desk and put it behind my back. I'm going to die here. I know it. *Why God, why? Why must I die on Valentine's Day?*

Ruth must have sent someone to kill me. It's a man. It's definitely a man. I can tell by the footsteps. I'll kill myself before he can find me. That's what I'll do. I'm hiding under my desk in a sweat. I'm breathing too loud. I can't take it. I want to turn myself in.

"Chloe, I know you're here. Chloe!!"

I jump out with the stapler.

It's Stan. He's wearing a tuxedo. He looks like Bond, James Bond.

"You scared the life out of me! How did you know I was here? I thought you were a murderer."

"Why?"

"Because who else would know I'm here alone, but a murderer?"

"Why would a murderer come looking for you?"

"I don't know. I thought maybe Ruth sent someone to kill me."

"Well, if she did, it's lucky for you that I got here first. I looked all over for you at the ball, and then I overheard someone say that you were working late."

My heart is palpitating and my back is sweating. Not only because I thought I was about to be killed but because Stan has the most beautiful black silk gown that I've ever seen draped over his arm and I'm almost positive it's for me.

"Is that for me?" I ask.

"Maybe. It depends."

"No, seriously, why are you carrying that?"

"Don't you want to go to the ball?"

"I do, but where did you get that gown?"

"I got it from the fashion closet. It's all yours . . . for tonight."

"I'm not supposed to wear anything from that closet."

"Says who?"

"Says Ruth."

"That nut?"

"That nut is my boss and she can make my life very miserable if she wants to."

"I also got you these," he says.

Stan holds out a pink flannel drawstring bag, and I take it from him. I open it up and pull out one black patent leather Mary Jane lined in pink velvet.

"Where did you get these?" I ask him.

"A friend of mine made them for me . . . I mean for you."

"You have a friend who makes shoes for you?"

"Just this once. She did me a special favor."

"What's your friend's name and how can I find her?"

"Emma Hope. She leaves near The Kings Road in London."

I'm still standing, but I'm not sure how much longer I will hold out. I can't believe what I'm looking at. I slip the other shoe out of the little bag. I'm holding a piece of my childhood. My most precious memory is in the palm of my hand, and it's real, and it's so incredibly beautiful that I have no idea what to say. It's like playing "make-believe grown-up" in reverse.

"They are exactly as I remember them. How did she know?" I whisper.

"I just repeated everything you said to me that day in the closet, and somehow she got it right, I guess. They even have pearl buttons. These are real pearls. I bet yours didn't have real pearls on them, did they?"

"No, they definitely didn't. These are even better than the ones I had."

"Try them on," he says.

I unbutton the pearl from the little black silk loop and slip my foot into the shoe. It fits me perfectly. I wonder what size it is. I press my hand against its buttery soft leather sole. It feels so incredibly new. Then I slip my other foot into the other shoe and stare down at them. They are perfect. I close my eyes and try to remember that feeling I used to get whenever my mom said I could wear my party shoes. I feel like a princess.

"On the other hand, the dress has to be back in the closet by Tuesday. It's going to Italy to be shot on location. It might be a little long. The model who will be wearing it is five feet ten."

"Wait a minute. You came here knowing that I would be here, and you just happen to have these shoes and this dress? This doesn't make any sense. I hope this isn't a dream. I will be so mad if these shoes aren't real." I slip them off my feet to get a closer look at them.

"No, I grabbed the dress right before I came down to get you, but I had the shoes made for you the same day you described them to me. They've been in my desk. I was just waiting for the right moment to give them to you."

"Any moment would have been perfect," I say. "I can't believe you were actually listening to me that day, and I can't believe how much trouble you went to, and I can't believe how much trouble you could get *into* for letting me wear this dress before the shoot."

"Don't worry. It's no big deal. I know how to cover myself around here. Put it on," he says.

I hand him my shoes and let him drape the dress over my arms. It's much heavier than I expected. I start to walk toward the ladies' room.

"You're leaving the room to change? Do you have any idea how many models change in front of me every day?"

"I'm not a model."

And I'm wearing panty hose. I would never let anyone see me in my panty hose. No one should ever have to see that.

Just then my phone rings. "The ladies' room is locked," Stan says and turns around to answer my phone. He sits on the corner of my desk and takes his jacket off with his back to me.

What underwear am I wearing? Oh God.

In less than a second, I have the dress on, and I'm frantically pulling my own clothes out from under it. By the time he turns back around, I'm pulling my skirt out and I'm ready to be zipped up.

"Zip me up, please," I say.

"Someone named Zoe is on the phone, and you're pretty good at that."

I grab the phone while Stan zips me up, and I tell Zoe that I called her because I thought there was a murderer in the building but it turned out to be a friend and that I can't talk because I'm changing into a gown. For some reason this is enough of an explanation for her and she says, "I guess you'll give me more details later." She's getting really good at letting things go.

The gown is pure silk. The chiffon straps dip loosely off my shoulders. The bodice is a corset, which gently flares out and slides down my hips like two sheets of rain. Whoever made this dress is a genius. I look like I'm wasting away in this thing. I could have easily left all of my clothes on and this dress would still fit me.

It was designed for a very large person. I face Stan and twirl a little, waiting for his reaction. I always forget. Men don't clap.

Instead, he puts one hand on his heart. He reaches out to me with his other hand and pulls me onto his lap. Then he whispers in my ear, "Beautiful Chloe."

Something about the way he says that makes me want to rush to the phone and thank my mother for naming me Chloe. I hug him around his neck and he says, "Stand back up. I want to see you spin around again."

After a few seconds, I get up to do a quick twirl and walk

over to the mirror. The dress makes the most incredible swishing sound as I walk. Even for one night, this is the greatest gift I've ever received. Then I step back a little. The dress is not only way too big, but it's about eighteen inches too long. I'm staring at myself in this incredible dress, trying to calculate how many hours of alterations it would take to shrink it down to human proportions.

Stan sees the expression on my face in the reflection of the mirror and laughs, "Okay, I think we've looked at this dress long enough. Go ahead and take it off."

"Why? I love wearing this dress," I say. Clearly, he's never played dress-up or he would understand that size doesn't matter.

"Really? Great. Then put on your new shoes and let's go."

"Put my Mary Janes on with this gown?"

"Yeah, why not?"

"They don't go."

"What do you mean, 'they don't go'? You said Mary Janes were party shoes and that's a party dress, so put them on."

I slowly walk over to the shoes and unbutton them again. If I didn't know that I had a much smaller foot when I was seven years old, I would swear these were my original shoes. I take one shoe and slip my finger inside and push against the velvet. I love velvet. The white pearl button is glazed in oyster pink. The toe shape is exactly the way I remember it. It's sort of square with rounded edges. I pick up both shoes and hold them to my heart. I want to tell them, "*Look at me in this movie star dress, look at my desk and look at that piece I'm working on. See that? It says Shoe Issue. I'm almost there.*"

I slip them on and button the little button on each shoe. I walk back to the mirror, holding the sides of my dress up. The shoes are so flat that they point up in the front. The only other shoes that ever did that were my original Mary Janes and I hated that about them. I try to curl my toes down, but the shoes won't move.

What could I possibly wear with these shoes, besides a little jumper?

I don't know what to say.

"Okay, here I come!" I'm walking toward him in what suddenly feels like house slippers and an old nightgown.

"Perfect, let's go," Stan says, standing up.

I can't be seen in public like this. It's fun to dress up in big, fancy dresses and everything, but not outdoors.

"Um, I know! Let's stay here and dance," I say.

"Are you sure?"

"Oh, I'm positive. I have to finish this project anyway and I don't want to waste an hour getting there and back. I'll have to come back anyway and I don't want to spill anything on this dress and risk having the editors get mad at me for ruining something I wasn't supposed to wear in the first place."

"Are you sure it's not because the dress is a little long and you don't think the shoes look right?"

"Of course not! The dress is fine, if I pick it up on the sides, and the shoes, the shoes are perfect. I would just rather stay here, that's all. We can dance all night, right here. Let's get started. I'll hum."

"What if we get caught in this building, dancing alone? We're taking a big chance by staying here, don't you think?" he asks.

I take another glance at myself in the mirror, just to make sure that I'd rather slit myself in half with a dull blade than step foot outside looking like this.

"No one will come back to the office at this hour. I'm perfectly willing to risk it."

"Really? That's funny, because I remember hearing you say that you can't be seen with me alone . . . ever. You got over that pretty quickly."

"Oh that? I was just kidding. So what would you like to hear? What kind of music do you like? I'm an excellent hummer."

"You don't have to hum. I'm just glad that you love the shoes and the dress, because I'd hate to feel like I went to ALL THAT TROUBLE only to have you decide that you don't want to go to the ball because you feel silly in that ridiculous dress with those dumpy shoes."

"These shoes are not dumpy! What is wrong with you?"

We both look down at my feet. It's impossible not to laugh.

"You look like a pilgrim," Stan says.

"That's it! You're absolutely right. I couldn't put my finger on it. But I still love them. I really do. In fact, I'm going to frame them in a shadow box and hang them in my room."

"When did you come up with that idea?"

"I came up with the idea of framing shoes the other day. I wanted to do a retrospective shoe exhibit at the Metropolitan Museum of Modern Art and call it, 'A Walk through Time' to promote our shoe issue. But Ruth hated the idea."

"She hated it? I think it's great," he says and kisses me. As soon as I feel his lips, I lose my hearing in one ear. The same thing happened when I won the jelly bean contest in sixth grade. I guessed it right on the nose. There were 1,465 jelly beans in the jar, and somehow I just knew, which is amazing, because my original guess was 185. But, luckily I erased that and wrote 1,465. From that day on, 1,465 has always been my lucky number.

"So when did you come up with the idea to frame *these* shoes?" he asks nonchalantly.

"What?"

"I said when did you come up with the idea to frame *these* shoes?"

"As soon as I saw them on my feet," I say. *I hope I'm not yelling. I can't tell.*

"So I guess we just discovered another pair of Mary Janes that should never be worn, is that it?"

"Pretty much."

"And I guess that also means that we're not going anywhere tonight," he says, leading me back to the desk. I sit down on the edge of the desk and he stands in front of me. He loosens his tie, unbuttons his collar button, and kisses me. Then he tilts my head back and kisses me again. There goes my other ear.

We're really kissing now. I mean, really kissing. I hope he thinks my lips are puffy enough. They feel a little skimpy compared to his. He's got my head between both of his hands. I can't even begin to describe how much fun I'm having. He stops for a second to pull a few strands of hair away from my face. For some reason, I use this little intermission to begin talking incessantly.

"We're much better off here than at the ball," I say.

"I agree with you there," he says.

"If we were seen together, it would be totally asking for trouble. Did you know that a few of the editors saw us in the shoe closet the other day? None of them like me anymore, after that. Did you see the article that was circulating around here about the horrible assistant? That article was about me."

More kissing. Maybe he didn't hear me. I pull back a little and say, "That's what I couldn't tell you the other day, because they were all standing right there. I have no idea how I suddenly became the villain around here. I didn't even do anything."

I'm sitting all the way back on the desk now. The kisses are getting a little harder, so the back of my neck is sort of pressing into the wall. He is so good at this. If my neck does, in fact, break, it would actually be worth it. He stops kissing my lips for a second, kisses my forehead a few times and sits down next to me.

Please don't stop, professional kisser. I'm finished talking. I promise.

"They're just jealous. And for your information, that article got cut. But you're going to have to learn how to deal with jealousy, sooner or later, because that's something that's never going to go away. Every successful person has to deal with jealousy, in one form or another. That article should have made you realize that you're considered serious competition around here.

"Once you prove to them that they can't ruin you, and that you're in it for the long haul, they'll have no other choice but to accept you. You'll never get anywhere if you let other people's insecurities get in your way."

Okay, fine. I won't let anything get in my way. Now, get back to work.

I must be staring into space like an idiot, because the next thing he says is, "Are you listening to what I'm saying?"

What was he saying? Oh right. We all have to learn to deal with jealousy. I actually have an answer for that.

"That's easy for you to say because you don't know how it feels to be hated by them. I wanted them to like me so badly. I wanted to be part of their little group, and the sad thing is, I thought I was. It's amazing how quickly I ruined everything. One minute in the closet with you, and it was all over. They are so possessive of you. Are you even aware of that?"

Actually, I don't really care. Just do that thing again where my neck almost breaks.

"I've worked with all of them for so many years. We have a long history together, and they depend on me. But the truth of the matter is, they know I report to corporate, and they are smart. They are not as possessive of me as you may think. They just want me to like them."

"For professional reasons?"

"Yes, exactly, and there's nothing wrong with that. Business is business."

"So what kind of things do you report to corporate, and what do you really do here?"

"Mostly I report people who hang around the shoe closet

for no reason. But first I force them to try on every single pair of shoes in the closet, and then I have them reorganize everything, over and over again, by color. In your case, you made my job easy because you volunteered. Still, I should have fired you on the spot. I made an exception for you because I couldn't resist you in those velvet shoes."

"You said you thought they were ugly."

"Yeah, well, I lied. Besides, the more important question is, what do *you* want to be doing here? Because I heard through the grapevine that you are being considered for a promotion, very soon."

"Really? I can't imagine why anyone would recommend me for a promotion. I hardly even know what I'm doing."

"Then I'm sure you'll be surprised to know that it's the publisher who wants to promote you," he says as he removes his cuff links and rolls up his sleeves. "He's looking for an idea person to fill the creative services director position. You'd be perfect for it."

"Well, I hope he changes his mind before it's too late," I say, trying not to stare at Stan's neck. He has the most amazing neck skin.

"Why?" Stan laughs.

"Because then I'll be stuck here forever. We don't do anything that really promotes the magazine. The whole department is a total waste. We design folders. Do you really think the sales people want to take those folders with them on sales calls? Because I don't."

"The salespeople need to bring information with them. The research numbers are probably their most valuable tools. Most of the time they're just looking for a creative way to present those numbers. But I think you're right. Your department could use a lot more energy, and that's exactly what Rob is hoping you'll bring to the table. He talks about you and your ideas all the time. He knows the department is weak at the moment. That's the whole purpose of making a change."

I'm sitting right next to him, but he pulls me even closer and takes my hand.

"I wish he would just promote Ruth and move me somewhere else. I can still give her ideas from anywhere in the building. She won't even have to know they're my ideas. I can send them to her anonymously and she can say that they're hers. In fact, I'd be glad to do that. Ruth doesn't deserve the torment she's going through. She's suffering and I'm partly responsible."

"Chloe, I think there is something about climbing the corporate ladder that you're not quite getting."

"Oh, no, you're wrong. I get it perfectly. I'm just not interested in climbing the corporate ladder. I've had a dream, ever since I was a little girl, and the only ladder I want to climb is the one that will get me to my dream."

"What is it? I've got to hear this," Stan says.

"Promise you'll keep it a secret? I've never told anybody."

He lets go of my hand and crosses his heart.

"Okay, here I go. Ready?"

"As ready as I'll ever be," he says.

"I want to be shoe editor."

He's biting his lip. Now he's covering his face with one hand, but I can still see a big vein popping out on the top of his forehead. I'm pretty sure he's trying not to laugh. Either that or he's having some kind of seizure. I don't know how much longer he can hold out. . . .

"Shoe editor! What the hell is that?"

"I made it up and it's not that funny," I say, standing up.

"Why would you want to be called shoe editor? It's so demeaning."

"I don't think it's demeaning. I think you are. I would never laugh at someone else's dream or their ideas. Don't you even realize that magazines need shoe editors? In fact, that's the whole problem with magazines today! The shoes are all wrong. If you knew anything about this magazine, you would have realized that this is a huge problem a long time ago!"

"I'm sorry. I think it was the way you said it."

"No, it's because you think I'm some stupid girl with a stupid dream but it's still my dream and I would be really good at it, too. I care more about shoes than anyone else in this whole entire place. And if you think I needed you to come rescue me with this enormous dress, you're wrong! I don't need anyone." I pull off the dress, right over my head, which isn't that difficult considering that it was designed for a giant.

"I've wanted to work at a magazine like *Issues* all my life. Every time I walk through those doors downstairs, I feel like I'm walking onto a movie set, starring me as the girl I always dreamed I'd be. This is all I ever wanted. The fact that I hate my job doesn't even come close to ruining it. And the fact that my fantasy job doesn't exist in real life doesn't bother me either, because I'm here. And that's all that matters."

I'm standing here in my matching bra and panties from the Ruby Valentine Fun & Frilly Collection. It's the same bra and panty set that Jen picked out as an example of ridiculous lingerie. It's covered in a smiley-face heart-shaped balloon print. There's an oversized smiley-face balloon right smack in the middle of my . . . you know. It's a very festive set. The balloon strings are twisted into letters that say, "Happy Valentine's Day, Honey," if you look very closely.

So help me God, I will never buy another holiday promotional lingerie set again as long as I live. Even if it's two-for-one.

I quickly pull on my skirt and my sweater. He's apologizing like crazy, but he keeps ruining it by laughing in between apologies. He's trying to make it up to me by describing a pair of SpongeBob SquarePants boxers that he got as a gift from his nephew. I'd love to tell him that my Happy Valentine's Day bra and panties were a gift too, but no one would ever buy either of these items for anyone.

After a while, I manage to relax and make a legitimate excuse for my overly enthusiastic underwear by calmly explaining how excited I was for the Valentine's Day Ball. I think he
is beginning to understand how much I love it here and how
desperately I want to be a part of it. I'm not really mad at him
anymore. He's looking at me the same way he looked at me
the first time we met, in the shoe closet—right after he overheard me talking out loud to a pair of boots. This is the man
who brought me back a piece of my childhood. He's not judging me. He just thought shoe editor was a funny title. I totally
forgive him. You can't get mad at a person for thinking a word
is funny. I can't help it when I crack up every time someone
says *bunion*.

It's taking several hours for us to make up from our little argument. At one point, Stan thought he remembered seeing a
tag with a really big pin still stuck to my bra. He checked
everywhere, but it turned out to be his imagination.

As it turned out, he really liked my smiley face bra and
panty set, and he made me promise to wear it as often as possible. We tried at least fifty times but finally gave up trying to
let go of one another. He is by far the most edible creature on
the planet. I would gladly give up the remainder of my life to
stay here until the morning, but I feel too guilty about the fact
that I have to finish Ruth's Christmas list project.

"This is it. I really have to go now. If I stay here any longer,
I'm definitely going to do something that I'll regret."

"Like what? Give me an example."

"I can't. I really have to get Ruth's list finished. I mean it,"
I say.

"At least let me take you home. You can't stay here all night.
Take the address book with you. You don't have to finish it here."

I didn't let him come up, which is definitely for the best, because now I have all night to think about what just happened

and attempt to finish this list. It would have been impossible for me to get any work done with him around, and the kissing was becoming a safety issue. I came this close to blacking out at least three or four times. I've never been kissed like that in my life. He didn't bite me once.

CHAPTER THIRTEEN

~

When You Find Yourself Being Helpful, Try Not to Get Caught

It's Monday morning. I managed to copy every single name into Ruth's new address book, and I typed up a copy for her. The messenger never showed up, and I spent the rest of the weekend recuperating from what I thought was carpal tunnel. It turned out to be a small blister, but I bought one of those paraffin machines, just in case. Jen and I used it all weekend. We dipped everything. It's a great machine.

Stan called to see if I finished the project and to see if I wanted to have Sunday dinner with him and his sister and her family in Connecticut. I had just invited Jen over, and the machine was heating up when he called. I was about to tell Jen, "I'm sorry, but we'll have to play with this dumb machine one night during the week because the greatest guy in the world is on the phone and he just invited me to have dinner with him and his family in the country." But Jen was so excited about it that she kept yelling out the digital temperature reading while I was still on the phone with him.

"It's up to one hundred and one degrees!" she yelled. Five minutes later, I heard, "One hundred and ten!!" I finally told him that all the yelling was my best friend who was on my couch with the flu, and that I just couldn't leave her home sick with such an incredibly high fever. I didn't want to tell him that I couldn't take a two-hour drive with him to meet his sister and her children because I just bought a home paraffin machine, which will most likely wind up in the garbage as soon as I come to terms with the fact that I have no place to keep it.

"Ruth, good morning! I'm so sorry, but the messenger never showed up and I still have your address book. I transferred all the numbers and made you a file copy."

"What messenger?" Ruth asks.

"The one you said you were going to send to my apartment on Saturday to pick up your address book."

"Oh right. I should have called you. I got an unexpected visitor, and I decided to put off my early Christmas list project. After all, it is only February. I hope that little misunderstanding didn't ruin your weekend."

"No, it was fine. I didn't really want to go to the ball anyway," I say unexpectedly.

"You what?" Ruth asks.

"I mean, I *did* want to go, but it was no big deal. There's always next year's ball."

"I'm sorry, Chloe. I didn't realize you were planning to go to the ball. I can assure you, you didn't miss much. You'll be able to read all about it on Page Six anyway, and besides, what did you think would happen if you went to the ball? Did you think you would meet the man of your dreams?" She turns around laughing, then walks in her office and slams her door. A few minutes later she walks back out, and to both of our surprise, I'm still standing there with my mouth open.

"Chloe, why are you still standing here? Is there nothing for you to do? Where's the booklet for the fragrance piece? On second thought, I have something more important for you to work on. I'd like you to make me an entrance poster for the lobby introducing the *Portrait of a Lady* luncheon. Get an easel from upstairs and make it spectacular. I want it in the lobby as soon as possible. Don't ask me any questions. Just get it done. We should have had something downstairs over a week ago."

I walk into the art department and stand around for a few seconds wondering which one of them I should approach. Unfortunately, Rhonda is on the phone. Trai has his headphones on, and Ali is standing in the corner. I think she's looking into a hand mirror or something. She's really digging herself into that corner. Poor thing. She probably has a pimple.

"Hey, how's it going?' I ask, as though they are regular people.

Hallie comes running over.

"Can I help you with something?" she asks.

"Actually, yes, Ruth wants me to make a poster for the lobby to introduce the *Portrait of a Lady* luncheon." I roll my eyes a little so she won't think I want to do it. It's my way of letting her know that I realize a poster is an art thing and that I have no business taking on this type of project.

"Great, let's get started," she says, falling all over herself to help me. Just then, Rhonda slams the phone down and mouths the words "Don't talk" behind Hallie's back.

"What do you want it to say?" Hallie asks.

I don't answer.

"What do you want it to look like?" she asks.

I don't answer.

This is an impossible working arrangement.

Rhonda walks over to me and says, "You can talk about the poster." Then she whispers in my ear, right in front of Hallie, "Just don't say anything bad about Ruth. Not one word."

Oh! *Why would I say anything bad about Ruth?*

"Well, I guess it should look like a giant invitation, with a date, a time and a place, and a picture of a bunch of ladies lunching."

"Why a *bunch* of ladies?" Hallie asks. She looks confused but relieved that I'm talking again.

"I don't know. It's a women's magazine. We're doing *Portrait of a Lady* as a theme. It's a luncheon. The idea of ladies who lunch just popped into my head."

"But the article is called *Portrait of a Lady*. That means it's only one lady," Hallie says.

"I know. But that's just the title of the article. I'm assuming that the article will be about ladies in general. You know, on second thought, we could do a still shot of Nicole Kidman from *Portrait of a Lady*. That's a better idea anyway. I'll go and download something, and if you could show me how to get it blown up, that would be great."

"Well, don't you think that everyone will think that they're being invited to a showing of the actual movie if you do that? Or they might even think that they are being invited to a luncheon with Nicole Kidman, if you put her picture on the poster," Hallie says.

"That's true. Let's just get a photograph of someone dressed up like a lady."

"You mean to look like Nicole Kidman?" Hallie asks.

"Not necessarily, we can dress up anyone like a lady. Preferably an old-fashioned lady."

Trai takes his headphones off and says, "Let's dress you up, Chloe. I'll take some digitals, and we'll blow it up right now and see how you look as a lady."

I guess he had his music turned off.

"I'll blow in some kind of Victorian-looking copy and there's your poster," he says. I love the idea, but I wouldn't dare put a picture of myself on a poster that's going to be sitting in the lobby. Trai turns to Ali and whistles. She drops the mirror, which miraculously doesn't break, and takes two steps forward.

"Ali," he says, "today is Monday. You work at *Issues*. Your job is art assistant, and I'm going to give you an assignment, so pay attention. Here are your instructions: Go upstairs to the seventh floor and ask the first person you see to please help you. Whoever she is, tell her that you work in the art department, on the sixth floor, and that you need some kind of an old-fashioned pin or cameo and some old velvet ribbon. Then go to the fashion closet and take any kind of shirt that you can find with a ruffled collar, and then ask someone where Courtney sits. When you find her, tell her that Rob asked her to come downstairs immediately and help with hair and makeup. Can you do that, Al?"

I'm amazed at how quickly he is pulling this together. But poor Ali is all worked up. She's frantically writing it all down, and she has to change pencils twice. She presses very hard. She takes her notes and runs out practically in tears.

"Do you think she'll be okay?" I ask.

"People get lost all the time here, Chloe. It's a chance we have to take."

"Listen," I say, "I think we should dress up Ali. She has such a classic look and she's so pretty and she is sort of old-fashioned looking. I think her face would be perfect for the poster. If she's too uncomfortable to do it, then let's get some shots of Rhonda. You'll do it, won't you, Rhonda?"

"Are you kidding?" Trai says. "Rhonda looks like a man. You really want to put a picture of a man on a poster that says *Portrait of a Lady?* That makes a lot of sense."

I look at Rhonda to see if she's insulted. She's not. She just shakes her head and says, "Grow up already, Trai. I've had it with you! And I wouldn't let you take my picture if my life depended on it."

She does sort of look like a man. I never noticed that.

"Let's just do Ali," I suggest again. "Nothing is more lady-like than that blonde hair and that fair skin and those blue eyes of hers."

"I can't photograph Ali. She always starts crying whenever I come near her with any type of electronic equipment. You should have seen her react when I brought in my Game Boy two years ago. She thought it was a gun," Trai says.

"What's wrong with her?" I ask.

"I think she was in Nam," Trai says, seriously.

"She's too young to have been in Vietnam," I say.

He seemed so smart just a minute ago. How could he not know that?

"Not Vietnam, you idiot. Nam!" he yells at me.

"Whatever. We need to choose someone for this poster. I guess I can just pull someone from the hall if I have to."

"You're in the poster or I'm not doing it," Trai says. He puts his headphones back on, and Hallie turns her chair around to face me.

"Trai likes you, Chloe. Are you aware of that? He didn't even suggest using me for the poster."

"He probably just assumes you wouldn't want to do it. I still think Ali has the right look for this," I say.

"No, Ali will ruin it. It should be you. Do you like him back?" Hallie asks.

At this moment, I realize that Hallie likes Trai. This is all so grim, and I need to somehow convince Trai to photograph Ali.

"I'm sorry, Trai," I shout, "but you have to shoot Ali. I can't be in the poster. We need a blonde," I say with absolute authority.

"Okay," he says to me and then turns to Hallie and says, "Hallie, you shoot it. I don't feel like doing it." He puts his headphones back on. He's done.

Miraculously Ali returns with a really pretty tan cameo on a cream velvet ribbon and a white shirt with a ruffled collar and cuffs, but no Courtney.

"What happened, Ali? You couldn't find Courtney?" I ask.

"I asked for her, but one of the editors looked at me and I thought she was about to yell so I apologized for asking and came back down without her. I'm so sorry. I'm really so sorry." She's going to cry.

"Stop, don't cry. We don't need Courtney. I'll do your hair and makeup," I say, even though I can't even make a decent ponytail.

"*My* hair and makeup? Why mine? I'm going to be on the poster?" Ali asks. She's terrified.

"Ali, I really need you to do this. You are perfect for this. You look like a lady."

She lets me take her into the ladies' room, and I grab my own makeup bag on the way. I can't really do hair, so I ask her to help me, and in about twenty seconds, she's created a truly elegant swirling French twist. Her hair is so silky and golden that it doesn't even feel like hair. I start putting some blush on her, and then I stop. There's no reason to go any further. She's so incredibly beautiful, but she's always hiding her face.

"No one even knows how beautiful you are," I tell her.

"I'm not beautiful. I look like a canary," she whispers.

"Ali, you should be a model. You don't belong in the art department. It's hazardous to yourself and those around you. I think someone should introduce you to the editors."

"Oh, I don't think so," Ali says, slipping into the ruffled blouse.

She slides the ribbon through the cameo pin and ties a knot in the back. Her neck is so long and perfect; it's an incredible transformation. I unbutton her collar to let the choker show. The ruffles graze her jawline on both sides. She looks at herself for a second, and I realize that she's not seeing what I see. She really has no idea what she looks like.

I walk Ali back into the art department. All she did was pull her hair off her face and add a choker, but she looks completely different.

"Wow," Trai says. "You look good as an old lady, Al."

She's trembling. I wouldn't dare let go of her. She would immediately fall to her death.

"Just take her picture and get this over with," Hallie says.

I can't believe how much she likes him. How could she? He's practically a troll.

Trai takes about ten shots of Ali and a few of Rhonda and me and none of Hallie.

"Take one of Hallie," I whisper to him.

"No fucking way," he says sweetly.

"Give me the invitation copy. I'll print this, blow it up, and I'll even frame it for you. How's that?" Trai offers.

"You would do that for me?" I ask.

"I'm only doing it because I'm really looking forward to the *Portrait of a Lady* luncheon," he says.

"What are you going to use for a frame?" I ask.

"Just leave it to me, okay?"

"How about an easel?" I ask.

"Yeah, get me one of those," he says.

When I walk back into the art department with the easel, everyone is gone, except for Trai. He has one of the photos of Ali on his screen. She looks amazing. I want to call someone upstairs, but it's not exactly my job to recruit models.

I know!

"Trai, can you do me a favor?" I ask.

"I'm already doing you a favor, so no," he says, without turning around.

"I really want some of those photos that you took of Ali. I want to do something with them. Can you just print me out a few?"

"What are you? A lesbo?"

"I think it would be great if some of the editors got a look at her. I'm going to leave a couple of pictures of her on their desks with her extension number. I think it's worth a try," I say, attempting to ignore the way he's looking at me.

"I should have known you were a fucking lesbo."

"Okay, I am. Now will you do that for me?"

"I can't believe I didn't see that," he says.

"See what?"

"That you are a les-bi-an."

"I'm not a lesbian."

He's mad at me again.

"Trai, don't be mad at me. If you want me to be a lesbian, I'll be one, okay? Just do me this one favor."

"I don't want you to be a lesbian."

Hallie was right. He does like me. How gross is this?

"You know I like you, Trai. It's just that I have a boyfriend. I couldn't let myself *really* like you. You know that, right?"

I realize that was wrong of me, but I'm sort of in a rush here.

"So will you do that for me?" I ask.

"I think it can be arranged," he says.

Now he feels like he's got the upper hand, and it's really annoying.

I return to my desk. At that very minute, my phone rings, and it's Stan. We talk for a few minutes, and he asks me to meet him for lunch in the closet, which we now affectionately refer to as The Shoe Inn, but I can't today. We decide to meet on Wednesday because he has a lunch meeting tomorrow. Wednesday sounds so far away.

I miss him so much. I wish I could go home and go to sleep until Wednesday, but there's no way I could ever pull something like that off.

The only time I even came close to staying in bed all day was when I faked sick in fourth grade. My mom let me watch TV in bed, but I got up during every commercial to change into a different pajama outfit. I eventually got bored with my sleepwear theme and started trying on every single thing in my closet. I was wearing such a cute outfit at one point that I begged my mom to take me to school. I could just see that same thing happening all over again.

~

CHAPTER FOURTEEN

Right Now She Plans to Use You on the Front Line

I'm fifteen minutes late for work and I really need to get upstairs, but there's a little crowd in the lobby blocking the entrance to the elevators.

The frame is a glossy white Victorian masterpiece. There are fresh flowers scattered around the base of the easel, and there is a pair of white gloves draped over one corner of the frame. Everyone is crowded around the poster. As soon as the girl in front of me steps away, I get a glimpse of the top of the photograph. It's an enormous headshot. All I can see is Ali's hair, which looks like spun gold. The presentation itself is a work of art. I'm sure it's an incredible portrait. Trai is a genius in his own right. He understood the look I was going for, and he nailed it perfectly. You'd never believe he could pull this off by having a conversation with him.

As I move in closer, something looks odd. The hair and the face don't quite go together. Oh my God! That's me! He put my face inside of Ali's hair. I'm sort of smiling and looking away.

So that's what I look like as a blonde.

I am going to kill him! He made a complete fool out of me. Everyone is going to think it was my idea to put my face over Ali's, on a poster, in the goddamn lobby! I run to the elevator.

As soon as I reach the sixth floor, I can feel trouble. When I get to the art department, it's empty, except for Ruth and Hallie. They are sitting together very quietly.

"That poster is a disgrace!" Ruth says, the second she sees me. "It doesn't send the right message. You obviously dropped in your own face after the photograph was blown up, and you didn't even have the decency to have it approved. I think we need to talk, Chloe."

Halli and I follow Ruth into her office as I prepare myself for another routine decapitation.

"Ruth, there's been a terrible misunderstanding. I didn't want my picture on that poster. I wanted to use Ali's picture. Trai transposed Ali's hair onto my face or my face under Ali's hair. I have no idea why he did it. Please Ruth, you have to believe me. Ask Trai."

"Trai isn't in this morning," Ruth says.

"He stayed home to shave his head," Hallie says.

You can tell she's really excited about it, too. Personally, I think it's a terrible mistake. His hair was his best feature.

"Then ask Rhonda," I plead.

"Rhonda isn't here at the moment, either, as you can see," Ruth says.

"Then ask Hallie," I say.

Ruth turns to Hallie and asks, "Who chose the photo for the poster?"

"Chloe came in here demanding that we get her a poster immediately. Trai sent Ali upstairs to borrow a necklace and blouse from the fashion closet, and then Chloe asked Trai to take pictures," Hallie says.

There's nothing like leaving out a few million details.

"Where's Ali?" I ask.

"I'm afraid she's not here either. It looks like you have no one to blame but yourself, Chloe."

"Ruth, you have to believe me. This was not my choice."

"Chloe, I think it's time that you start facing facts and begin taking responsibility for your actions. Hallie and I know what happened here.

"If Rhonda, Trai, or Ali choose to defend you by lying, I really don't think that will help you grow as a person in the long run."

Ruth turns to Hallie and tells her to redo the poster immediately.

"Just blow in a headshot of one of our models. The rest of the poster is fine," Ruth says.

I sit in my cubicle for about an hour trying to figure out how to prove myself to Ruth. I wish I had Trai's home phone number. I decide to instant message him instead.

CHLOE:	Sup Skinhead? Do u have any idea what u did 2 me?
TRAI:	What I do?
CHLOE:	U put my pic in Ali's head.
TRAI:	Tru dat. My bad.
CHLOE:	Y? Y? Y?
TRAI:	Cuz Ali is mental.
CHLOE:	But I asked u not 2. Now Ruth hates me.
TRAI:	Ruthless always hated u.
CHLOE:	Now she hates me more.
TRAI:	My head is bleeding. Got 2 go.

What made me think talking to him about this would make me feel better?

"Chloe, get in here!"

Ruth wants me. I can't believe she is even talking to me.

"I need you to fill in for me today. Do you think you can

handle that? I need you to take a client to lunch. His name is Bruno Calabrese."

"Bruno Calabrese? The fur designer? Oh my God. His stuff is amazing. That's so exciting. Thank you, Ruth."

"Well, I'm glad you're excited about it. As it turns out, I've been invited to an editorial lunch, so you'll have to take care of Mr. Calabrese. He's a very important man, Chloe. Do not blow this for us. His account is worth several million dollars a year. He's one of our largest advertisers. You'll be meeting him at Nanni's at noon."

"I can't believe you're trusting me with this. I mean right after what just happened! I really appreciate this. What exactly is the purpose of the lunch?"

"The purpose of the lunch is to keep Mr. Calabrese happy. He loves promoting the fur industry. Any ideas you can give him would be greatly appreciated, by him and me."

"Wow. This is such a great opportunity. Mr. Calabrese is so famous. Thank you so much."

"Just make sure you're on time. He's expecting me, so he'll be a little disappointed to see you, but he'll be even more disappointed if you're late."

"I won't let you down, I promise."

As soon as I walk into Nanni's, I feel like a woman of the world. The restaurant is charming and elegant and buzzing with beautiful people. I see a lot of familiar faces from the magazine. The whole place smells like warm olive oil and garlic and perfume and flowers, and I am just so glad that I'm not a little kid anymore. Little kids never get to do stuff like this. I'm dressed perfectly, too. I'm wearing my new little black dress. I only wore it because I was thinking about that whole 'Lady' thing. I never expected to be going out to lunch with an important client. In fact, I thought I was overdressed when I left the house this morning in my black suede stilettos that I swore I'd never wear to work. Look how it all worked out. Amazing.

I head over to the maitre d' and I tell him that I'm Ruth Davis's assistant and I'm here to dine with Mr. Calabrese.

"Right this way, madam," he says.

Madam. Can you believe that?

When I arrive at the table, I see that Mr. Calabrese is quite a gargantuan human being. He stands up to greet me. He is easily six feet seven. I've never been this close to such a large person before. I feel childish and silly all of a sudden. It feels like he's one of my parents' friends and that he's going to take me out to a nice lunch and then, perhaps, the circus. I walk over and shake his hand. "I'm Chloe Rose, Mr. Calabrese."

"It's lovely to meet you, Miss Rose, and to what do I owe this tremendous pleasure?"

"Well, Mr. Calabrese, Ruth is unfortunately tied up for the afternoon at an editorial lunch meeting, and so she asked me to meet with you. I hope you don't mind," I say, as though I just graduated from charm school.

I love my dress. I love being here. I love Issues. I even love Ruth.

"Have some wine with me, will you? And please, call me Bruno." He motions to the waiter, and within seconds there is a bottle of wine chilling in a silver wine stand next to our table. His lips are enormous, and his voice is so loud and hollow. I think he is a real giant. I never thought I'd ever meet a giant.

Mr. Calabrese pours me a glass of wine, and I could swear that he winked at me, but that's probably just his way. He is such a grand old gentleman. I take a sip and try to pretend I like it. The truth is, I can't stand drinking wine.

I'll never understand how it became so popular. It's amazing how many people are willing to sit around drinking spoiled juice all night and talk about how delicious it is when everyone knows it tastes terrible. I hold my breath and somehow manage to finish my glass almost immediately. Bruno does the same and proceeds to pour us both another glass.

I wonder if Zoe's advice about dining out applies to clients as well as bosses. If so, I guess I'll have to eat whatever Bruno eats and then . . . what was I supposed to do? . . . Oh right . . . lodge it in my teeth somehow. Zoe gives the worst advice.

"So, tell me, Chloe, what sort of things do you enjoy?"

"Well, believe it or not, I love fur, and of course, shoes, and I like to read. And I love tennis, I mean I adore it. And I enjoy fur, of course, and horseback riding, and I occasionally play some croquet. I also enjoy traveling and meeting new people. Nothing terribly exciting."

Mr. Calabrese is smiling at me. I sure developed a whole new crop of hobbies.

"Well, I find everything about you terribly exciting. As a matter of fact, why don't we finish our business here and go across the street for a drink."

"Is there a better place for drinks across the street?" I ask.

"My hotel room is across the street," Mr. Calabrese says.

Oh my God.

"Oh stop it, Mr. Calabrese," I say, pretending that he's joking and that I know how to handle myself in this situation.

"Stop what? You think I don't know why you came here today? Bruno understands women better than he understands fur. You like fur, don't you, Chloe?"

"Yes, of course," I say, wondering if it's too soon to scream.

"Then why don't you do as I ask? Let's get out of here and I'll show you some things from the new collection in my hotel room. There's nothing to be afraid of. You're a woman. I'm a man. And I'm a very busy man. I don't have time for games."

"I'm sure you are, Mr. Calabrese, but—"

"Call me Bruno, Chloe. Mr. Calabrese is so formal," he says, patting my hand.

"If you'll excuse me, Bruno, I have to use the ladies' room." I get up from my chair and turn around and there's Sloane and Blaire and Ruth! They were only two tables away, all along. I'm so relieved to see them. I can hardly control myself.

"Mr. Calabrese, there's Ruth. What a surprise. I'm sure she'd love to join us."

"Sit down, Chloe. We are having a private lunch."

He grabs my hand and squeezes it until it just starts to hurt.

I pull my arm away from him and manage to stand up. The force is so great that when he releases my hand, the whole table shakes.

I feel my head spinning, and I'm not sure what to do. I turn to look at Ruth, and she mouths the words "Don't you dare leave," but I can tell by her expression that she is both afraid for me and very worried. Maybe she's devising a plan to get me out of this. She probably wants to kick herself for getting me into this mess in the first place.

I turn back to Mr. Calabrese and he's standing up. I'm about to turn and run when Mr. Calabrese says, "If you run out of here, I will hold you personally responsible for losing my account. I don't take no for an answer, Chloe. That's the kind of man I am. I know what I want when I see it, and I always get what I want. And something tells me that this little game you're playing means you want me, too. So, just settle down and have a nice lunch with me, and then we'll go across the street, just like I asked, okay, sweetheart?" He grabs my hand again and squeezes it so hard that I hear something crack. I think he broke my pinky. I pick up a fork with my other hand and push it into his hand and tell him, "If you don't let go of me, I'm going to start screaming for the police, okay, sweetheart?"

A moment later, Stan is at my side with two other men. I drop the fork and stand next to him, and he puts his arm around me. I can't believe how many people from the magazine eat here. The food must be very good.

As soon as Bruno sees the men, he stands up to greet them. They all seem to know each other.

"Well, hello there, gentlemen. Is this lovely lady a friend of yours? She's absolutely charming. Now don't go and steal her away from me. We're having a wonderful time. Aren't we, Chloe?"

"Get out," Stan says.

"Don't get excited; we're just getting to know each other. There's no hanky-panky going on, if that's what you're afraid of. Now, if you don't mind, we're discussing business. I hope you haven't forgotten who I am," Bruno adds with another one of his little winks. As soon as he's certain that Stan will leave him alone, he walks around the table to pull out my chair, indicating that I should sit back down.

"I know exactly who you are and I want you out of here, Bruno. *Issues* doesn't need your business anymore," Stan says, as calmly as he says everything.

"That's nonsense, you're overreacting. We're having a nice lunch."

"Don't make a scene, Bruno. Just get out or I promise you, I'll have you thrown out."

Big Bruno gets up and charges out like an injured elephant, mumbling something about Stan being irrational and me being a little bitch. Stan calls for the waiter and tells him to put Bruno's wine on his tab. Then he tells the other two men to carry on without him. *Stan really is a troubleshooter!*

As we leave the restaurant, Stan is pulling my arm, and my hand still hurts.

"What are you mad at me for?" I say as we're walking out the door.

"I'm not mad at you at all. I'm mad at myself. I should have come over to your table immediately. I thought he was behaving himself until I saw you stick that fork in his hand. I should have known he'd pull something the second I saw you two. Why in hell were you out to lunch with that guy in the first place? Everyone knows what he is."

"Ruth sent me. She wanted me to give him some ideas to promote the fur industry. He seemed like such a gentleman at first. But then he invited me up to his hotel room. I almost panicked, but then I spotted Ruth just in time. I tried to signal to her that I was in trouble, but she made it clear that I couldn't leave. I'm sure she would have done something if she'd sensed that I was in any real danger. He's a huge advertiser, Stan. You should have never done that. I was handling myself pretty well on my own. I hate to say this, but if you hadn't interfered, we might still have his business."

"Chloe, you were stabbing him."

That's true. I was stabbing him. We probably would have lost the account either way.

~

CHAPTER FIFTEEN

If You Do Fall for Some Guy at Work, Make Sure He's Worth Losing Your Job Over— Just in Case

Rhonda and I have decided to take a quick peek at Barney's biannual shoe sale. Everything is thirty to fifty percent off, and, as it turns out, we're not the only ones here. Most of the staff of *Issues* has shown up, along with the entire female population of Manhattan. It's so crowded. It's almost impossible to walk around in here. It's especially difficult for me because I'm wearing the Lulu Guinness shoes from the shoe closet. I've worn them out a few times over the past several months and not one person has ever noticed that they are both lefties.

"Oh, look who's here!" I say to Rhonda.

"Who?"

"That guy over there. He's a friend of mine, from work."

"Really?" Rhonda says.

"He works in editorial. His name is Stan."

"Are you kidding?" she asks.

"No, I'm serious. Isn't he so cute?"

"I still can't tell if you're kidding or not."

"Why? You don't think he's cute?"

"You're not kidding, are you?"

"Kidding about what?"

"What did you say his name was?" Rhonda asks.

"It's Stan."

"No, it's not. It's Dan."

"That's what I said, 'Stan.' I've been seeing him, sort of, secretly. I've been dying to tell you, but I haven't told *anyone*."

"How did you meet him?" Rhonda asks.

"Promise you won't tell a soul?"

"Hope to die, stick a needle in my eye," she says in her deadpan voice.

"Okay, remember the first time I visited the shoe closet? Well, I got myself locked in there somehow and Stan got me out. And then we got really friendly, and then . . . he gave me my own key! I'm wearing a pair of shoes from the shoe closet right now." I whisper the part about the key.

"Well, now I have a couple of things to tell you," Rhonda says. "Number one: Those shoes don't look right on you. Number Two: Your cute friend, who works in editorial, who got you out of the closet, and who gave you your own key, is the editor-in-chief of *Issues*. Besides that, he owns it. His family is the Princely family. Your little secret boyfriend is Dan Princely, as in, 'The Prince.' He never mentioned that?"

"No, of course not, because his name is Stan."

"Chloe, his name is Dan, Dan with a D. Trust me."

"How come everyone always calls him Stan?"

"I can honestly say, I've never heard anyone call him Stan until just now, and I've been at *Issues* for eleven years."

"But I've been calling him Stan for almost a year."

"Well, you've been calling him by the wrong name. Dan and Stan sound similar. It's an honest mistake."

"Are you sure?"

"I'm positive."

"I feel like a complete idiot. It's like finding out your mom is really a man . . . or something. Why didn't he ever correct me? I feel like I don't even know him anymore."

This changes everything. I quickly slip off both shoes and shove them into my bag. I'll just act like I'm waiting for the salesperson to come back from the stockroom with a pair of shoes that I asked to try on. That's all. No big deal.

"Look who's headed our way," Rhonda says.

"Hello, ladies," Stan—I mean, *what's his name*—says to both of us.

"Hi, Dan," Rhonda says. "It's good to see you. Shop here often?"

He didn't correct her, and she definitely called him Dan. That settles it. Rhonda really does know everything.

"Well, it just so happens that I have a very good friend who confessed that this is her favorite place in the entire world to come and think. I have a few things to sort out, so I thought I'd try this place myself. Besides, I had a feeling she'd be here today. Although, I must say, I can't imagine getting any real thinking done in here."

"Well, I guess it all depends on what's on your mind in the first place," Rhonda says.

She's very quick, that Rhonda.

I shouldn't be obsessing over the fact that Dan never mentioned to me that I've been making a fool out of myself, pretty much every day, since we met. Nor should I be nervous or uncomfortable about the fact that I'm carrying a pair of shoes in my bag, with two left feet, that I promised to return about six months ago. St . . . Dan and I are close enough to laugh about something like that.

It's just that, part of me feels as though I should have known who the editor-in-chief of Issues *is, even if I'm not that great with names. Most people seek out that kind of information right away. It just never occurred to me that I would ever meet him. No one ever pointed him out to me, and the fact that he's been lying to me about his name didn't help either.*

The same thing happened to me when I changed schools in third grade. On the last day of school, my friend Lisa Collins was talking to an old lady out on the blacktop, and they shook hands. I asked Lisa if the old lady was her grandmother and she said, "No, that's Mrs. Dixon. She's the school principal." I had no idea. I had never even seen her before.

I'm all conflicted inside. I wonder if it shows. I can't really move, not even my lips. I can't even lick them. I'm so confused, and I realize now that I'm also extremely dumb. I hope no one is talking to me. Emotions can be paralyzing, but I do feel my underarms sweating. If my underarms are able to soak my T-shirt, does that mean I'm not paralyzed?

"Chloe, hello?"

Who said that? Why am I so nervous? What's wrong with me? I know these people.

"I'm not wearing any shoes," I blurt out in a desperate attempt to hide the fact that I'm not wearing any shoes. I have every right to be nervous. This is a very awkward situation, but Dan isn't uncomfortable at all. He's not looking at my feet or the little pointy heels of my shoes, which are sticking out at least two inches from my handbag. He's looking right at me, and I no longer care about the shoes, the editor-in-chief thing, the uncanny similarity between the words Dan and Stan, my inability to control my own voice, or the fact that Rhonda seems to have drifted off somewhere. I don't care because I realize that Dan smells like some kind of woodsy, spicy fig leaf and he's wearing perfectly worn in, taupe suede bucks. He's got the kind of arms and blonde arm hair that make my lips burn (maybe that's why I can't move them), and he's smiling that Dentyne smile. He's a perfect man. Even if I get fired for having stolen a pair of shoes with two left feet, I will go knowing that I have met and loved the perfect man.

He's looking at me with those aquamarine eyes, and he's whispering a question in my ear, but I can't even hear him. I can't hear anything, as a matter of fact. Either I'm having some kind of an emotional breakdown in my own little world or I'm really going deaf this time.

It's like we are the only two people here, silently considering what we've become to each other without ever realizing it. It's just the two of us, in this store, on this street, in this city. It's just him and me and we're standing so close we're practically touching.

I can see him and smell him, and oh! What are those? Those are the boots I was looking for in brown! I didn't even know they came in brown.

"Excuse me, *Dan,*" I say, and run after the salesperson, who is carrying the open box of brown boots back to the storage room.

"What size are those, please?" I ask.

"These are the last pair," the lying salesperson says, as though he plans to keep them. "What size were you looking for?"

Ha!

"Whatever size is in that box is fine," I say, with my hands on my hips, feeling a little pushy and wishing I weren't tapping my foot.

"They are a six and a half," he says, looking down at my feet.

"Perfect!" I say, while attempting to take the box out of his hand. I really have to pull it away. Clearly, he doesn't want to let them go. He can't possibly wear a ladies size six and a half. "Is there a problem?" I ask.

We're both holding the box now.

"Not really," he says. "It's just that I saw you put a pair of shoes in your bag, and I was just wondering—"

"She probably took her own shoes off because they don't fit her," Dan interrupts. "They're right here," he says, reaching into my bag.

He pulls one out and looks at it for a second. "You wore these?" he asks.

The lying salesperson reluctantly hands me the box and hovers around me, just in case I suddenly run away.

"How is that possible?" Dan whispers.

"I wore them by accident," I whisper.

He leans over to kiss me, but the boot box hits him in the stomach before he can reach me. He tries to grab the box, but I won't let go. We wrestle with it for a second, then he impatiently hands it to the hovering salesperson and says, "Can you send these to her apartment, please? Her name is Chloe Rose and I'm sure her address is in your computer." Then he takes out his credit card and hands it to the salesperson, who seems to like me a lot better now.

"Wait, I don't want you to do that, *Dan*," I say.

"But I want to buy them for you," he protests.

"Oh, that's okay. It's just that I wanted to wear them now."

As we turn to walk out, I realize that I totally forgot about Rhonda. I check all the dressing rooms and walk around every inch of the fifth floor, but she's gone. I try her cell phone.

"Hello?" Rhonda says.

"It's Chloe. Where are you?"

"I walked home. I couldn't watch you two anymore. I've never seen such a perfect couple. It's sickening. I'll see you at work on Monday. Call me if anything exciting happens. Actually, don't."

Dan and I head to the first floor, and I ask him what cologne he's wearing. He says that he doesn't know because he got sprayed by accident while walking by someone who was dousing himself with it from head to toe.

I walk up to the most knowledgeable-looking fragrance specialist I can find and ask him to smell Dan. He agrees wholeheartedly and starts sniffing Dan.

"By the way, I know your name is *Dan*, not Stan."

"I realize that."

"But everyone calls you Stan. Why is that?"

"Nobody ever calls me Stan."

"I do."

"I know. You're the only one. It's pretty funny, don't you think?"

"What's funny about it?"

"I don't know. The first time you said it, it was *really* funny."

"How come you never corrected me?"

"I never had a nickname before. I was sort of enjoying it."

"Well, don't expect me to ever call you that again. For now on, I'm calling you Dan."

"That's fine. I really don't care what you call me."

"Obviously."

The salesperson is about five feet six with bright orange spiky hair. He's wearing a bright pink shirt and lime green corduroy jeans. He looks like a really big Gerber daisy. Dan pulls his body back a little as the salesperson sniffs his neck.

"Don't worry, handsome, you're not my type. But you're wearing Helmut Lang. It's fabulous on you." Dan doesn't say anything. He's sort of being a baby about this.

"We'll take a bottle of that," I say, and I hand the fabulous daisy *my* credit card. *Please let them accept it by mistake. Please God. Please mess up.* You can do it . . .

I can't believe it! It's a miracle. My card is completely worthless, and it worked!

As Fabulous hands me my card and the little black shopping bag, he leans over to me and says, "You can stop by tomorrow and pay for this. And good luck with that gorgeous piece of—"

"Thanks for your help," Dan interrupts, and we head out, holding hands.

I love Dan's hands. They are so big and dry and warm. I wish I could keep one.

We go to his apartment, which is exactly how I picture my apartment would be if I were the perfect man. It's all brown leather and mahogany, and the whole place smells like him. His kitchen is amazing. Everything is stainless steel, and there are pots and pans hanging up over the island. Used ones. I wonder if he cooks. That would be too good to be true.

As soon as we sit down, I ask, "Do you cook?"

"A little," he says. "Do you?"

"A little," I say.

"How much is a little?" he asks.

"I have an ice cream maker," I say.

"Well, why don't I make us some pasta with a mushroom and shallot sauce and a really big salad with baby pear tomatoes and feta cheese . . . oh, and for dessert, I make a really amazing chocolate cake."

How much can a person be expected to take? I'm only human. I have needs, and a man who can cook is . . .

It's four o'clock on Saturday afternoon. We never ate dinner or breakfast or lunch, but we are ready to get out of bed.

We've decided to spend the rest of the afternoon walking around Central Park, in my new brown boots, figuring out what to do with our relationship at work on Monday. I know it's going to be difficult, but there is nothing about this man that I don't love.

He's warm and sweet and funny and generous and incredibly polite to the elderly, and he doesn't own one pair of ugly shoes. I checked all of them. He really is a prince.

"How come you never told me who you were?" I ask.

"Because you liked me without knowing," he says.

I can't wait to introduce him to Zoe.

~

CHAPTER SIXTEEN

Everyone Is Guilty Until Proven Innocent

"He's really sweet and funny and incredibly generous and adorable. And he has the absolute best shoe collection of any man I've ever known," I say, attempting to get them both in the mood to meet Dan.

"He sounds like a complete asshole," Zoe says. "He didn't even have the decency to tell you his real name. There's something very disturbing about that."

"Give the guy a chance," Michael says. "He probably found it amusing that she thought his name was Stan. I wish you had called me Stan when we'd first met."

"He didn't want me to know who he was. He wanted me to like him for himself, not for his position in life. I think that's incredibly sincere," I say.

"What is it exactly about *lying* that you find incredibly sincere?" Zoe asks.

"I don't know. All of it," I say.

"Don't judge him until you spend at least a couple of hours with him," Michael says.

"Forget about the fact that he never told her his real name. I can almost deal with that. But how can you possibly expect me to ever accept the fact that my sister is having a relationship with a guy who deliberately disseminates information intended to weaken the female psyche by comparing normal, healthy women to unattainable images of twelve year olds dressed up like working women, thereby forcing them to drag their frail, damaged spirits to the marketplace in a meager, pathetic attempt to buy back their self-worth? The guy is a misogynist. I hate him." Zoe is in a bad mood.

"It's just a fashion magazine," I say, "and it's not Dan's fault that some women enjoy shopping."

"Oh, yes it is," Zoe says, pushing Michael off the bed.

For some reason, she's directing all of her anger at Michael. I think it's because he let his beard grow into a little goatee. Zoe and I are not big on facial hair. He let the hair on his head grow really long, too. I wonder why she hasn't said anything about his new look. She's usually not one to hold back. Personally, I think Michael's hair looks great long. They almost look like brother and sister now. Except that he's so tall and she doesn't have a little beard.

"Stop pushing me," Michael says.

"I'm not pushing you. You're taking up the whole bed," she answers.

They are both lying on my bed while I pull several outfits out of my closet. Michael doesn't love any of my choices and Zoe keeps telling me that I look too thin. I love the idea that I look too thin, but I think she's wrong. I'm never too thin.

I know Zoe is going to love Dan, as soon as she gets to know him.

"I understand your concern, but you have to take into consideration the fact that he is a businessman. His job is not to save the world," Michael says.

I wish he would stay out of it. Every time he tries to stick up for Dan, he incites her even more.

"Whose side are you on?" Zoe asks Michael.

"I'm not on anyone's side. I just think you should hold off judging this guy until you meet him."

"I already know what he's all about. And Chloe, you should go weigh yourself. You're too thin." She's worried. Maybe I am too thin.

I step on the scale. *Please let me be too thin. Please, please, please. Just this once. Oh my God. I weigh 115.*

"I weigh one fifteen!" I yell.

"Never mind, maybe it was my imagination," Zoe says.

"What do you mean?" I ask, "I said I weigh one fifteen!"

"That's what you always weigh," Zoe says, unimpressed.

"No, it's not. I always say I weigh one fifteen but I usually weigh between one twenty-two and one twenty-five . . . or so."

"You lie to me about your weight?" Zoe asks.

This amazes her.

"I pretty much lie about everything, Zoe, you know that," I say to console her.

"Yeah, but your weight? That's a health issue. Do you lie at the doctor's office?"

"If they ask me without checking, I always lie. If they tell me to hop on the scale in front of the nurse, I move it over a tiny bit when she turns her head. But if they weigh me and write it down immediately, I never change the number—even if the nurse leaves the room for a long time."

"You scare me," Zoe says.

"I do the same thing," Michael says.

He's not funny anymore. It's the goatee. It ruined his personality. He almost looks like he's not feeling well with that thing on his face.

"I hate the goatee," I blurt out.

"Are you lying about that?" Michael asks.

"No, I'm actually telling the truth. You don't look healthy anymore. You look like you've been sick or in jail, but I like your long hair."

"I agree," Zoe says, "but I think your hair is too long. You look like a girl."

"I do not. Why do you say stuff like that?" Now Michael is upset. "I look like a girl with a beard," he mumbles to himself.

"You just look terrible. It's the whole combination and you're too thin also," she says.

"What the hell is wrong with you? What are you, a weight expert now?" He's really mad.

"Well, she knew *I* was too thin," I say proudly, in Zoe's defense.

"Yeah, well, I think she's fucked up," Michael says. "What do you weigh, Zoe? Ninety pounds? That's a good weight. I weighed ninety, too. In sixth grade," he says sarcastically.

"That's great, Michael. You were also six feet tall in sixth grade. You're just mad because you don't look good with a goatee," Zoe says.

I think the idea of meeting Dan is too much for them. It's making them hate each other.

Zoe and Michael take their disagreement into the other room while I get dressed. I've decided to wear my new jeans and my new putty-colored suede jacket and a brown leather cord around my neck with a small, silver, rectangular medallion that says HEART. I'm so excited to wear my new brown boots.

Damn, I left them at Dan's!

~

CHAPTER SEVENTEEN

Keep Your Mouth Shut and Your Head Planted Firmly on Your Shoulders at All Times

We arrive at the restaurant a little early, and I go in first. It's very crowded. Zoe and Michael are way behind me.

There's Dan at the bar! He's talking to a girl. That's not good. She's a blonde girl. This is awful. Her hair looks a little dry. He'd never be interested in a girl with dry hair. They are probably just . . . oh no, she's standing up behind him and giving him a little neck massage. This is horrible. I should leave.

Where's Zoe? I want to go home.

"There you are, Chloe, come over here, I have a surprise for you," Dan says. The surprise better be that the blonde girl is his mother.

As I get a little closer to them, I realize who the surprise is.

"Chloe, you know Courtney. Courtney, you know each other, right?"

"Hi! You look amazing," Courtney says.

"So do you," I say. "Amazing!"

She looks the same as she always does. Blonde, dry, and overly enthusiastic.

"I brought your boots," Dan says, hoping that it makes up for the fact that he showed up with one of The Girls. He's standing there holding the boot box.

"Thank you. Thank you so much," I say, as though I'm talking to a bank teller. I take the box from him, paying careful attention not to grab, and sit down to unzip my old, ugly boots and change into the new beautiful pair. At this point, they are the only reason I'm staying. I put my old boots in the new box and leave them under a bar stool. I hope someone steals them.

Zoe and Michael have caught up to us now, so I turn to them and say, "Zoe, Michael, this is Dan and Courtney."

We're all a little confused, but Courtney clears up the confusion almost immediately. She's not an ex-psychiatric social worker turned mental health editor/makeup artist for nothing.

"I can't believe I ran into Dan here. I was supposed to meet someone, but he never showed up. I'm Courtney! You know, *Courtney*, Courtney, from 'Don't be Afraid To Ask Courtney'?" she says, waiting for applause from Michael and Zoe, of all people.

"You write that column?" Zoe asks, pointing at Courtney as I lightly step on her toe, indicating that she should stop talking now.

"Guilty," Courtney says, having no idea just how much.

"I really have to know," Zoe continues, as immune to a light toe-stepping as ever, "is the whole column supposed to be a joke?" I should have kicked her unconscious.

"You know, it's so funny that you're asking me that. When I first started writing the column for Dan"—she looks up at him as she says that—"I wasn't trying to be funny at all. I was totally serious. But then, a few people started telling me that they thought it was funny, which was sort of weird, so then I started exaggerating a little bit here and there, and it just gave the whole column a totally different feeling. I guess, in a way, it became totally funny," she says, in an overly animated, fifteen-year-old-girl-at-an-all-boy-party kind of way. No wonder they all hate her. She's totally annoying.

Still, I hate to see anyone suffer at the hands of Zoe, so I say, "I love your column. I think it's very honest in a very amusing way. You really offer very honest advice and you do it very amusingly," I say, noting to myself how many more words there are in the dictionary than the ones I've chosen to use.

"I agree," Dan says.

"You do?" Zoe asks Dan.

Dan is not sure what to make of Zoe. He can't quite figure out if she is mad at him in particular or just looking for a fight in general. Wait until she takes her coat off and he sees what she's wearing. That should set him straight. The whole outfit is army green, including her little green suede combat boots. She looks like a little GI Joe. An actual size GI Joe.

What is it with my family and all one color?

"Why don't we see if our table is ready?" Dan asks. He's completely in control of this totally uncomfortable situation. It's obvious that he has no interest in Courtney, and it's not uncommon to run into coworkers at a bar. I just love everything about him. I love his jacket, his smile, his sweetness, his . . .

"Can I join you guys?" Courtney asks. "I'm definitely not doing anything tonight."

Dan looks at me and I say, "Of course, sure, yes, absolutely."

Dan looks relieved, and I'm pretty sure I don't like him anymore.

Zoe and Michael quietly argue the whole way to the table, and I think Courtney is wearing white shoes. And not cool ones either. Something about her really bothers me. At the moment, Dan bothers me too. And Zoe and Michael are the worst couple. I feel like getting drunk. I hate everyone here, and that column of hers isn't amusing or honest. It's just boring and stupid, like her and Dan and Michael and Zoe.

As soon as the waiter comes I order a green apple martini, and Zoe looks at me as if she's going to laugh.

"Make that two," I say to the waiter.

"Two what?" the waiter asks.

"Two martinis," I say.

"Two for you?" he asks.

"No, one of them is for me," Zoe says.

"No, I want two," I say.

"Fine, have two. I'll have a beer," Zoe says.

"Make that two," Michael says.

"Two for her?" the waiter asks.

"No, one for her and one for me," Michael says, not even noticing that the waiter is a little bit of a moron.

"And one for me," Dan says.

"I'll have the green apple thing," Courtney says.

Copycat.

Whoever invented the green apple martini was an amazing inventor. If the bartender knows what he's doing, the alcohol is completely unnoticeable.

When my martini arrives, it's sweet and frothy, like a lemonade smoothie. I could drink ten of these. I finish the first one immediately and start on the second one. It's gone in way under a minute. Drinking is so easy if you stick with the right drink. I motion for the waiter to bring another two. Dan is truly the most handsome human being I've ever known. *His lips are like Angelina Jolie's. That was a weird thought. Maybe Trai was right about me being a lesbian.* I'm a tiny bit drunk. I realize that now. Not *drunk* drunk, but just drunk enough to wonder what went awry with Courtney's implants and if she ever slept with Dan. I also wonder what everyone at the table is talking about.

I think I might have fallen asleep. Nope, I'm up.

When my next pair of drinks come, Dan picks one up and drinks it almost immediately. I motion to the waiter to get me another one and I point to Dan so the waiter won't think I'm drinking too much. The drink comes, and Dan and I practically fight over it.

Why doesn't he just order his own drink?

"Have we ordered yet, Stanley?" I ask, sloshing down my third or fourth martini.

"And Courtney, may I ask what exactly happened to your bosoms?"

At first I think I may have spoken out of turn, but then I remember that famous line, "Don't be Afraid to Ask Courtney!" so I lean in a little closer to get her answer.

Something isn't right, though. I can feel the vibes. Either the food is taking too long or the conversation isn't going right or I've just peed a little. I really shouldn't drink. I have no idea how this evening is going. I wonder if Zoe likes Dan and if Michael is going to shave after all.

"Chloe!" Dan says, as though he knows I peed.

"Oh, that's okay, Dan," Courtney says, hitting him and laughing, as though someone made a joke. She's such a playful girl.

Did someone make a joke?

"As a matter of fact, Chloe, I did have my breasts done, but I had them done years ago, and they are unfortunately a little lopsided. But I just heard about a surgeon who is doing the most gorgeous, natural-looking breasts. I get so many questions about breast implants, I'm thinking about doing a whole page of Q&A devoted entirely to breasts."

"What the hell is she telling me that for?" I ask, out loud by accident.

"Because you asked her," Dan says to me. He's rather stern. I never noticed that about him. You see? You never know about people. You can think you know a person, and then, when you least expect it, it turns out that they're stern.

The food comes, and it seems I've ordered a salad and a humongous steak. Poor Zoe, I think she might throw up from the smell of all that meat wafting from my plate. I'm sitting right next to her. She's eating a veggie burger and so is Michael. So is Courtney and so is Dan.

"Why am I the only one with a steak?" I ask. Maybe out loud, maybe not.

It's hard to tell, because no one answers.

I was probably just wondering internally . . . in my head.

They are all talking right over me, and Dan keeps rearranging my plate and my whole eating area. His hands are giving me shooting pains in my stomach. Shooting stomach pains are a sure sign of love.

Could it be that I'm in love with his hands and that's it. Nothing else?

I reach over to hold his hand, but he's a lefty so he can't very well eat now, can he? He squeezes my hand a little and tells me to be quiet. I didn't even say anything.

I feel so left out. It's almost like I'm being allowed to sit with the grown-ups if I promise not to talk. Dan takes my hand off the table and puts it in my lap and puts his hand over it. Then he continues eating as a righty. He's a wonderful person.

Zoe and Dan are finally talking. No, they're fighting. Zoe is fighting with everyone today.

"Do you really think that magazine empowers women in any way?" Zoe asks.

Here we go again.

"I can only tell you that our editorial is an offshoot of what our research indicates our readers want. My objective is to target and respond to their requests. If they want to know what the best hemline is to flatter their figure, we tell them. If they want to know how to write a better résumé, we tell them. I can't dictate what they want. Of course I don't always agree with the direction of editorial, but my job is not to redirect my readers' thinking. My job is to respond to the way they already think."

"That is the most irresponsible thing I've ever heard." Zoe is turning red.

We should leave. I start to get up and say, "Waiter!" but then I fall back down and my hand hits my plate. Some of the food jumps up a little.

Dan turns to Courtney and says, "Courtney, why don't you take Chloe to the ladies' room?"

He knows I peed! I didn't, though! I'm sure of it!

On the way to the bathroom, I sense that I'm not walking properly and that I might be very, very ill. I want to tell Courtney that I might be having some kind of an allergic reaction to something I ate, but instead I say, "Once we restore our country's faith in our financial system of rewards, those noncontributing members of society who once felt that the odds of success were against them because the game was rigged by thieves will once again become active achievers, thereby reducing the need for social and welfare programs to extend their services to those individuals who had the ability to sustain themselves all along."

I can tell immediately that she didn't understand any of that, because as soon as we get inside the bathroom, she changes the subject completely.

"Would you like to see my breasts?" she asks.

"No thanks," I say, making a mental note of the fact that she is extremely self-absorbed. *Why would she ask me a question like that?*

"I just thought you'd be interested in seeing them. I don't mind showing them to people. My left one is beautiful. It's the right one that's a bit of a problem. When I first got them done, I couldn't resist lifting up my shirt every time someone glanced at them," she says with pride.

"I used to lift my shirt up a lot, too . . . in kindergarten. The teacher finally called my mom, and I haven't done it since. I actually forgot about that. Thank you for reminding me. So, how do you think the evening is going? I can't really tell. I think I might be a little drunk. What's everyone talking about?" I ask.

"Well, Michael is mostly listening. You can tell he's a really smart guy because he makes these really big points with only a word or two. I love that. He pretty much agrees with Dan about everything, from a business point of view, but he agrees with Zoe that the media has an obligation not to feed off human weakness, or something like that. And Zoe and Dan are sort of arguing, even though Dan sort of agrees with her, too, from a philosophical point of view, but Zoe doesn't really understand the magazine business very well, and I think she might be a communist or a feminist or even a combo of the two. I also think that Michael is totally hot, way hotter than Dan."

I'm not sure how I should react to that last statement because I don't really feel anything. I'm just grateful for the fact that I haven't peed in my pants, and I agree with her about Zoe. She is a communist. I never noticed that before. Courtney is much wiser than people think.

I decide to go back to the table. Once I'm seated, it doesn't take long for me to realize that my drink tastes funny.

Where is that waiter? What did he put in my drink? Why is everything turning black? This feeling can't be good for me.

CHAPTER EIGHTEEN

~

Beauty Is the Icing — It's Not the Cake

I have magically appeared in my own bed, and I have grown another tongue. At least it feels that way. I go to the bathroom to check it out, but I only see one. Maybe it's swollen. It's very dry, that's for sure. The size of my tongue, however, is nothing compared to my hair, which has spun itself into a giant beehive. I could easily walk right out of here and audition for *Hairspray.* I can't wait to show Zoe what happened to my hair. I'm just about to walk into her room when I remember that she doesn't live with me anymore. I'll just take a shower. I feel so sad all of a sudden. I want to show someone my funny hair.

"Chloe, are you up?"

"Dan? You're here?"

"Come on out," he says.

"I can't," I say. "I look like Phyllis Diller."

"Who?"

"Never mind. When did you get here?"

"I brought you home last night . . . after you passed out."

"I passed out? Really?"

"Really. Don't bother drinking anymore. You're terrible at it. I've never seen anything like it. Was that your first time?"

"Of course not. I drink all the time. I just never really got the hang of it. I didn't insult anyone, did I? Sometimes I say the wrong thing when I've had a few too many."

"Well, at one point, you called me a fairy, but don't worry about it. I'm pretty sure I'm in love with you anyway."

"I used the word 'fairy'?"

"I was surprised, too."

"That's so funny of me. I thought I forgot about that word. People should say *fairy* more often."

I shower and brush my teeth and tongue and come out wrapped in a towel. Dan is wearing the same clothes that he wore last night, including his belt and shoes. He's a very neat guy.

We spend all of Sunday wrapped in each other's arms and a huge blanket and Dan tells me some funny stories about last night, some of which may or may not be true, but I love the one when I asked Courtney about her wayward implants and the one when I took a sip of a Diet Coke and then accused the waiter of trying to kill me. I wish I had been there . . . more. Dan asks me if I want to come back to his place for dinner, but I can't.

"I have to pull myself together and get mentally ready for work tomorrow. Then I have to call my mom. Then I have to call Zoe and Michael and tell them that you casually told me that you love me, and then I have to ask them if they like you and then I have to pick out my clothes for tomorrow and I should have started all of this a long time ago."

Dan is already packing up a little overnight bag for me, so we decide that I'll call Zoe and my parents from his place instead. I can always get up early and come back here in the morning.

"Hi, Mom."

"Hi, honey, where are you?" she asks. She doesn't have caller ID. She just knows.

"I'm at Dan's," I say.

"Oh?"

"THAT'S RIGHT," I answer, indicating that we will now be talking in code for the rest of the conversation. She will ask me several questions and I will answer yes or no. In a few minutes, she'll know everything there is to know.

"Someone new?"

"Yes."

"Someone from work?"

"Yes."

"The publisher?"

"No, but you're mysteriously close."

"Ah! The editor-in-chief!"

"How could you possibly know that?"

"I spoke to Zoe already. I just couldn't remember whether it was the publisher or the editor. Is he handsome?"

"Very. What did Zoe say about him?" I ask, and then I whisper, "Does she like him? Just say yes or no."

"Yes and no."

"What does that mean?"

"She likes him but she doesn't like the magazine. She thinks she can convince him that it needs to be reworked."

"The magazine is fine. I wish she didn't feel the need to fix everything!"

"You know your sister. She always wants everything to be perfect. She can't help it. And she did say that *he* was perfect. It's the magazine that's not perfect."

"I know she loves me, and she wants everything in my life to be perfect, but would it ever occur to her that she could be wrong about something? The magazine is not that bad, and you should have seen what she wore out to dinner with us. She looked like a Green Beret."

"Did you wear your new suede jacket?"

That does it! I just bought that jacket two weeks ago, and my mom never saw it.

"How do you know about that jacket? I just bought it. Do you have someone following me when I shop? This has been going on for too long. You know everything! You know I have things that I don't even know I have. Do you know that I bought a new pair of boots too?"

"No, as a matter of fact, I didn't know that. I hope they're brown, though. Your other brown ones are going to ruin your feet."

Just then my dad cuts in and tells my mom to hang up so he can talk to me.

"Hi, Chloe."

"Hi, Daddy."

"How's the job?"

"Good and bad."

"Need anything?"

"Not really," I say, surprising both of us.

"So you're making good money now?"

"Not really."

"So what's good about the job? Did you meet someone?"

"As a matter of fact, I did. Mom will tell you all about him. She already spoke to Zoe."

"That's wonderful, sweetheart. Does he play golf?"

"I'm not sure. Hold on."

"Do you play golf?" I yell to Dan.

"I try my best," he answers.

"He tries his best," I tell my dad, knowing that I just described his idea of a perfect man.

"Good enough. He's perfect for you," my dad says.

"I love you, Daddy."

"I love you, too."

"Hi."

"Hi!"

"So?"

"So, I like him. No, that's not true. I love him!" she says.

"Does Michael?"

"Yup."

"Anything you'd like to change?" I ask, getting right to the point.

"You spoke to Mom?" she asks.

"Yup."

"Actually no, I think he's perfect for you. But I just think that, with a little convincing, that magazine could really be great. I was thinking that . . ."

She's about to go off on a tangent, and I don't have time now. "It would probably be better if you write it all down," I say.

"I really should, but I doubt I'll get to it. I have a ton of work," she says. She definitely will.

"I have another question for you, and then I have to go. How does Mom know everything I have in my closet? Don't you think it's a little weird when she asks me if I wore something that she can't possibly have known that I bought because I live in New York and she lives in Florida? I just bought something two weeks ago and she asked me if I wore it last night. Don't you find that just a little spooky?"

"No, not really."

"Why not? Please tell me why that's not spooky."

"Because you probably put it on her credit card. She collects all the receipts, and then she makes little outfits out of them. She's been doing that ever since you got your own apartment."

I never would have thought of that. Of course those bills have to go somewhere!

"Well, I just wanted to say goodnight and I'll speak to you tomorrow. I'm glad you like Dan, and I'm sure he'd love to hear your ideas for the magazine. Just don't get carried away. It is what it is. It's not supposed to be *The Radical Mind*."

"Like I said, I have a ton of work, so we'll see. Anyway, have fun with him. He's great. Love you."

*   *   *

"Are you almost finished talking about me?" Dan calls from the other room.

"Zoe likes you and so does Michael," I yell back.

"Really? Zoe likes me? Even though she hates the magazine?"

"She's not letting that get in the way because she's planning to convince you to change it," I say.

When I walk into Dan's room, he's at his computer, and he's wearing glasses. I've never seen him in his glasses. He looks so different. He's got so many disguises.

"Read this," he says.

It's a mission statement called New Issues.

As the editor-in-chief of *Issues,* I spend a good portion of my time trying to figure out what women *want.* My job is to offer information. I try not to influence, but I realize that information and influence are natural reciprocates by virtue of the fact that all forms of communication are intended to have an effect. Our loyal readers interpret everything we print in *Issues* as "truth," and we are therefore more inclined to sell the brand of truth that best serves our needs.

Until now, we have always interpreted and translated our readers' needs into advertising dollars, but everyone has a wake-up call at some point in his or her career, and I've decided to answer mine. I am therefore proposing a relaunch of *Issues.* We are headed in a new direction.

From this point forward, we will now give our readers what they *need.* The voice that speaks to our readers will no longer reek of competition or an obsession with appearances. We will begin to tackle the issue of beauty, less in terms of change and more in terms of enhancement, and at best, acceptance.

We will focus on the idea of women advancing themselves in the workplace as more of a collective concern. Gone are the days when we taught our readers how to size up and undermine the competition. Our advice will now teach women how and why they need each other and what they can do to help themselves by helping each other.

Somehow we've gotten off track and forgotten the purpose of this magazine. I think we've been feeding into human insecurity instead of attempting to foster independence and growth.

I'm suggesting a total redesign of the cover of *Issues,* as well as an entirely new editorial approach, both in terms of the issues we will now cover and the way we will cover them. The new voice of the magazine will be more respectful and intelligent. My editors and I need to rethink who our reader is and how she deserves to be addressed.

I'm not saying that we should deny the fact that fashion and beauty are important factors in women's lives, but somewhere along the line, we've gotten confused. Beauty is the icing. It's not the cake.

"Wow," I say.

"Wow good or wow bad?" he asks.

"Wow number one: Zoe said that exact same thing about the icing and the cake and wow number two: I can't believe how easily she convinced you to take all the good stuff out of the magazine."

"I'm going to make the magazine better. It's going to be even more beautiful and a lot more intelligent and exciting. I want women to feel good when they read the *New Issues,* not 'not good enough.' "

"I like the way I feel when I read it," I say, in defense of what used to be my favorite magazine.

"Hopefully there are millions of readers who feel good when they read *Issues.* But there is no question that the magazine could do more for more women. Right now it's like a Band-Aid, and it should be more of a cure. We need to get to the bottom of what causes women's issues—especially the ones that they have with one another."

"So what are you saying? You want to give the magazine more substance by focusing on more serious issues?" I ask.

"Pretty much."

"Bad idea. No one will read it anymore. Except for maybe you and Zoe."

"No, I think Zoe made some good points last night. We can reach even more women if we start giving them something to sink their teeth into besides another teeth whitening kit," Dan says.

"The magazine is what it is. Zoe has a way of making everyone want to be a better person. She's always had that problem. Don't let it get to you. Although I do think *Issues* hit a low point when Courtney suggested a new under-eye concealer to a woman who was clearly suffering from depression and perhaps malnutrition."

"So in some ways you agree with Zoe?" he asks, pulling me onto his lap.

"Not really, but the eye-concealer suggestion was the funniest thing I ever read. I don't take *Issues* as seriously as Zoe does. I like getting fashion and beauty advice. I don't take it as an insult to feminism or my rights as a female. I feel that I have the same rights as anyone. If I want to climb a mountain, I'll climb it. If I want to climb it in a dress, that's my right. I like being a girl, and I don't think *girl* is a dirty word. I think some people find fashion and beauty magazines offensive because they show women how great they could look if they lost a few pounds or put on a little makeup. Sometimes that's scary too, you know.

"Some women deliberately ignore their appearance to convince themselves that they don't care, but they do. Everyone cares. One woman might hide behind an 'au natural' appearance the same way another woman might hide behind a face full of makeup. They are both overly concerned with what their looks say about them. They both have issues. They're simply different issues. Not all women have these issues, but enough of them do to warrant racks and racks of beauty magazines.

"Magazines in and of themselves are harmless. They don't say, 'You look terrible.' That's just what some women automatically hear when they see a photograph of a beautiful woman. That's the real issue.

"How could anyone get mad at a magazine? All it wants to do is help. If you really want to help women feel good about themselves, don't stop offering beauty advice. Teach women that it's okay for them to *want* to be beautiful and that it's okay for other women to be beautiful, too.

"Zoe is right about a lot of things, but there are millions of girls out there who want to look their best in every possible way. Do you have any idea how many hours of shopping that involves? Sure, they'd love to have other hobbies or perhaps start a family, but there just isn't enough time. I think it's pretty obvious that these girls are responsible for the bulk of our nation's wealth and that these are definitely the girls who advertisers need to reach. But it's your choice. You have to pick your reader. Just remember, girls who don't want to care don't want to shop either."

~

CHAPTER NINETEEN

At Some Point, You May Be Forced to Make a Lateral Move

After five consecutive nights at Dan's apartment, I have insisted that we spend the night at my place for a change. Now I see why we don't come here very often. There is nothing to eat.

I'm watching *The Mary Tyler Moore Show* and Dan is sitting and reading a stack of essays that Zoe wrote. Every now and then he says, "What's this one about?" and I say something like, "Some kid who called me fat," or "Some girl who went to our high school who had a pierced vagina."

He loves the way Zoe writes, and he wants to read them all. Lucky for him there's about three hundred of those things. We order in, and Dan reads all night. After about two hours, he says, "Chloe, this stuff your sister writes about girls, especially when she's sticking up for you, is really funny." He's flipping through the pages like he can't believe how many times she felt it was necessary to defend me.

"She worries about you a lot, doesn't she?" he says.

"All the time," I say.

"Well, I have to be honest. I'm worried about you, too."

"Why?"

"Well, there's sort of a problem here, and I'm not sure what to do about it."

"What is it?" I ask, hoping he hasn't suddenly developed a sexually related problem. I'd hate to have to work through something like that so early on in a relationship. Or ever.

"We never talk about the fact that *Issues* is a family business, but it is, and in principle, I shouldn't be having a relationship with you. To make matters worse, I was perfectly serious when I said I'm in love with you."

"In principle, meaning you signed something that said you wouldn't have a relationship with anyone who works in the building, or it's just frowned upon?" I ask.

"It's more than frowned upon. It's forbidden."

"Don't you make the rules?" I ask.

"Not all of them. Not the ones that come from corporate."

"Is corporate your mom and dad?"

"And an uncle or two."

"So what do you want to do about it?"

Please God. Don't let him break up with me. I'll never lie or eat candy for breakfast for the rest of my life. I'll never buy another pair of shoes that I can't afford and I'll devote my life to the hungry from this moment forward.

"Well, since you're unhappy at your job and you're not interested in the promotion that you are going to be offered very soon, why don't I see if I can find you something somewhere else that you would really love doing?"

"You want to find me another job so that you can continue to go out with me?"

"I don't know what else to do," he says. I feel my nose start to burn, which means I'm about to cry. My eyes are welling up and my throat has that enormous bubble in it that makes me sound like Gomer Pyle.

"Zoe is going to kill you for this," I say in my Gomer voice.

"I don't think so. I think she'd agree that, at the moment,

Issues isn't the healthiest place for anyone, and until I can make it better, it's the wrong place for you. Ruth is a problem for all of us. That incident with Bruno was horrible for you. You complain about the way the editors treat you, and the truth is, you don't even like your job or your whole department."

Dan walks over to me and takes my head in his hands. *Please don't kiss me.* If he kisses me, I'll agree to anything. I'll probably offer to fire myself.

"Dan, please don't do this to me. I love *Issues*. I want to stay there. I won't complain ever again." I'm in a begging/praying position now, which, unfortunately, is a very weak and typically unsuccessful pose for winning an argument of any kind. He's looking at me with his piercing blue eyes, and I feel my knees cave in a little. They're practically touching now. *Am I sitting or standing? I guess I'm sort of kneeling and falling.*

"I love you, Chloe. You know I love you."

There's a little awkward moment here because I did sort of topple to my knees. It wasn't like I came crashing down or anything. It was sort of a slow drop.

"Chloe, what are you doing?" Dan asks as he pulls me back up onto the couch.

"I don't know. You were looking at me funny. So I fell over."

He starts kissing my face and my hair, pretty much . . . my . . . everything.

Who really needs a job anyway? I mean, really. You wouldn't believe how good he smells.

He stops for a minute to look at me and says, "Chloe, I refuse to give you up, and I can't have a relationship with you if you're working there." He puts his arms around me and hugs me so tight that my back cracks. The cracking noise snaps me out of my stupor and I manage to pull myself together.

"I'm calling Zoe. I feel sorry for you when she hears about this. I really do. I've wanted to work at *Issues* my entire life and now you're taking it away from me because you love me.

Nothing could be more unfair." I stand up and walk over to the phone.

"Go ahead and call her, Chloe. I guarantee she'll agree with me. You know she doesn't like the idea of you working at *Issues*. It goes against everything she stands for, and she knows how difficult it is for you. She wants what is right for you and so do I, and who knows? Maybe we'll start our own business one day. Maybe we'll go into the shoe business, but as far as *Issues* is concerned, it can't work. I've made my decision. It's final."

"I'm still calling Zoe, and you better not try to use the fact that I hate my job as an excuse to fire me, because that has nothing to do with how I feel about *Issues*. Tell Zoe the truth. Tell her that it's because of the *rule*. Then we'll see what she says!"

By the way, thank you God for the fact that he didn't break up with me. You're amazing. Can you just forget the part about the hungry for now?

"She'll probably write a whole book about you!" I continue. "Chloe, it's for the best. The discussion is over."

"But I belong at *Issues*." I put the phone down for a second and walk over to my portfolio. I take out the drawing of the human brain that I designed for the shoe issue. When I look at it again, I realize that there is a lot more to that drawing than I thought. It's a true testament to the fact that "the shoe issue" is actually a very complex psychological condition. I hand it to Dan. He looks at it for a second and asks me what it is.

"It's a picture of a brain," I tell him.

"Oh. Did you draw it?"

"Yes, why? Doesn't it look like a brain? It's supposed to be a brain deciding what shoes it's going to wear. See? Think of it as a map that leads you through all the various factors that are involved in the decision-making process.

"All you do is pick an activity or an event, all of which can be found lined up in the pre-frontal cortex area (commonly known as the forehead) and trace it along, until you reach the shoe that the brain chose to wear for that event or activity. It's easy. Look over here where it says, 'Need to lose five pounds. Go running.' Now just follow along the brain wave.

"At first the brain chooses the red-and-white leather Nike Shocks, but then the brain remembers (see the tiny lightbulb) that she will most likely run into a certain guy, who she likes and who is very cute, on the way to the park. So . . . she decides to wear her Sergio Rossi black leather six-inch stacked-heel boots instead. But then, it occurs to her that she will most likely fall and kill herself right in front of him if she attempts to walk on anything but a completely flat, unpolished surface in those boots (see the little tombstone there). So . . . she puts on her Oscar de la Renta over-the-knee chocolate brown Napa boots, with the detachable D-ring belt and three-and-a-half-inch heel, instead. And of course, she brings her sneakers to change into when she gets there."

"Wow. I honestly had no idea the decision-making process was so multifaceted. But seriously, this is very good, Chloe. All of your ideas are funny and great, and I was in complete agreement with Rob that you would be perfect as the director of creative services."

The shoe brain wasn't supposed to be funny. What's he talking about?

"But you don't want the job and I can't go over this any more." He hands me back the drawing, and I take another look at it. I guess it's not that great. It's sort of childish in a way, now that I think about it.

"Why can't they give that promotion to Ruth? She wants it so badly. It's driving her crazy. Why would they crush her by giving it to me? She thinks promotionally all day long. Her whole life is devoted to getting herself promoted. All I ever think about is shoes."

"And all I ever think about is you. At one point, I wanted to rename the magazine *Chloe*. I don't know how I let things get this far, but I've never felt this way about anybody. I swear,

Chloe, I don't know what it is, but some of the things you do just kill me. That day when we first met in the shoe closet, I had been listening to you in there for so long. I kept thinking, 'When I open that door, if she's even a little good-looking, I'm a dead man.' And then, there you were, standing there with a shoe in each hand, and I knew I was in love with you, right then and there."

"But that's not a good enough reason to fire someone!"

"Chloe, I want us to be together. I will find you another job!"

"I have a job. Please let me keep it."

Dan gets up and walks over to the window. He looks out and continues talking without turning around. "Believe me, as much as I don't want to lose you, I don't want the magazine to lose you either. Just when I was convinced that you had absolutely no interest in being at *Issues,* aside from the shoe closet, you come up with these great ideas and I know I'm making a mistake. I don't know what to do with you anymore, and I certainly don't know what to do about us. I don't know anything anymore."

~

Every No-Win Situation Can Be Won

Zoe has agreed to meet Dan and me at a coffee shop. When she sees me through the window, she gives me a big smile, and you can tell that she can't wait to get inside.

"Is she always this happy to see you?" Dan asks.

"Always. If I walk out of here and walk back in, she'll get happy all over again. I'm pretty much her favorite thing. So I suggest you choose your words carefully."

"I think I can take her if things get ugly," he says.

"Hey guys!" Zoe looks cute, as usual, and she smells like her delicious shampoo. She's wearing Michael's big leather jacket. I love the way she looks in his clothes.

"Hungry?" Dan asks her.

"Just coffee for me," she says.

He turns to me. "Chloe, hungry?"

"I'll just have a piece of that coconut pie," I say, pointing to the spinning glass case.

We order quickly and Dan is about to present our little dilemma to Zoe, but she's already off and running.

"Dan, I've been thinking. I know Chloe loves *Issues* the way it is, and I love the idea that the magazine attempts to deal with women's issues. In fact, I'm sure the original intention of the magazine was right on target. Women do have issues with their bodies, their clothes, their careers, and their overall self-image. Of course they have other issues, too. They have health issues, legal issues, political issues, hormonal issues, issues in the military, eating disorders, immigration issues, tax issues, financial issues—"

"You want to improve the magazine by printing articles about hormones in the military?" I interrupt.

"No, not at all. I'm just getting to my point."

"Don't bother. You already talked him into changing it. Once he makes up his mind, it's pretty much a done deal," I say.

"Really? That's great. Because I've given this a lot of thought and I put together a little synopsis of my ideas. First of all, I strongly believe that the biggest issue that most women face is their inability to understand and get along with other women," she says. "Of course, a perfect example of that is Ruth—"

Before she can say another word, I take the ten-page list out of her hand and start reading it.

How to Get A Green Card
How to Defend Yourself in a Rape Situation
How to Prepare Your Own Taxes
How to Form a Coalition of Women

"Zoe, are you out of your mind? Who the hell cares about any of this stuff?"

"Excuse me, but I have something to say," Dan says.
Nice try.

"Zoe, *Issues* is supposed to be light and happy," I explain.

"You were reading the wrong page. Those were my notes for something I was working on for my own magazine. My idea for *Issues* is a totally new concept that's never been done before by any other women's magazine. Here's the idea: Teach women how to laugh at themselves. That's all there is to it. Start running articles that teach us what we are really all about. It's time to hold up a mirror to the inner workings of the female mind. For the first time in magazine history, instead of showing them what they are supposed to look like, show them how they already look—on the inside.

"*Issues* has the potential to be a truly unique, inspiring, and highly entertaining literary magazine about 'girls' and the underlying issues that cause them to react to one another. And don't be afraid to use the word *girl*. In fact, celebrate the fact that it is okay to be girly and feminine.

"The magazine can still be filled with tons of fashion and beauty advice, but it should be intelligent, thoughtful, realistic advice that celebrates our femaleness without making a mockery of it. In other words, it's time to give girls advice with respect to how they really look and how they really think.

"Shine some light on the fact that most girls don't walk around all day thinking pretty thoughts—but that doesn't mean they are bad. It means they are real and very funny. Once women and girls come to terms with the fact that we don't have to be perfect little angels all the time in order to be acceptable, we will find it easier to tolerate the natural behavior of the other girls around us.

"Somewhere along the line, someone set the bar for female behavior way too high. That's why girls are so hard on each other. They can't possibly measure up to the unattainable physical and moral standards that society has created for them. It's time for them to accept the fact that they are only people.

"The problem with many women, especially in the workplace, is that they get offended when they see another woman trying too hard. They feel threatened and angry when they should be rooting her on. A victory for one woman is a victory for us all.

"We need to allow each other to be competitive and beautiful and still respect each other in the morning.

"Print articles that tackle the female boss issue one month and the female assistant issue the next month. Get the best writers and comedians to dissect these relationships, one after the other, and create a little literary show each and every month. Cover best friends, siblings, mothers-in-law, you name it. It's time to lay all the cards on the table, once and for all, and teach girls how to play and enjoy the game. Accepting the truth is the only way to grow, but the real challenge is finding access to the truth. And that's where *Issues* can shine. Slopping on more lipstick and exposing more cleavage is not advice. It's a Band-Aid."

Oh my God. They've merged.

"It's time to break into the locker room of the girl psyche and expose the mystery once and for all. If you can do that, and prove to girls how valuable they are to one another and how lovable and 'acceptable' they are, then I think you will have really done something for everyone.

"Oh, and one more thing. I think you should call the magazine *Miss Understanding: A Girl's Guide To Girls.*"

She does get it. She totally gets it.

"Listen, I hate to interrupt. But I do have something to say, and I think you'll both find it of interest," Dan says. "First of all, Zoe, I love your ideas and your whole approach. The magazine does need to be more literary and more socially responsible, and I agree with you, the thing it needs most is a sense of humor. The exploration of female relationships is a perfect vehicle for change. I think if we follow your advice, we will most definitely be headed in the right direction. And that brings me to my next point.

"Zoe, I want to offer you the position of deputy editor. I think the work you do at *The Radical Mind* is really impressive, and the essays you write for your sister are even better—especially the stuff about other girls.

"I want that kind of writing in my magazine. I want relevant, cutting-edge humor, and I want you to write it. I want that voice. I think you have a way of making people think and laugh at the same time. That's exactly what I want the magazine to do."

"I don't know what to say. This is unbelievable. Thank you, Dan, thank you, thank you, thank you," I say, even though the offer technically went to Zoe. I get up to sit next to Zoe on her chair. "I can't believe it. It's so unexpected," I say.

Zoe is speechless for the first time in her entire life.

"She's perfect for the job! We can go out to lunch every day!" I continue.

"Dan, wow. That's an incredible offer. You really didn't know about this, Chloe?" Zoe asks.

"I had no idea. I love you, Dan. This is perfect. Now Zoe and I can be together all the . . . oh, right . . . never mind . . . this is awful."

"What's the problem?" Zoe asks. She's already got that look on her face when she senses I'm in trouble.

"Dan, you tell her," I say.

"*Issues* has a very strict policy about romantic relationships. I'm in love with your sister, and rules are rules. We cannot be involved with one another if she works at the magazine. I'm not giving her up, so I don't see any way that she can stay. And the truth is, I don't love the idea of her working for me anyway, even if it's in another department. I also think that, at the moment, it's not the best place for her."

"So you want to fire her so you can continue to go out with her?"

"I told you she'd be mad," I lean over and say to Dan.

I'll just sit here quietly and wait and see how this whole thing unfolds. It's really between Dan and Zoe at this point. I know I'm in good hands, because I can already see my sister's eyebrows analyzing the situation. They're bouncing around like crazy. They say the eyes are the window to the soul, but with Zoe, it's all in the eyebrows.

"I love your sister, Zoe. I'm at a complete loss for a solution. She wants to stay, but I can't allow it. I know she's a tremendous asset to the company and I'm being selfish here, but I just think it's for the best. I know Chloe will be upset with me for a while, but I really believe that she will be much happier at another magazine."

I doubt I'll be able to sit here and keep my mouth shut much longer. He can't just decide to fire me and keep me. Shouldn't I have a say in the most important decision of my life? *Oh look! Here comes my pie. . . . This is a huge piece. . . . I'll never be able to finish this. . . . I should really offer them a bite— but they're busy . . . and neither of them are really pie people. It's funny because I usually order chocolate layer cake in diners, but the coconut looked so fluffy. I'm not even listening to them anymore. I'm sure they'll work out something. This is the kind of pie that you could never get sick of. Even if I had, let's say, two pieces like this one, I'd never get tired of it. Listen to them . . . Dan just keeps saying the same thing over and over again.*

Oh wait. He's leaning back in his chair now with his arms folded. It looks like it's Zoe's turn to talk. I'm sure Zoe will figure out some brilliant plan that will make it impossible for Dan to fire me. She always comes through for me. I have the best sister in the world. I put my fork down so I can give her my full attention.

"This is a tough one; there's no question about that," Zoe says, "but you're absolutely right, Dan. You have to fire her."

"WHAT??" I cry. I take a deep breath and immediately begin choking on a giant crumb that must have been just sitting there on my lip waiting to be inhaled.

"Hold on, Chloe, I'm not finished. Dan, both of your parents work at the magazine, is that correct?"

"That is correct," Dan says as he hits me on the back a few times to dislodge the crumb. *Phew! That's better.*

"And they are married to one another?" she asks.

"As far as I know," Dan says.

"Fine. Then I guess there is no rule about being married to an employee. Fire Chloe, marry her, and rehire her."

Oh no. Here comes the coughing. How could she do this to me? This is so humiliating. It seems like everyone in the whole diner suddenly froze. The silence is closing in around us like quicksand. I guess everyone turned around to see if I'll choke to death. The air temperature must have risen like thirty degrees in three seconds. Something must be burning in the kitchen! Maybe if I yell Help!! it will distract Dan from having to respond. What if he starts laughing at the two of us? I want to crawl under the table and out the door. Dan hands me a glass of water, and I gulp it down. Zoe finally lost her mind. I knew this would happen. She's . . . she's. . .

"That'll work," Dan says, while patting me on the back a few more times.

"Zoe! You can't just talk people into marrying me!"

"I wouldn't waste time arguing with your sister, Chloe," Dan says, as he gets down on one knee. I forget everything and immediately get down on one knee, too. I'm not sure why exactly.

"Chloe, will you marry me?"

I can't believe this is happening. His eyes are looking right through me. I feel a little light-headed. I ate much too fast. My whole body is shaking. I have to answer him, but nothing will come out. I think I'm coming down with something. He takes my head in his hands, the way he always does. I hope I never forget this moment for as long as I live.

"Yes, yes, of course she will!" Zoe says.

It's a good thing someone said something. I wasn't even close to coming up with anything that resembled an actual word.

"And Zoe, will you take the job I offered to you?" Dan asks.

"Yes, yes, of course she will!" I say.

"But only under one condition," Zoe interrupts.

Oh no. Here we go again. She better not blow this whole

thing right now with some lame idea for the magazine like turning the cafeteria into a soup kitchen.

"I want you to approve my first decision as deputy editor. After the wedding, and the rehiring of Chloe, I want to officially appoint her shoe editor."

"What? Wait a minute. How did you know I want to be shoe editor?"

"You talk in your sleep," Zoe says.

"But there's no such thing," Dan says.

Zoe quickly glances at her watch to indicate that her work here is done.

"There is now," says my sister.

❧

CHAPTER TWENTY-ONE

No One Ever Said the Subway Makes Sense for Every Occasion

Zoe and I have decided to meet for breakfast every morning and commute to work together every day. Dan goes in about two hours earlier than everyone else, so his morning routine doesn't get mixed up with ours. I'm running a little late today because I don't have anything to wear. I'm all showered, and I did my hair and makeup over an hour ago. Unfortunately, all of my clothes shrunk in the closet while I was on my honeymoon. It happens to a lot of people. Rhonda claims that it's caused by quick changes in closet temperature. I also might have put on a pound or two in Italy. The pasta is very good there.

I try on a few outfits but nothing looks right, so I try on my wedding veil instead. The headband is made out of tiny white enamel flowers with a diamond chip in the center of each flower. I'm thinking about making it into a necklace or something because Dan says I should really stop wearing it out all the time.

Sometimes I sit here for hours looking at our honeymoon photos. There are no wedding photos, in the traditional sense, because we eloped. It's a long story.

Actually, I could write a whole book about it, but the important thing is that I got to wear my dress and the white satin toe shoes I dreamed of wearing my whole life . . . if I ever got married . . . or decided to become a ballerina.

It's getting late. I don't want to keep Zoe waiting. I'll just throw on these old black Moschino wool gabardine flared trousers and my black washed-silk button-down shirt and . . . oh my God! I have the perfect shoes for this outfit. I just bought a new pair of ivory Sergio Rossi spectator pumps with polished black trim and a bow on each strap. I can't believe I didn't think of them sooner! My adrenaline is really kicking in now, which is good, because I'm going to have to run as fast as I possibly can to meet Zoe on time.

I get dressed, run a brush through my hair, slip on my new pumps, and grab my bag. As soon as I take a step, I realize that I have to really curl my toes to keep these shoes on. If I remember correctly, one of them is an eight and a half and the other one is either a nine or a ten. I never should have agreed to take them when the salesperson announced that there were two different size shoes inside the box marked six and a half— and that he was very sorry, but neither shoe was close to a size six and a half—or even a six or a seven.

It's amazing that I'm able to keep up this pace in such a difficult walking shoe. It took over two million teeny, hurried steps to get this far, but I can already see my sister waiting for me at the end of my block.

When I finally reach her, Zoe looks down at my feet and shakes her head. Then she smiles at me and gives me a big hug. We are both so excited to be together again. We walk one more block to the subway station, run down the stairs, and then run back up. We might as well take a taxi . . . just this once.

To: Production
From: Daniel Princely, Editor-in-chief
Re: Masthead Changes

Editorial

Deputy Editor	Zoe Rose
Shoe Editor	Chloe Rose-Princely
Cover Model	Ali Rhodes

Advertising

Creative Services Director	Ruth Davis
Art Director	Rhonda Gold

President of Maintenance Operations	Joseph Paglione
President of Cafeteria Services	Liz Jabonowsky

Want More?

Turn the page to enter
Avon's Little Black Book—

the dish, the scoop and the
cherry on top from

STEPHANIE LESSING

Introduction to *What a Doll!*

My sister Zoe did not believe in dolls. She felt there was something artificial about them. "How could you hold that thing and pretend it's a baby?" she would ask me.

"I don't know," I'd say. "It looks like a baby." But she was right—I was kidding myself. And it was only a matter of time before every single one of my baby dolls was cast aside on the grounds that it was a poseur with no personality. Still, I hated saying good-bye to them. They were so young and overdressed, but what could I do? I typically went along with whatever my sister suggested, pretty much until I went to college, and according to Zoe, the only cool doll was Barbie.

Zoe didn't single out Barbie because she was incredibly beautiful or because she came in a hot pink box—both of which seemed like damned good reasons to me. And she certainly didn't choose Barbie for the hundreds of opportunities she offered us to live vicariously through her sporty, sexually active, and yet surprisingly career-oriented lifestyle. The truth is Zoe chose Barbie for one reason and one reason only. Barbie needed a bra.

I think my sister felt that Mattel played a malicious trick on Barbie by giving her . . . well . . . hooters instead of regular breasts. And Zoe was determined to make it up to her. Her first crude attempt at ameliorating Barbie's breasts was to file them down with an emery board. When that didn't work, she tried binding them with Scotch tape. She even tried filling in the rest of Barbie's torso with silly putty to even things out.

My sister, who grew to be four feet eleven with a 34DD chest, must have seen it coming. I can think of no other reason why she would have spent the best years of her childhood trying to make a doll's breasts disappear. And yet, as much as she loved Barbie and sympathized with her, the idea of *playing* with her never crossed Zoe's mind. I'm not sure, to this day, if my sister even realized that Barbie was a toy.

Zoe wasn't big on playing. Imaginary games, of any kind, were completely out of the question. She refused to make a fool out of herself, even in front of me, who had no qualms about parading around the house laughing and pretending to smoke, wearing a housedress and a shower cap, convinced I was a dead ringer for Phyllis Diller. Instead, my sister preferred to watch me from across the room and occasionally remind me not to poke my eye out with my cigarette holder.

My idea of "playing Barbie" was to dress her up as a slut in every conceivable color combination and then, as a grand finale, dress her in her Executive Barbie outfit and have her fire all the other dolls in the room. In all of my firing scenarios, Barbie worked at a fashion magazine where she held the title shoe editor.

My sister couldn't bear to watch other children talk to themselves. She found "make-believe magazine office" to be an excruciating embarrassment. All she wanted to do was wash Barbie's perfectly straight hair, marvel at the fact that it dried without getting frizzy, and then get down to the business of fitting her for a bra with proper support.

I'm convinced that Zoe's guarded personality and her desire to save the world, one pair of breasts at a time, is what turned her into a writer. Now that she's an adult, she works for a magazine called *The Radical Mind,* where she uses her pen to expose injustices, defend the innocent, and lobby for human rights. When she's not working, she uses her pen for the sole purpose of making sure that no one hurts my feelings. Actually, she's been doing that all of my life. If you don't believe me, take a look at my baby pictures, mention to Zoe that I was fat . . . and then wait. There's an excellent chance you'll get a twenty-page letter in the mail that will make you wish you'd never laid eyes on me.

When all of my friends went to sleepaway camp the summer before I turned nine, I thought it was just an ordinary summer. I had no idea we were supposed to grow up that year and suddenly start hating Barbie. Because I was unaware of the transformation I was supposed to undergo that summer, I made the mistake of taking out my Barbie case filled with dolls, clothes, and shoes the second they returned.

I'll never forget how they immediately fell on the floor laughing. I remember laughing with them, pretending I was just kidding around, but they knew. Years later, when I told my sister about my little faux pas, she reacted the same way she always does. She got out her pen.

Chloe Rose
September 27, 2004

An excerpt from *What a Doll!*

from *The Complete Works of Zoe Rose*

I like to think back to the time in my life when the only girls I knew were little girls and my closest friend was the prettiest thing I had ever laid eyes on. I adored her, idolized her, and longed to be with her every waking hour of the day. She let me do anything I wanted to her, which included a habitual strip search and a series of wash and blowouts that were so ruthless, it's a wonder her head remained intact for as long as it did. And all she ever did was smile. She smiled as I tried to pry the little diamond off her finger day after day. She smiled at every single one of my attempts to give her breast reduction, and she smiled when I trimmed her bangs—right down to their holey roots. The more I tried to dissect and desexualize her, the more she offered herself to me . . . again and again and again.

Of course we were little girls in different ways, and the fact that I knew she would never grow beyond eleven and a half inches tall gave me an edge. Also I had skin. And although I didn't grow up to be the equivalent of five feet six with an eighteen-inch waist and I don't bring in over a billion dollars a year, I don't resent her. Because Barbie was the best friend I ever had.

No matter how many defamatory books they write about her or how many times they post her image on the web pinned to a cross with birthday candles protruding out of her breasts, she will always be my girl.

Always in a good mood, never jealous, never angry, never competitive or edgy about being cloned over and over again—and talk about a willingness to share! Who else would clomp around in one purple pump after a full day of water skiing on an asphalt cul-de-sac all because another Barbie needed to borrow her shoe?

Bring in a third friend and still, no problem. Temporary rejection for another, cooler Barbie? Bring it on. You could flush her down the toilet and it was like she knew she had the best hair and that was enough to assure her that you would want her back again—even when the Barbie with the hair down to the floor came out. She knew you would eventually see through that flash in the pan and come running back. Somehow she just always knew. Damn, she was something.

We all know there will never be anyone like her, ever again; and yet the world continually mocks her, reducing her to the likes of a boozed-up trailer park party doll—a rubberized sexual icon of depravity.

I just can't figure out why everyone is always so mad at her—unless it's the no-cellulite thing. If it is the no-cellulite thing, I think she deserves a break on that one. Her thighs are made of poly-vinyl chloride. No one is expected to compete with that.

Maybe it's the cloying, slightly bucktoothed smile that turned you against her. That's certainly understandable, and I can see how that could easily be misconstrued. I just see it as more of a defense mechanism than a perpetual come-on.

Is it because her feet have holes in them? Again, there's a reason for that. I can only assume there's a reason for everything Mattel does.

Is it because she's always just a little too tanned? Granted, tanning is a health issue, but has anyone been to Malibu lately? Is it not as hot as hell over there in the summer?

Let's face it; the only thing Barbie ever did was help you make friends, and now you won't even admit that you slept with her.

Nice.

STEPHANIE LESSING

STEPHANIE LESSING is a freelance writer who lives in Demarest, New Jersey, with her husband, Dan and two children, Kim and Jesse. Stephanie was formerly the Promotion Copy Chief for *Mademoiselle* magazine and traveled with *Mademoiselle* to co-host fashion and beauty events, going on to freelance for magazines such as: *Vogue, Glamour, Vanity Fair, Conde Nast Traveler, Self* and *Women's Wear Daily*. While attending the American College in Paris, she interned for the *Herald Tribune* and then graduated from Boston University with a B.S. degree from the School of Public Communications.

She's Got Issues is her first novel; a sequel is in the works.